Book Two of the Modern Prophet Series

# The Reluctant Prophet:

# A Love Story

## Karl J. Morgan

Book Two of the Modern Prophet Series

*The Reluctant Prophet:*
*A Love Story*

Copyright © 2014 by Karl J. Morgan



*The Reluctant Prophet: A Love Story* may be purchased or ordered through booksellers or at www.karljmorgan.com, or www.sacredlife.com.

ISBN: 978-0-9860270-8-6
ISBN: 0986027081
Library of Congress Control Number: 2014953911

*Cover and Text Design By: Sabrina Lueck, SLdesigns54@gmail.com*

*Sacred Life Publishers*™
*www.sacredlife.com*
Printed in United States of America

*Dedicated to Aida, my wife of 25 years*

*This book is lovingly dedicated to my wife, Aida, who has stood by my side for the last twenty-five years. While she and I have not gone through the same adventures as Bea Watson and Zeke Thompson, we have experienced and learned from everything that life has given us. We have learned as do the protagonists in my books that life is a much more magical and mysterious journey than most folks could ever imagine.*

*At one point in the tale, Bea tells Zeke that there is much more going on than just a love story about them, but in reality that is never true. If we can just hold on to the love in our hearts and share it with those around us, just maybe the love can grow and eventually cover the planet. If our faith in God and each other was only strong enough, there may never be a need for time travelers like Bea to save us from ourselves. It is up to each of us.*

*Aida, thank you so much for making me the person I am today and enabling me to craft and share stories such as* The Reluctant Prophet. *Thank you for helping me to see the beauty around us and for traveling with me along the winding path that is life.*

# Contents

# Chapter 1

Zeke Thompson was exhausted. He had been searching for work after graduating from college for months, and now spent most of his days pouring over job postings, looking for some light at the end of his tunnel. He wanted to sleep, but today he needed a haircut, so he drove the half mile to the local strip mall and walked into the barbershop he frequented when his mane of brown hair became unmanageable. He sat in the barber chair with the cape cinched around his neck and Sheila busily cutting away at him. He closed his eyes, hoping to rest a bit since there was little else he could do at this time. He almost jumped out of the chair when he felt a hand on his knee. When he opened his eyes, a thin woman with a wrinkled face and a tattered mini-skirt was looking at him. "What do you want?"

"Come on out back, honey, and let me rock your world for fifty," she grinned. The smell of alcohol on her breath was overwhelming.

"Leave me alone," Zeke barked.

"Get out of here!" Jack, the owner of the shop exclaimed as he hurried over. "I'm not going to tell you again, so get out and stay out of my business!" He took her arm and started dragging her toward the front door.

"A girl's got a right to make a living, Jack," she argued as she tried to wriggle herself out of his grip.

"Not in the middle of the day and not inside my shop!"

The prostitute turned her head back toward Zeke and shouted, "I'll be waiting outside if you change your mind!"

A random thought shot through Zeke's head and he replied, "Wait!"

Jack froze and turned back to glare at Zeke. "What the hell do you mean by that? If you want this whore, do that outside my store."

The prostitute pulled her arm free and rubbed it with her other hand. "You see, Jack, your customer likes me."

"No, it's not that at all," Zeke groaned. "Just let her go out the back door."

Jack hurried over to Zeke and pulled him up from the chair and shook him. "You stinking pervert. Take your shit out of here and never come back." He started to push Zeke toward the door.

"Zeke's a good kid, Jack," Sheila called out.

"Shut your mouth, Sheila. This is my shop and my rules. No perverts and no hookers!"

The prostitute opened the front door and began to walk out. "Wait, not the front door!" Zeke yelled after her. She only winked at him and walked outside.

Jack was pushing Zeke toward the same door when his eyes opened too wide and his jaw slackened. There was a loud crashing sound and the front windows exploded as a car jumped the curb and sideswiped the storefront. The patrons and customers dived for the floor. Both men saw the car slam into the prostitute. Her body contorted and her face slammed into the hood just before the car passed the storefront and they lost sight of it. There was a second crashing sound and then quiet. "How the hell did you do that?" Jack gasped. He released his grip on Zeke and climbed over the broken glass and crushed door frame. Zeke followed behind him.

The car had crashed into one of the pillars supporting the overhanging roof of the mall. The prostitute was pinned between the car and pillar. She did not move and they assumed she was dead. An elderly man sat behind the wheel of the car. He wasn't moving either. Zeke looked around but could not see any other injured people. He pulled the phone from his pocket and dialed 911.

When the police had been notified, Zeke sat on the curb next to Jack, who was holding his head in his hands and breathing heavily. "It's okay, sir, it's all over now," he said.

"I'm sorry. I never should have assumed you were her client," Jack replied. "You're welcome back to my shop anytime." He extended his hand and said, "I'm Jack Watson. Please call me Jack."

Zeke shook his hand and said, "Thank you. I'm Zeke Thompson. Please call me Zeke."

"Zeke, tell me one thing. How did you know the car was coming?"

He sighed and replied, "I didn't. I just had a feeling in my mind that something bad was about to happen outside. I didn't know what it was, but it was like a flashing red light and siren telling me to keep everyone inside."

"Do you have a lot of these visions, Zeke?"

"I'd rather not talk about it, if you don't mind," he replied. "What a nightmare!"

"Have you ever seen that woman before?"

"No. I've been getting my hair cut in your shop for years, and this was the first time."

"Well, we have seen her a lot recently. But she's usually around here at closing time. Today was the first time she was here so early."

"It's too bad she changed her schedule," Zeke noted.

"You got that right," Jack agreed. "Come on inside and let me finish your haircut, Zeke. You look like shit right now."

§

It was 4:00 p.m. and Zeke was sitting at a small table in an interrogation room at the local police station. Everyone in the barbershop had told the police about him warning the woman not to go out front. It had already been reported in the local media that the driver had had a fatal heart attack just before the accident, causing him to press down on the accelerator and veer the car onto the sidewalk. The woman was also pronounced dead at the scene. Zeke had no idea what information he could provide, but here he sat and waited. He waited another ten minutes until the door opened and two detectives walked in and sat across the table from him.

"Good afternoon, Mr. Thompson. I'm Detective George Summers and this is Detective Sam Wainwright," the taller, blonde officer said. The officer with the dark hair and eyes only nodded his head.

You guys can just call me Zeke," he replied.

"Mr. Thompson, as you can imagine, this accident was a terrible tragedy. The driver died before the accident and the woman was killed by the impact," Summers said. "To me, it's an open and closed case, except for you."

"I don't understand."

"Mr. Thompson, everyone in that barbershop has stated that you warned that woman not to go out the front door more than once," Summers continued. "Did you have advanced knowledge that this would occur? Were you involved in this incident in any way?"

"Of course not! I just went to get my hair cut. Next thing I know, she's grabbing my knee and trying to solicit me," Zeke answered.

"Why did you warn her, Zeke?" Wainwright asked.

"Have you used her services before, Zeke?" Summers quizzed.

"No, I have not used her services!" Zeke exclaimed. "Listen, right after she touched my knee, a random thought went through my mind. I didn't see the car crash coming. I just had a feeling that no one should go out front at that time. That was it."

"Did you hear that, George? We've got a freaking prophet in our office," Wainwright grinned. "Are you a prophet, Zeke?"

"No, I just had a feeling, that's it. It's never happened before and I doubt it will happen again."

"Mr. Thompson, we have nothing on you, and you are free to go," Summers stated. The two officers stood up. "But do you mind if we try a little experiment, Zeke?"

"What are you talking about, George? This is very irregular," Sam noted.

"Hey, it's just in fun. I already told him he could go," Summers laughed. "Zeke, shake each of our hands and tell us something about our futures." Zeke stood and backed up to the mirror behind him.

"Just go, Zeke. Don't listen to my partner," Wainwright said.

"What's the big deal about shaking the guy's hand?" Summers argued. "You go first, Sam."

The other officer glared at his partner for a moment, and then extended his hand. "Zeke, it was a pleasure to meet you."

Zeke inched forward as though the man's hand was a ball of fire. He raised his right arm slowly and slipped his hand into Sam's and shook it. "Pleasure to meet you too."

"Anything?" Summers asked. Both men were staring at Zeke.

"I think your wife is pregnant," he squeaked.

Both officers laughed out loud. When he could speak, Wainwright said, "That's a good one, Zeke. My wife and I have been trying for years and nothing. Her gynecologist told her we should give up and consider in vitro."

"I'm sorry," Zeke sighed.

"Now it's my turn," Summers grinned, shoving his open palm toward Zeke, who took it gingerly and shook it. "Well?" he asked as they separated.

"I don't think I should say any more," Zeke groaned as he walked backward toward the wall behind him.

"Oh come on! You told Sam and it was hilarious. You have to tell," George begged.

"I don't know. Can I leave now?"

"It's okay, Zeke," Sam interjected. "We laughed about mine. Tell us."

Zeke looked down at the floor and mumbled something under his breath. "What did you see?" George urged.

"Your wife knows all about Stacey," Zeke sighed.

George's face turned bright red, and he started to move toward Zeke. "You son of a bitch! I'll get you for that!"

Sam grabbed his partner and pushed him to the opposite wall. He turned his head to Zeke and said, "You better get out of here now!" Zeke moved toward the door, staying as far from the police officers as possible. He left the room and closed the door behind him, making a beeline for his car. "What the hell is wrong with you, George? Do you want to get fired and lose your pension? Forget it. That stupid kid doesn't know shit."

George's arms went limp, and he leaned back against the wall. "I'm sorry, partner. I just couldn't believe what he said."

"He made it up, George, just like he made up the story about Shirley being pregnant!"

"No, Sam. The kid was right. I've been having an affair with Stacey Jones for almost a year now. How could Zeke know that?

And if he's right, and Maryann knows too, my marriage is over," George groaned.

"Our Stacey Jones? Detective Captain Stacy Jones?" Sam asked. George only nodded his head. "Oh my God!"

§

Zeke arrived at his parent's home in Chula Vista, California, in ten minutes flat. The traffic lights seemed to change to green just as he approached each intersection. He unlocked the front door and flew up the stairs and into his room, locking the door behind him. Zeke kicked off his shoes and climbed into bed, pulling the covers over his head. "What is going on with me?" he thought. "I must be losing my mind!" After a few minutes, he heard familiar scratching at the door. He rose and opened it for his dog, Chachis. The small poodle jumped up on the bed and waited for him. When he had climbed back into bed, the dog began to lick his face and jump about, wanting to play fetch, but Zeke was not in the mood. He rolled onto his side and the dog curled up next to him. Chachis was lucky, though. She fell asleep in a minute, while the memories of his day kept rattling around in Zeke's head. After ten minutes of fighting the thoughts, he stood and walked over to a small bookcase and removed the last of a long line of notebooks. He opened it to the first blank page and wrote:

"September 21, 2014. A horrible day, first I was propositioned by a hooker while getting a haircut. Then she was killed by a car, and I ended up in the police station. I don't think those guys will be very friendly in the future."

He stared at the words and considered tearing out the page. He took his pen and wrote a final sentence.

"Three visions, one of which came true already. RIP."

He closed the notebook and pressed it back in its place on the shelf. He pulled the notebook next to that one and looked at the cover. It read, "ZT Journal. August 2012 to November 2013. 684 visions; 317 known true." He let his fingers run over the indentations in the cover from his writing and smiled.

"Zeke, how are you?"

He looked up and saw his father standing in the open door. "I'm great, Dad, but I had kind of a tough day." Abe Thompson was fifty-one years old, married to Sarah for twenty-five years with one son and one daughter named Rachel. He had been an accountant since he graduated from college, twenty-nine years ago.

Abe walked in and sat on the bed and started to pet Chachis, who was thrilled for the attention. "Do you want to tell me about it?" Zeke pulled the other notebook from the shelf, opened it and handed it to his father, who read the new posting. "Yikes! I heard about that accident in my car on the way home. Why did you go to the police station?"

"I warned that woman not to go out of the barbershop, but she wouldn't listen. I guess the cops thought I knew something, but it was just one of those vision things," he replied.

"Why won't they be friendly now?"

"They made me shake their hands and tell them something about the future," Zeke said. "It didn't go over well at all."

"You know, all of these things could be lucky guesses," Abe noted as he stood. "If not, you have a pretty miraculous gift, son."

"Thanks, Dad, but it doesn't feel special to me now. It's a pain in the ass."

"There's a reason for everything, Zeke. We just have to follow our path until we understand."

"Did they teach you that at the University of Iowa?"

Abe laughed. His laugh was deep and throaty and reminded Zeke of his childhood and how much he and his father loved to watch stand-up comedians on television. They would sit together laughing until they could not breathe. What happened to those times, he wondered.

"Dinner will be ready soon," Abe noted. "You can tell us more about everything downstairs."

"Okay, Dad," he replied as his father walked down the hall and then down the stairs. Chachis jumped off the bed and followed Abe, hoping to get a treat.

Zeke sat quietly for several minutes as he usually did after being faced with the truth of his visions. By forcing his mind to be quiet, eventually he would remember that he saw something, and he was not the cause of the incident. He remembered his vision of Detective Wainwright's wife being pregnant. That was a good thing, he thought. Why did that vision not come true? Why was it always the bad ones that had a habit of being verified? What could possibly be wrong with more good visions? He stood up and stretched his aching back, and then headed downstairs, summoned by the smell of freshly baked lasagna coming out of the oven.

§

After dinner, Zeke and his father sat in the family room, watching Sunday Night Football, another father-son tradition that Zeke loved. Abe had a ravenous appetite for professional football. Zeke preferred the opportunity to just hang out with his dad. He knew he would move out soon. He was twenty-two already. If not for the terrible economy, he'd already be working and earning enough to rent his own apartment. He wanted to stay in the area, unlike his sister who had moved to southern

Florida three years ago when she graduated. "How's the job search going?" his mother, Sarah, asked from across the counter in the kitchen, where she was washing the dinner dishes.

"Okay, I guess," he replied. "I'm hoping to get a second interview with one company. I thought the first went great!" he replied.

"You'll land on your feet, son," Abe stated. "You're my son, so you're smart. It's just a matter of time. Why don't you get us a couple beers, Zeke? It's not football without a cold one."

"Sure thing," he replied as he stood up and walked toward the kitchen. He pulled open the refrigerator just as the doorbell rang.

"Who the heck would be coming here at this hour?" Abe complained. "It's freaking eight o'clock."

"It's okay, Dad, I'll get it," Zeke said. He closed the refrigerator and walked away toward the front door. He switched on the porch light and opened the door. The two detectives were standing outside. "What is it now?"

"Zeke, we want to talk to you for a minute on non-police business if we can," Sam said. "For one thing, George wants to apologize." Zeke stepped out of the way so the two men could enter. He led them to a couch in the living room and sat on a chair across from them.

Abe joined them, saying, "What's the meaning of this? Who are you guys, and what do you want from my son?"

Zeke stood and said, "It's okay, Dad. These are the two detectives I spoke to earlier. Guys, this is my dad, Abe Thompson."

After the officers introduced themselves, Abe stood next to his son. "We're listening."

George cleared his throat. His eyes were firmly fixed on the floor. After a moment of silence, he began, "First of all, I'm sorry for being angry down at the station. That was totally unprofessional, and I apologize." Zeke smiled and nodded, while Abe looked totally confused. "But most of all, I want to thank you for saving my marriage."

"What?" Abe gasped.

"Mr. Thompson, your son told me that my wife knew I was having an affair," George started. Abe looked back and forth between Zeke and the officer. "At first, I was pissed off, like he was telling on me. But I was the one having an affair. I went home and talked it out with my wife." He chuckled softly. "She's known about the whole thing for months, but never hinted at it. I apologized to her over and again. I don't know what will happen, but at least she and I aren't living a lie anymore. Tomorrow, I'm asking to be reassigned, so Maryann and I can try to work things out."

"I hope you two can reconcile," Zeke said.

"Thank you."

"My turn," Sam said, grinning from ear to ear. "He pulled two cigars from his jacket pocket and handed them to Abe and Zeke.

"She's pregnant?" Zeke asked.

"Yes, isn't that a miracle?" Sam exclaimed. "I stopped at the drug store on the way home and bought one of those pregnancy tests. When I gave it to my wife, I could see the daggers coming out of her eyes. She told me I was being hurtful and cruel. I told her about your vision, and she laughed at me. Truth be told, I felt pretty damned small at that point."

"This doesn't seem like a happy story, Detective," Abe replied.

"But it didn't end there," Sam continued. "For some reason, she went ahead and tried the test. I was just washing the dishes when she ran out of the bathroom crying. I felt like shit. I was certain the test failed and she was really pissed again. But then she told me it was positive! I couldn't believe it. Thank you, Zeke."

"I didn't do anything really," Zeke said. "She was pregnant whether you two knew it or not."

"You don't understand, Zeke. Because of you, we know now, not tomorrow or three weeks from now. You gave us hope."

"You're welcome," Zeke smiled.

"We'd better get going, partner," George said as he stood up. "We've both got wives who are anxious to see us." He shook hands with the two Thompson men. "You've got a great son, Mr. Thompson."

"Thank you, Detective," Abe replied. "Thanks for stopping by."

"We'll let you get back to your game now. Who's winning?" Sam asked.

"Chargers are up by seven, the last time I looked," Abe replied.

"Take care," Sam said as he shook the men's hands, and then the two officers walked out.

As he turned the lock in the door, Zeke said, "Let's get back to the game, Dad."

"Don't you need to update your notebook, son?"

"It'll wait. The game comes first," Zeke replied as he hugged his father.

# Chapter 2

It was 7:00 a.m. when Zeke woke to the sound of the front door opening and closing. He stood up and looked out front to see his father climbing into his car, backing out of the driveway and driving off to work. With no job and little prospect of finding one soon, he lay back on his bed and dozed off. Within a minute, he was fast asleep again.

In his dream, Zeke woke to the sound of his mother crying. He hurried over to the master bedroom where he found her sitting on a chair by the window sobbing. His sister, Rachel, was sitting on the opposite chair with reddened eyes and the tracks of teardrops on her cheeks. He walked over and tried to comfort his mother by touching her cheek, but could not feel her. It seemed as though either he or the two women were ghosts, oblivious to the presence of the other. "When did they tell him?" Rachel asked.

"About ten o'clock this morning," Sarah replied. "Jack asked him to stay a little late so he could remove his things when the rest of the staff weren't around."

"What a heartless bastard!" Rachel exclaimed. "Dad's worked for that man for more than a decade and this is how they treat him?"

"It will be okay, Rachel," her mother sobbed. "Companies reorganize all the time. That's the way things are. Unfortunately, the economy still isn't good, but we have money for a while. We just have to have faith."

"Mom, you know how hard Zeke has been looking for work. There aren't any jobs anymore. You can all move to Florida and stay with me."

Sarah smiled warmly and held Rachel's hands. "Thank you, sweetheart, but we'll wait a while to see what happens. I think things will work out."

"I don't know how you can rationalize that, Mom," Rachel argued. She turned to stare at Zeke with her dark blue eyes. "What do you think, Zeke?"

Zeke's eyes popped open and he sat up in bed. The dream was still locked in his mind, replaying over and again. He looked at his bookcase and thought about writing down this dream, but then changed his mind. "Dreams are just dreams," he said out loud. He looked at his alarm clock and saw it was 7:20 a.m. He climbed out of bed and walked to the bathroom to get ready for his day. He had an interview later this morning and needed to look his best.

Seconds later, he rushed back into the room and grabbed the last notebook and began to write: "September 22, 2014. Dad fired, please God, don't let this one come true. 7, 21, 23, 38, 41, 46." He looked at the words and thought about marking them out. Instead, he slipped the book back in place and went to take a shower.

§

Three hours later, Zeke was sitting across a conference table from Mr. Smith, the human resources manager for a small local firm. Their ad said they were looking for a junior accountant to supervise accounts payable and the general ledger. Zeke was hopeful, but all too often, there were hundreds of applicants for every job, and his prospects were not great. Smith sat quietly reviewing Zeke's resume. Every few seconds, he would look up and smile thoughtfully at the young man. Finally, he said, "Mr. Thompson, let me be totally honest with you. Yesterday, a major firm made a purchase offer to our CEO. While it is too early to know, if this sale goes through, this office will likely reorganize, so I can't say how permanent any jobs are."

Zeke felt his phone vibrating in his pocket. It was after ten o'clock now and Zeke had a feeling his father was calling him about the layoff. "Mr. Smith, I understand the state of the economy, and that nothing is really permanent nowadays. I just want to work hard and help out where I can."

"That's admirable, Zeke. I'll hold on to your resume, and once things calm down a bit and we decide to move forward, I'll let you know," Smith said as he stood and extended his hand. Zeke stood and shook his hand. "Have a good day."

"Thank you for your valuable time, Mr. Smith," Zeke said, and then turned and walked out of the room and out onto the street. A new thought buzzed in his head, starting when he touched Smith's hand. He leaned back against the building and pulled out his phone. He saw a voice-mail from his father, but first opened his notepad and typed, "Balmore Enterprises acquired by First National. San Diego office to close by end of year." He closed the app and tapped the key to play his voice-mail.

His father's voice said, "Hey, Zeke, it's the old man. Things are kind of shitty here today. I just got laid off. Don't worry, son. Everything will be okay. I sure hope you didn't have that vision! That would really screw up your day. I'm looking forward to watching the game with you tonight. I love you. Bye." He sighed heavily, overwhelmed by the confirmation of his dream. Noticing a coffee shop just down the block, he headed toward it.

Minutes later, Zeke was sitting at a small table near the front windows of the Starbucks cafe, taking sips of his venti cafe latte. The store was mostly empty at this hour, sometime between the morning commute and lunch hour. He glanced back at the clerk behind the counter. She appeared to be about his age, very cute with black hair in a pixie cut, and bright red lipstick. She glanced over at him and smiled. Zeke quickly turned to look away and blushed slightly. Two men sat at a second table close by. They were in a deep conversation about something, but Zeke tried hard not to listen. Just beyond them, a tall, leggy blonde was sitting and typing on her laptop. Zeke focused on his drink, faced with the realization that his father was now out of work too and there was no way he could help out the family. His brain sped up with thoughts of losing the house and even living on the street. There had to be something he could do! But there was no way his finding a job could make up for Abe's income. Things were about to become really bad.

"Hi there," said a voice to his left. He turned to see the clerk standing next to him. She extended her hand and said, "I'm Bea Watson."

Zeke stood and shook her hand. "Zeke Thompson. It's nice to meet you."

"I hope I'm not being too forward, but would you like to join me for lunch?"

"Sure!" he exclaimed. "How long do you have for lunch?"

"My shift just ended. It's that twenty-nine hours per week thing. Fortunately, I have another source of income, but it still makes the paychecks pretty small."

"You're lucky, Bea," Zeke replied. "At least you have two jobs. I'm having a hard enough time getting one."

"After we eat, I'm going to buy a Powerball ticket. Maybe you should too. I've been told that I'm pretty lucky." The realization struck Zeke's mind like a lightning bolt. The six numbers he wrote down in his journal earlier. Could they be lotto numbers? The woman took his hand and began to pull him toward the door. "There's a great burger joint down the block. Let's go."

A man's voice said, "Don't forget our appointment, Bea?" Zeke noticed that the two men at the nearby table were watching them. "Be ready in an hour, okay?"

"You got it, Granddad!" she smiled. "I'll be ready."

As they moved down the sidewalk, Zeke began to engage his mind in a moral dilemma. Would it be cheating if he used his unique ability to win the lottery? Some people already knew of his gift and might make the connection. There was the physical proof on the page of his journal. On the other hand, there was no way anyone would know whether other lottery winners did the same thing. If he did not follow the vision, what would his family do for income? The warmth of Bea's hand in his brought him back to reality as they stepped into the small restaurant, the smell of frying potatoes filling the room.

They sat at a small booth. Bea began to flip through the menu while Zeke contemplated his situation. Why was this pretty woman so interested in him, he wondered. Rather than asking directly, he took another tack to learn more about her. "Bea, you called that man Granddad. He didn't look that old."

She set the menu down and smiled slightly. "Actually, both of them are my grandfathers. I'm sorry. I should have introduced you. Dave and Charlie are great guys." She picked up the menu again and said, "I recommend the black and blue burger, if you like blue cheese, that is."

"You didn't answer my question," he replied.

The server was standing at their table. "What can I get you folks?"

"Black and blue for me," Bea said. "Medium. Well-done fries and a Diet Coke."

"I'll have the same," Zeke noted as he handed the menu to the server. She thanked them and walked away, returning moments later with their drinks.

Bea took a sip of soda and looked at Zeke. "Let's say my grandparents and parents got married very young."

"Is that the truth, or is that just what you want me to believe?"

"Well, it is a bit complicated, Zeke. I'd say it's true though. Why are you so interested in them?" she asked.

"Frankly, that's the only thing I know about you. I am a bit surprised you asked me to lunch."

Bea cleared her throat and looked down for a moment. Then she raised her head and looked at him again. "Let me lay it on the line, Zeke. I know all about your visions, and I came here specifically for this chance to meet you." He stared back dumbfounded. She opened her purse and removed a folded sheet of paper, unfolded it and handed it to him.

Zeke looked at her in disbelief and then looked at the paper. It was a copy of the sheet in his journal he had written only a few hours ago. "Where did you get this? This is impossible." The part of the page below the lottery numbers was blacked out.

The server returned and set their plates in front of them. "Anything else?" she said.

"No, thank you. This looks perfect like always," Bea replied. Zeke remained staring at her. The server walked away. Bea cut her sandwich in half and then took a bite. "Man, these things are great!" She looked up and saw him just staring blankly. "Zeke, please eat your food before it gets cold." He looked down and seemed surprised as though the plate had suddenly materialized in front of him. "I'm from the future, Zeke. My job is to keep an eye on the course of time. People in your century are just beginning to realize that time is not a straight line that only goes forward. There are eddies and bumps in time, going in both directions. Just like what happens today affects tomorrow, what happens tomorrow affects today."

Zeke focused on his burger, which was spicy, cheesy, and excellent. He tried to understand the woman's words, but they were too strange to believe. Why would this person come from the future to see him? That didn't make any sense. "Assuming any of that is true, what has this got to do with me? Why don't you take me to your future so I can believe you?"

"I wish I could, but that would defeat the whole purpose for me being here," she replied while dipping a fry into a puddle of ketchup. "Zeke, you need to buy that lottery ticket. My world depends on it."

He laughed out loud. "What? That's crazy! The future depends on me buying a lottery ticket. That's absurd."

She reached across the table and took his hands in hers. "Zeke, I don't have much time, so let me lay it out for you. That ticket wins a 200-million-dollar prize. That money resolves the money needs of you and your family. That's good, right?" He nodded. "But there's more to it than that. Without having to worry about money, your father begins to write books."

"He has always loved to write. He showed me a bunch of poetry he wrote back in high school once."

"His novels talk about the fragility of time and how people might use it as a weapon. The more he writes, the more the scientific community starts to play with the concepts. Over the years, it leads to the discovery that time is as fluid as water. It can be dammed up, diverted, and even changed. Centuries later, it leads to a global war that almost destroys the planet!" she exclaimed.

"You want him to start a global war?"

"Abraham Thompson didn't start the war, Zeke. That happened hundreds of years later. It was the abuse of time and thirst for global domination that started the war."

Zeke shook his head. "I still don't understand why you want a war."

"You're missing the point," she scowled. "The horror of the war led to the first extraterrestrial contact. The Kalideans could not stand by and watch us destroy ourselves. They came to Earth to stop us. That ended the war and led to the advances that became my Earth. If Abraham doesn't write those books, the war will not occur."

"But the war did occur, or else you wouldn't be here."

She sighed heavily. "I know it's complicated, Zeke, but you have to trust me. There are others who seek to change the line of time in order to prevent the war. There are civilizations in the galaxy who would love to conquer this planet. Without the war and the intervention by the Kalideans, Earth will be enslaved."

Zeke pushed the plate away. "I think I lost my appetite. Bea, I think you are a beautiful woman, but certainly you must be nuts if you expect me to believe that tale."

"What's the worst that can happen?" she asked. "You don't win, and you can forget me forever as the crazy girl from Starbucks. Or you do win, and your parents don't have to lose their house and live on the street."

"They'll lose the house?"

"I don't know that, Zeke. Honestly, in my history, you buy the ticket and win. But are you willing to take that risk with your family?" She opened her purse and removed three twenty-dollar bills. She slipped two into the folder containing their check and handed the third to Zeke. "Here, now you won't even be out the cost of the ticket."

Without his noticing, Bea's two grandfathers had entered the restaurant and strolled over to their table. "You about ready?" one of them said.

"All set here," she smiled. "Let me introduce you two to Zeke Thompson. Zeke, these are my grandfathers, Dave Brewster and Charlie Watson."

"It's a pleasure to meet you both," Zeke said as he shook their hands.

"I've read a lot about you, son," Dave said.

"Take care of our future," Charlie added.

"Huh?" Zeke squeaked as Bea stood up.

"I'll see you later, Zeke," she said as she bent over and kissed him on the cheek. "Can you believe it? I kissed Ezekiel Thompson."

"Wait, can I ask you another question, Bea?"

"Make it quick. We only have a couple of minutes," Dave replied.

"Let's say we win the lottery, and my dad writes all of those books. What happens to me?" Zeke asked.

The two men chuckled. Bea sat down next to him and held his hand tightly. She leaned in and whispered in his ear, "There are a lot more notebooks to complete. You'll be a busy guy, believe me."

"And why was the rest of that page blacked out?"

She took his head in her hands and turned it to face her. She pressed her lips lightly against his and then stood up between her grandfathers. "You're so silly, Zeke. You haven't written the rest yet. We don't need to tell you the future. That's your job." The three walked out of the restaurant and down the sidewalk.

The server walked up to the table and took the folder and slipped it in her apron. Then she began to gather the dishes. "Where can I buy a Powerball ticket around here?" he asked.

"Right across the street and a couple doors down, there is a liquor store. Good luck!" she grinned and walked away.

He left the restaurant and walked toward the store. He realized he did not know which of the six numbers was the Powerball number, so he decided to buy six tickets, just to be sure.

§

As Zeke pulled his car onto the driveway, he noticed his father's car already there. That seemed odd. In his dream, Abe's boss asked him to stay late so as not to upset the rest of the employees. Now it was two o'clock in the afternoon, and he was home. That discrepancy made Zeke very happy. Perhaps Bea really was a crazy person and the rest of her story was just a fantasy. His father would not be responsible for a world war after all. He pulled the tickets from his pocket and considered tearing them up. He thought better of it and shoved them back into his pocket. He walked into the house and found his mother sitting at the table in the breakfast nook, watching her husband sitting out on the patio. Zeke kissed her on the cheek and then walked out back.

Abe sat there silently. Chachis was sitting on his lap and he held a glass with whisky over ice in his left hand, slowly swirling the liquid. Zeke patted his father on the shoulder and sat next to him. Abe's eyes were bloodshot and teary. "Everything will be okay, Zeke," he sighed.

"I know, Dad. I need you to sign a few things for me, okay?" He pulled the lottery tickets from his pocket and handed them to Abe.

"Is this our investment portfolio?" Abe laughed.

"Just sign them on the back, Dad. It's for good luck."

Abe began to sign them dutifully. After the fourth signature, he dropped his pen and looked up at his son. "These all have the same numbers, except they're moved around. What's this about? This wasn't another of your dreams, was it?"

"Not every vision I have comes true, Dad. And besides, with neither of us working, I figured we might as well take a shot."

"I'm not sure this is ethical, son."

"What are we going to do for money if neither of us can get a job?" Zeke asked.

Abe thought about what to say next, but then signed the last two tickets. "Let's never do this again, okay? I appreciate what you're trying to do, but it scares me a bit. It's almost like stealing in a way."

"Never again, cross my heart," Zeke said. "You keep the tickets, Dad. It's your money, if we win."

"Our money, son," Abe noted as he put the tickets and pen back in his shirt pocket. "How was your day? As you can see, mine was awful." He took a sip of whisky.

"The interview was a bomb. That company is on the verge of being bought out. I saw the press release in my mind saying that office was closing. Then I had lunch with a gorgeous, but completely insane, woman who works at the nearby Starbucks."

"Insane in what way?"

"She said she came from the future, Dad. She talked about a war that leads to the first contact with extraterrestrials. But she first told me to buy these tickets. She even gave me the money to pay for them."

"That's pretty crazy, alright." Abe took another sip of his drink.

"There was one thing that made me sort of believe her," Zeke noted. His father set his glass down and looked at him. Zeke pulled the folded paper from his pocket and handed it to his father.

Abe looked at the page in disbelief. "This is your handwriting, right?" Zeke nodded. "Did you write this today? You saw that I was being laid-off and here are those lottery numbers too! This is unbelievable. Did you give this to her?"

"She gave it to me, Dad!" he exclaimed. "I've never seen that woman before or even been to that Starbucks. Also, no one ever looks at my notebooks. I know you and Mom would never mention them to anyone. Rachel knows about them, but I wrote this page this morning! Isn't this weird?"

"I just don't understand. But maybe there is hope for us, even with me out of work. Just maybe there's a chance it will all work out, even though I have no idea what to do next."

Zeke smiled and said, "Maybe you should write a book."

# Chapter 3

Zeke watched the first half of the football game with his father. As the game progressed, Zeke began to remember something. At first, it was just an impression in his mind. With each play on the field, it became a little clearer. There was something in one of his old journals that was nagging at him. What was it, he wondered. When the game stopped for the two-minute warning, the thought resolved in his head, as though he had wiped the steam from the shower door on a cold morning and was able to see the rest of the room. He stood up. "What's up?" Abe said. "You're not going to watch?"

"I just remembered something in one of my old journals. I'm going to go check it out. I shouldn't be long." He left the family room and headed up the stairs and into his room. He pulled a chair in front of his bookcase and froze. One of the notebooks was slightly pulled out. "Who did that?" he said aloud. Zeke knew someone had been in his room and looked through his notebooks. That was a terrible invasion of his privacy. He felt betrayed. Only his mother was there all day. How could she do that? He pulled the notebook out and noticed a page was marked with a paper clip. Zeke never did that. He wondered what was going on. He opened the book to the marked page and noticed a small piece of paper was held in place by the clip. His head turned to mush and he almost passed out when he read it, "Thought you'd be looking for this. XOXO, Bea." He stood and raced over to his parent's room where his mother was sitting and reading a book. "Mom, did anyone come over today?"

"No, not a soul," she replied. "I was here all day and the doorbell never rang. Is something wrong?"

"No, it's okay. Thanks," he stated and walked back to his room and closed the door behind him.

Sitting on his bed with the book in his lap, he pulled the slip of paper from under the clip, folded it and placed it in his wallet. Then he read his posting:

"September 10, 2001. Horrible dreams about planes crashing into buildings, death and destruction. What is wrong with this world? The good news is we had a substitute teacher in math today. She was so cute with short, black hair and red lipstick, and her name was Bea Watson. Too bad she's too old for me."

He removed the clip and slipped the notebook back on the bookcase. He held his head in his hands and tried to rationalize what was happening. That memory was thirteen years old and yet he was convinced it was the same Bea Watson, even though she looked exactly the same age. If that was true, then the rest of what she said had to be true too, but it was too bizarre. He thought about discussing the situation with his parents, but quickly realized he would not believe it if someone else had told him either. He changed into his pajamas and headed downstairs for the second half.

When he entered the family room, the DVR was on hold and Abe was talking on his cell phone. His father motioned for him to bring a couple of beers and Zeke happily complied. He brought the bottles over and handed one to Abe and then sat down on the other couch.

"Yeah, Jack, I understand what you're saying, but it doesn't make any sense," Abe said into the microphone. "Why does Fred Drake want to talk to me? You guys fired me and now the CEO wants to chat me up? What's going on, and be honest." After a minute of listening, he said, "Okay. I've got a lot of free time, as it turns out. Just let me know. Bye." He disconnected the call and turned to his son. "Can you believe the audacity of those guys?

They let me go, and now the CEO wants to talk to me about my experience at Reliant. Just leave me the hell alone!"

"That's unbelievable, Dad. Are they going to offer you money to keep quiet?"

Abe frowned. "No. I think that's very unlikely. It's more like salving their wounds in the market. Look how good we are to our former employees. We value their opinions. Bullshit. I had to sign a bunch of documents saying I have to be a quiet guy or I don't get my severance. I'm not stupid enough to lose the money over a couple minutes of payback. These Reliant guys are ruthless and they employ plenty of attack-dog attorneys."

"I'm sorry you have to go through this, Dad."

"Thanks Zeke, that means a lot. Let's forget about them and enjoy the game. Cheers." The two tapped their beers together and took a drink. Abe hit the play button on the DVR.

§

Zeke woke early on Wednesday and began jotting notes in his journal. He did not remember dreaming, but the words poured out of him. He wrote so fast he could barely understand where his thoughts had come from. He put the journal back in its place and set his laptop on his lap and opened it. After logging on, he opened his web browser and navigated to the California Lottery page. As Bea had said, the Powerball jackpot later today was $200 million. He smiled and closed the machine, setting it on top of his bookcase. Then he made his bed quickly and headed to the shower.

Standing in the stall with the hot water pouring over his head, he fondly remembered his life when Rachel lived at home. Too often, he would run out of hot water after her unending showers. Her cosmetics, creams and shampoos covered most of the counter space, forcing him into a tiny corner. Now the bathroom was his, but that made him more sad than happy. After drying himself, he got dressed and walked out of the bathroom. He heard his phone ringing and hurried to his bedroom to answer it. The caller ID said "Out of Area." He clicked connect and said, "Hello."

"Hey, Zeke, it's Bea," the voice on the other end said. "I was just calling to see if you got my note."

"How and why did you break into my room and rifle through my stuff? My mom said no one came over yesterday."

She laughed. "You're still thinking too linearly. How often do you go through your old notebooks?"

"What's your point?"

"Do you remember the last time you looked at that particular book?" she asked.

"No, but it was partially pulled out. I always leave my notebooks neatly aligned," he argued.

"Always?" she scoffed.

"Well, usually I do. But why did you do it?"

"I figured you'd put two and two together when we met again Monday. It could take you days or weeks to find that entry, so I marked it for you," she said.

"So you had to do it then, since that's the second time we met!"

She laughed again. "You're too logical, Zeke. Remember I'm from the future. I can go to yesterday tomorrow or to tomorrow a thousand years from now."

"Your time talk is making me nuts."

"It goes with the territory, believe me."

"When can I see you again, Bea?" he asked.

"Not for a while, I'm afraid," she replied. "But I will show up from time to time, I promise. First, your family needs to win the lottery tonight. Then you'll believe me more since you'll have proof positive. You're going to be very busy now, Zeke, but I will see you before you know it."

"Tell me where you are and I'll come over now."

She laughed again. "I'm afraid that's not possible."

"Where are you, Bea?"

"You'll think I'm crazy again, but I'm in my office at the main library of the Ezekiel Thompson College of Science and Prophecy."

"You're nuts and I'm even crazier because I want to see you."

"Take care, Zeke, and I'll talk to you soon." The line disconnected. He pulled out the notebook and wrote the name of the college at the end of his earlier writings.

"Let's go out for breakfast, Zeke," his father said from the other side of the door.

"I'll be right there, Dad," he replied as he slipped the notebook back into its place.

§

Cafe Jalisco was not crowded at this hour. Zeke fondly remembered coming here almost every Saturday morning since he was a little boy. Abe was always working, so it was a real treat to be able to go out together on a Wednesday morning. The server brought three cups of coffee along with chips and salsa and took their order. There was never a need for menus since they had been coming here forever. Abe always ordered pozole and Sarah usually ordered mole enchiladas. Zeke tended to switch between the pozole, an omelet and the green chilaquiles. Today was a chilaquiles day. Sarah put down her coffee and asked, "Zeke, what is going on with the lottery tickets?"

"Mom, the odds of winning are like one in fifty million. What's the big deal?"

"You don't think your journals make this a bit unethical?"

"Well, it's already done," Zeke noted. "I already promised not to do this again, but remember that we really need the money now that Dad is unemployed. Also, there's no way anyone would believe I knew the numbers ahead of time. I just wrote down six numbers in my journal. That could be a safe combination for all I know."

"Then why did you buy the tickets?" Sarah asked.

"It was the crazy woman he had lunch with who suggested that," Abe noted.

"Yeah, you mentioned something about that," Sarah said to her husband. "Tell me more about her, Zeke."

"First, she is very gorgeous and super smart. Except for her claim to be from the future, she's an ideal woman."

"That is a pretty big exception, son," Abe replied.

"Well, if she claims to be from the future, then I'm not worried about the tickets anymore," Sarah chuckled. "That's the most ridiculous thing I've ever heard."

The server arrived with their food which, fortunately, kept Zeke from talking more about Bea Watson. He was already starting to have feelings for this crazy girl from the future. She was either insane, in which case he would avoid her, or she really was a time traveler, and then Zeke might be able to travel with her and have a real relationship somewhere in the folds and eddies of time. He imagined what it would be like to live in the distant future with flying cars and interstellar starships discovering new worlds. Then he considered that Bea might have a boyfriend or husband in that time. He pushed that thought away.

"Oh shit," Abe groaned.

Zeke escaped his revelry to notice his father's former boss entering the restaurant with a couple of other managers for an early lunch. They sat at a table at the far end of the restaurant and did not seem to notice the Thompsons. "Do you want to leave, honey?" his wife asked.

"No way," Abe stated. "I introduced Jack to this place and I'm not running away from him anymore." He continued to eat his soup. "But let's take our time so they leave first and I don't have to talk to him."

They sat quietly eating their breakfast for several minutes. Abe was angry that his boss showed up and did not want him to hear his voice. Zeke did not want to discuss his journals or the time traveler. Sarah was satisfied to be together with her family. Their server came by to refresh their coffees and left their bill. While standing there, she inadvertently touched Zeke and the image of her accepting an engagement ring rolled across his mind. He smiled at her but did not say a word, although he did take his phone out and type in a quick note for his journal later. Zeke looked up from his phone to see Jack Lance walking toward their table. Both of his parents were focused on their plates, so Zeke cleared his throat to get their attention. As he stepped up to the table, he grabbed their bill. "That isn't necessary, Jack." Abe said.

"It's the least I can do, Abe," the other man smiled. "Hi, Sarah. Hi, Zeke. It's good to see you both again. You take it easy, pal." He turned and walked back to his table where the other two had already headed for the door.

Abe chuckled. "You know, I worked with Ken and Rick for years, and neither one said a word or even acknowledged me."

"They're probably too upset now, honey," Sarah said.

"Yeah, I guess you're probably right," Abe sighed.

"Dad, when Mr. Lance was here, he bumped up against me," Zeke said.

"Oh no," Sarah moaned.

"What did you see, son?"

"The whole site will be closed in six months. Mr. Lance has heard rumors, but Mr. Drake will make the announcement next week when he's out here to see you."

"Oh no," Abe agreed.

§

After breakfast, Zeke drove over to the barbershop to see how his new friend, Jack Watson, was doing. There was a large work crew removing the damaged plate glass and framing while a truckload of new materials sat waiting. Plywood sheets had been quickly assembled into a makeshift temporary wall so the store could open again. As he walked toward the store, he saw Jack standing outside with a cup of coffee in his hand watching the workers. Zeke called out, "How's it going, Jack?"

The other man turned around and smiled when he saw Zeke. "It's coming together, Zeke. You're not here for another haircut already, are you?"

"No, I just wanted to check up on you."

"That's very neighborly of you, Zeke. It will be another couple of days until the new storefront is finished. Thankfully, we're all renters here, so the landlord has to pay for everything. By the way, I should tell you that a reporter has been nosing around recently. She heard the story about you warning the woman before she died. She wanted to talk to you for a human interest story or something." He stuck his hand into his pocket. "She gave me a business card to give you when I saw you next."

He removed a card and looked at it, then handed it to Zeke. "This is it."

Zeke read the card: "Shannon Thorpe, San Diego Union-Tribune." He pushed it into his pocket and replied, "Okay, but I'm not sure I want to talk to a reporter."

"It's your call, man. Most folks would love to get their fifteen minutes of fame."

"I'll think about it," Zeke said. "Did anyone tell her my name?"

"Not me, but it's possible that Sheila did. She talked to the reporter more than most of us. Don't freak out, kid, all you have to do is say, 'No, thank you.' "

"Okay, I understand. Well, I'll let you get back to it."

"Zeke, let me ask you a question before you go. The day of the accident, I asked you if you have these visions a lot and you said you didn't want to talk about it. Do you want to talk now?"

"I've had them from time to time, but they don't come true that often. Most are like the one here. A feeling runs through my mind just minutes before something happens. They seem less likely to come true when I have them longer in advance," Zeke said.

"Makes perfect sense to me."

"How so?"

"The future hasn't happened yet, Zeke. At every second, people can change their minds and the wind can change. The more seconds between your vision and the event, the more opportunity for things to change," Jack said.

"That's brilliant, Jack," Zeke replied. "Something just crossed my mind and I need to ask you a question." The other man nodded and took a sip of coffee. "I met two people with your last name the other day. Do you know a Charlie and Bea Watson?"

Jack grinned and said, "I'd rather not talk about that right now." He laughed and walked back into his store.

§

Zeke and his father sat in absolute silence in front of the television. Neither moved a muscle and both held their breath as the Powerball numbers were called. The winning numbers were 7, 21, 23, 38, 41, and the Powerball was 46. Abe selected the ticket with the correct numbers and turned it over and over in his hands. Zeke sat bewildered with the recognition that Bea Watson was indeed from the future. She was the one who suggested the Powerball lottery. Perhaps he would have figured it out, but the idea of a ticket came from her. There was a pop in the kitchen and both men turned to see Sarah with a bottle of Dom Perignon champagne in her hand. "I put this in the refrigerator after breakfast," she reported with a beaming smile across her face. "Thank you, Zeke."

"I can't believe it," Abe said at last. "This is the winning ticket. This can't be happening. Can we keep this, Zeke? Are we stealing this prize?"

"We are absolutely going to keep it, Dad!" he exclaimed. "Neither one of us has a job and the economy sucks. When those numbers went through my head, I was no different from anyone else who picks numbers for a ticket. People win lotteries all the time from numbers they picked."

Sarah brought a tray with the bottle and three flutes and set it on the coffee table. Zeke poured the champagne and handed a glass to each, and then offered a toast, "To family!" They clicked their glasses together and took a drink.

"What do we do now?" Abe asked. "I don't even know how to cash this thing in."

"First of all, don't tell anyone about this until it's been submitted," Sarah warned. "If anyone knew we had this ticket, God knows what they'd do to get it."

"Dad, there is a lottery office in San Diego. I recommend we go there tomorrow morning and claim the prize."

"I can't believe this is happening," Abe sighed.

Zeke was also in disbelief, but not about the money. His visions had changed from random guesses that sometimes came true to highly detailed premonitions of things that were destined to occur. Six winning lottery numbers was not random. And then there was Bea Watson. How did she have that page from his journal? Could she really be working in a college named after him in the distant future? Would that institution have all of his journals preserved for their students? The lottery would change everything. The Thompsons were now newsworthy, and Zeke Thompson had foreseen the car crash just days before picking the winning lottery numbers. That woman from the newspaper had a big story, but did not know it yet. In days she would, and then she would chase him down. Suddenly, Zeke had a pain in his stomach, knowing that his invisible life in Chula Vista was now over.

# Chapter 4

There were two Starbucks cafes within a half mile of the Thompson residence. Zeke suggested that Shannon Thorpe meet him at one o'clock just down the hill. It usually had more customers and he thought he would be less conspicuous there. He sat quietly with his cafe latte steaming in front of him. He and his father had gone to the Lottery Office when it first opened and completed the forms and submitted the original ticket. Both men kept a photocopy of the ticket in their wallets. Zeke sipped his coffee and looked around the room. A man was busy typing into his laptop two tables to his left. He wore the headset from his iPhone, most likely listening to his favorite tunes. The sitting area was full of young women talking about a wedding or other event that was scheduled for that weekend. A line of five people waited patiently for their turn at the counter while looking at their smart phones.

A pretty young woman stepped through the doorway and walked toward the other man. She wore a knee-length skirt and white blouse. She was very fair with blonde hair and big green eyes. She approached the other man and said, "Mr. Thompson?" The man shook his head but never looked at her.

Zeke stood up and said, "I'm Zeke Thompson. You must be Shannon Thorpe."

She walked over and shook his hand. "Thank you for meeting with me, Mr. Thompson."

"Please call me Zeke."

"Okay, Zeke, and you can call me Shannon. Excuse me for a couple of minutes while I go get a coffee too, okay?" He nodded and she left her briefcase and handbag on the other chair and walked to the end of the line. As Zeke turned his focus back to his own coffee, he noticed the man two tables away was watching him. When their eyes met, the other man quickly turned his attention to his laptop. Zeke thought that was strange, but quickly forgot about it.

Shannon returned and set her coffee on the table. She opened her briefcase and removed a notepad and recorder and then sat down. "Do you mind if I record this, Zeke?" He shook his head. "Great. Sometimes I miss things in my notes, so this always helps. Tell me about yourself."

Zeke cleared his throat and began, "There's not much to tell, really. I'm twenty-two and just graduated from SDSU with a finance degree. I'm still unemployed. As you know, the economy stinks right now." She nodded. "I'm single and still live with my parents. I can't really think of anything else."

"Thanks. The accident was just at the other end of this strip mall. I was a bit surprised you picked this place to meet."

"My house is less than half a mile from here, so it's convenient."

"That makes sense. Zeke, I spoke to most of the customers and employees of Watson's Barbershop. Most of them mentioned that you tried to warn Ms. Smith about the accident. Did you know something was going to happen? Had you ever met her before?"

Zeke looked startled by her questions. "No, I had never met her before. Until you said it, I didn't even know her name."

Shannon replied, "Sandra Smith, age 37, never married, lived in an apartment a few blocks from here. Did you know what was going to happen?"

"No, not at all. I just had a feeling something bad was going to happen out front. When Mr. Watson started to push her out, I had to say something."

"Do you get these feelings often, Zeke?"

"Once in a while, I guess, but I was shocked that this one came true," he noted.

She clicked the off button on the recorder. "Zeke, let me be frank. I am looking at your story from the human interest angle. A young man has a vision that could save someone's life. That's big news."

Zeke looked crestfallen. "I'm sorry, Shannon, but I couldn't disagree more. If I had jumped from the chair and blocked the door, then maybe I'd be some kind of hero. Sandra Smith is dead. I had a random thought and that's it. I'm no hero. There was a doctor in another store who heard the crash and rushed over to check on the victims. He tried to save Ms. Smith, but it was already too late. His suit was soaked in her blood. Jack and I were there when the first responders arrived. The paramedics performed CPR on the driver, but it was too late for him too. Those are the heroes in this mess, not me."

"So, you're not some kind of psychic?"

"No. I just had a hunch. Today, I wish I had jumped from my chair, but I didn't. Everyone gets hunches, Shannon. I just wish more people acted on them," Zeke sighed.

Shannon smiled slightly. "So, it was just a hunch?"

"Just a hunch."

"Kind of like picking lotto numbers, huh?" she smiled.

Zeke blushed. "I guess so."

"I won't take any more of your time, Zeke," she said, extending her hand. "Thanks for your time." She stood and began to gather her things.

Zeke felt something when their hands met, like a tickle in the back of his head. He reached out and touched her arm. "Shannon, please wait a second. Sit down." She sat and looked at him. "I know what this is really about."

She looked back at him like he was crazy. "Huh?"

"You're trying to get ahead in journalism. In the back of your mind, you're dreaming of the Pulitzer Prize."

"We all have dreams, Zeke."

He smiled. "I have two stories for you, but I can only give you the basics because that's all I know. You'll have to do the research and follow it through."

She chuckled and opened her notepad and took her pen. "Okay, I hope you're not losing it, Zeke, but go ahead."

"There's going to be a fire at the Reliant Industries factory in Campinas, Brazil. It is going to be a huge story. Thousands of people will die and the reputations of many business and political heavies will be dragged through the mud."

She smirked at him. "Is this another hunch, Zeke?" He nodded. "Whew! When is this supposed to happen?"

"I don't know for sure. It won't be very soon, but it is going to happen."

"Zeke, I wrote it down, okay? What was this other revelation?"

Zeke looked at her, but tried to keep the man two tables away in his peripheral vision. "You've read all about the NSA spying on Americans and the FBI spying on the press, of course?" he asked.

"Everyone has."

Zeke noticed the man had stopped typing and was watching them. "Don't think that happened once or at random, Shannon. Everyone in the media is being spied on."

Shannon laughed out loud. "Zeke, you're such a card. What possible evidence do you have that someone is spying on me?" she said loudly, causing people all over the cafe to look in their direction. It became deadly quiet and everyone's eyes were on Zeke.

Zeke stared at her but pointed his left index finger at the other man and said, "I don't know, but you might want to ask him!"

The man stood up and slammed his laptop closed and grabbed it. He said, "Abort," and headed toward the door. As he opened the door, a black van pulled up in front and the side door opened. The man climbed inside, the door closed and the van rushed away.

Shannon was too stunned to move. Zeke noticed that patrons of the cafe had been snapping pictures of the event with their phones and the room was buzzing with chatter. "Shannon, give me your business cards!" he exclaimed. She pulled the card case from her purse and handed it to him. Zeke jumped to his feet and began to pass out cards. "This woman is a reporter from the UT. Send your pictures to the e-mail on this card. This is important."

Zeke returned to the table and handed Shannon her empty card case. She stood up and put her arms around him and hugged him tightly. She whispered in his ear, "Zeke, that really happened, didn't it?" He nodded. "How did you know that?"

He kissed her softly on the cheek, smiled, and replied, "It was just a hunch." He hugged her again and walked out of the cafe toward his car.

The black van raced through the red light, turning right on the street toward the freeway. Several cars slammed on the brakes to avoid colliding with it. The two men in the back held on for dear life. "What the hell happened back there, Jackson?" the man in the passenger seat shouted.

"I don't know, chief," Jackson panted. "I was monitoring the target when her companion started talking about the government spying on reporters. The next thing I know, he's pointing at me." The van roared up the on-ramp and swerved into the fast lane.

"Stan, I know you're new at this, but really?" Special Agent Bradley Marcus asked. "Is that what they're teaching at the academy now? Panic and run away? I hope you know that you've blown our cover."

"I'm sorry, chief. I just panicked. How did that guy know who I was?"

"Have you ever seen him before?"

"No, sir, but we have video of him now. We'll find out soon enough," Stan replied.

"I doubt it. This doesn't make sense, chief," the driver said.

"Yeah, I know."

"What are you talking about, Steve?" Stan Jackson asked.

"Put two and two together, Stan," the driver growled. "How would the average guy identify you when you're not wearing your badge? That guy has to be another spook."

"One of ours?" Stan asked.

"If he is, we'll get a match when we run the video. If not, we've got an even bigger problem."

"You think he's a Russian agent?" Stan gasped.

"Perhaps, but unlikely. With all the coverage of our espionage activity, he could work for anyone," Steve replied.

"Or it could have been a hunch on his part," Stan suggested. The other three men began to laugh.

"You'll learn, rookie," Agent Marcus said.

§

Abe Thompson sank his tortilla chip into the freshly made bowl of guacamole and then ate it. This was all part of the Thursday night ritual to mark the first game of the professional football week. His wife was sitting at the breakfast table looking at her laptop. All day she had been preoccupied with their newfound windfall. They had a comfortable life living in relative obscurity and all of that was about to change. She spent the day watching videos and reading accounts of lottery winners who ended up with nothing after only a few short years. She took upon herself the responsibility to keep that from happening to them. "Abe, you know we're not just going to split this four ways, right?"

"Huh?" he replied.

"If we split it, it will run out quicker. Also, we all have relatives and friends who will come begging for money. You, Rachel, and especially Zeke are pushovers. I'll be in charge of the money if you can live with that."

"That's okay with me, sweetheart. I know you'll take care of everything," he replied.

"Thanks for making that easy," Sarah smiled. "What do you think the kids will say?"

"It doesn't matter. They'll be taken care of. If one of them has a business or investment idea and they can get your approval, they'll get what they want. Sarah, kick-off is in a minute or two."

"Okay, but we'll be talking about this tomorrow," she stated.

"I know we will, dear."

The lock in the front door turned and Zeke came inside and locked the door behind him. He walked to the kitchen, grabbed a beer, and then went to his mother and kissed her on the forehead. "Hi, mom."

"I'm glad you're home, Zeke. Just so you know, your father wants me to be in charge of the money," she said.

"That works for me, Mom," he laughed and walked over to the family room and sat on the chair next to his father. "Has it started yet, dad?"

"They're lined up for kick-off now."

"Dad, I think I made things worse today."

Abe pressed the pause button on his remote and looked at Zeke. "What did you tell that reporter? You didn't tell her about the notebooks, did you?" Sarah had walked over and put her hands on Zeke's shoulders.

"No, nothing like that, but it might have been better if I had," Zeke continued. "There was this guy sitting close to our table. At first, I thought he was just doing work on his laptop. But then we made eye contact and I discovered he was an undercover FBI agent."

"What?"

"He was monitoring Shannon, the reporter."

"You have to be mistaken, son," Sarah said.

"When I pointed him out, he slammed his laptop closed, ran through the doorway and into a waiting black van which sped away. I don't think I was mistaken."

"What do we do now, Abe?" Sarah asked.

"There's nothing to do. Zeke didn't do anything wrong."

"Dad, I'm not so sure," Zeke argued. "There is no way some guy could identify an undercover agent. His bosses are going to be very interested in finding out what makes me tick."

"Well, son, if that happens, there's not much we can do. They are the government after all. It's not like the Russians or Chinese are trying to kidnap you," Abe replied. "What do you want to do, son?"

"I think I want to fly to Hawaii," he said. "If the FBI is going to lock me up somewhere, I might as well have a vacation first."

"Zeke, we won't get the lottery money for some time yet," Abe cautioned.

"That's okay, dad, I have some money saved up. I already bought my ticket with an open return. If I'm running out of cash before the lottery shows up, I'll just fly home."

"When do you leave, Zeke?" Sarah asked.

"Tomorrow morning at ten o'clock," he replied.

"Well, I guess that means we have time to watch the game then," Abe said as he pushed the play button on his remote. "Zeke, it's Jags versus the Saints. Who do you think will win?"

"Saints 24, Jags 21," he replied.

Abe hit the pause button and frowned at Zeke, saying, "Really? Now why should I watch this game?"

"Dad, press play, I just made that up. It was a joke!"

§

"Ladies and gentlemen, we have begun our final approach to Kahului International Airport. Please return your seat backs and tray tables to their full upright and locked position. All personal effects need to be stowed and electronic devices turned off and put away. The cabin crew will be picking up any remaining service items or other articles to be disposed. Thank you for flying with Hawaiian Airlines. Aloha," the voice on the loudspeaker said.

Zeke opened his eyes. His head was still cloudy after his nap and his neck ached. He looked across the people in the other seats to see blue skies and a few scattered clouds. Now, after five hours in the air, he began to panic that he had not made a hotel reservation. He had wanted to be spontaneous, but now he faced the real risk of sleeping on the beach or worse. "First time in Maui?" the man seated in the center seat asked.

"No, I came here a few years ago with my folks," Zeke replied.

"Where are you staying?"

"Not really sure," Zeke replied. "I sort of forgot to make a reservation."

"You're a brave man," the man said. "If you can get a room near Lahaina, I recommend it. Bar hopping is great there, if you ask me."

"Thanks for the tip," Zeke replied. "My name's Zeke Thompson."

"It's nice to meet you Zeke. I'm Peter Smith."

"I hope you have a nice vacation here, Peter."

"Well, it's not actually a vacation, Zeke. There is a spiritual retreat on the island that I go to every year. Here," he said as he reached into his pocket and withdrew a card. "This is the place. If you're a man of faith, you might check it out sometime."

The card read: "Sacred Life Tranquility Retreat. Maui, Hawaii."

"Thank you, Peter."

"No problem, Zeke."

Thirty minutes later, Zeke was walking down the concourse with his backpack and roller-board suitcase. His panic had faded when he remembered that most airports had kiosks or phones for many resorts. He was now confident he would find a room somewhere. He followed his fellow passengers into the baggage claim hall and noticed the hotel phones on the opposite wall. He headed toward them. He was passing a long line of limousine drivers holding name signs when he froze. Someone was holding a sign that said, "Z. Thompson". His shock dissipated when he realized it was Bea Watson holding the sign. A huge smile crossed his face as he walked up to her. She was stunning in her bright yellow sundress, floppy hat, and stiletto heels. She wore two flower leis around her neck.

Bea put the sign between her knees, removed one of the leis, and put it around his neck. She kissed him on both cheeks and said, "Aloha! I'm glad your flight was on time. Do you have any other luggage to collect?"

"How did you know?"

She giggled and took him by the arm and began to lead him toward the door. "Have you forgotten again? This is your time, not mine. To me, I'm walking along in a history book."

"I'm still trying to figure that one out, Bea."

"Zeke, you have to stop wasting your time analyzing everything! Just be in the moment and let your gift take over," she suggested.

"Did you tell me that in your history book?" he quizzed.

"In some of them, yes," she replied. He stopped and stared at her for a minute. "It's kind of complicated, Zeke. We can talk about it when we get home."

"Do you live here? I thought you said you lived in the future!"

She grabbed his arm and pulled him along. "For now, Zeke Thompson, you and I live here. Come on." He reluctantly followed her to a silver Bentley GT Convertible. She opened the trunk and Zeke put his bags inside. Then he climbed in and buckled his seatbelt. Bea buckled herself in and started the motor and lowered the roof. Then she pulled out into traffic.

"Nice wheels, Bea," he said.

"It'll do in a pinch," she laughed and winked at him.

# Chapter 5

"You expect me to believe that a foreign agent is uncovering our agents to let the American people know we're watching them?" Agent Tyrone Baker, head of the FBI San Diego field office, said to the conference table full of agents.

"We don't know what to think, boss," Agent Marcus replied. "All we know is this guy didn't show up in any scans of our people, the NSA, or the CIA. He doesn't match any federal, state, or local law enforcement profiles and doesn't have a criminal record."

"Agent Baker, I have another idea," Special Agent Stephanie Marshall said. The others turned to look at her. "I've reviewed the video from Jackson's camera, and it looks to me like this guy made a lucky guess."

"Go on, Stephanie," Baker replied.

"Let me put it up on the screen." She pushed a button and her computer screen appeared on the flat screen bolted to the wall. "On the left is the outbound video link. The camera looking back at Agent Jackson is on the right. After syncing both cameras, I see Stan making eye contact with the other man multiple times. It is possible that the man thought Stan was paying too much attention to them and that piqued his interest."

"Boss, I think we all know that is a possibility; after all, Stan is a new agent and doesn't have the experience we do. I'm just not willing to let it go at a theory," Marcus argued.

"Brad, I don't think I said I was certain. I agree it is only a possibility, although a significant one in my opinion," Marshall replied.

Baker sighed heavily. "So, you all say we need to turn this over to the NSA?" Everyone else in the room nodded their agreement. "Shit, this is the last thing we need now. If this story gets out, we're all going to take it in the can!" He sat and thought for a couple of minutes, looking at each of the others for new opinions. Most sat quietly with their heads down. "If this goes bad, you're all going down with me." Their heads snapped up and they were staring at him intently. "Sorry, forget I said that. Marcus, turn everything we have over to the NSA. Tell them to search all social media, school websites, and driver's license bureaus, whatever they've got. I want to know who this guy is. That's it." The other agents stood and began to file out of the room.

Marcus walked over to his boss and said, "It'll be fine, boss. Don't worry."

"With all due respect, screw you, Brad."

§

Zeke sat on the lanai outside the beach house where Bea took him. When they arrived, she showed him to his room, and then left on other business. She said she would return around nightfall. The house was magnificent, with ten bedrooms, and a massive open living/dining room surrounded by a library, a den, a theater, and a few rooms set up as offices. After unpacking, he had walked down to the beach and swam in the warm waters of the Pacific. It was so different from Southern California, where the Alaska current kept the ocean chilly year round. A man named Kally acted as butler and chef. He was aided by a guard, two gardeners, and a housekeeper. The home sat on an acre of beachfront property not far from Lahaina. Zeke looked across the infinity pool toward the sun setting into the ocean. He heard a sound behind him and turned to see Kally approaching with a tray, two bottles and two glasses. "Good evening, Zeke," he said. "Miss Watson will be arriving soon and thought I should bring you two a drink."

"Thank you, Kally," he replied. "When is dinner, by the way?"

"I'll be serving shortly after Miss Watson arrives." Kally opened the beer bottle and poured into the tall frost-encrusted glass. Then he opened the bottle of wine and poured the other glass. "Excuse me, sir, I need to prepare the oysters and lobster now." He turned and walked away.

Zeke turned to see the other man and said, "Thanks again." As he watched, a bright flash of white light shot from one of the small rooms inside. Zeke clenched his eyes against the intense light. When he opened his eyes, he saw Bea walking toward him. She was carrying several books under one arm. He stood and smiled at her.

When she arrived on the lanai, she set the books down next to the tray and kissed him on the cheek. "Always a gentlemen, I like that." Then she sat down and picked up the glass of wine. "Here's to us, Zeke." He took his glass and tapped it against hers and sat down as well.

After sipping his beer, he said, "Did you see that bright flash inside? What was that?"

"It was nothing to worry about for now, Zeke. How was your afternoon?" she diverted.

"Great. This place is amazing! Do you own it?"

She laughed. "No, I don't. It's for rent right now, but I have a feeling they will find a buyer soon. You did submit the ticket, right?"

"Are you implying that I'm buying this place?"

"According to my records, this residence was purchased by Abraham and Sarah Thompson on December 16, 2014," she stated as if that date was in the past. She picked up the top book from the pile and opened it to the marked page. "If I may, let me read a paragraph from this book." She cleared her throat. "If I recall the story correctly, Ezekiel told me how his father, of blessed memory, acquired the Maui house when he began to write novels. There was too much commotion and intrigue in the old neighborhood. Everyone Abraham had ever known came to the house over those first weeks, begging for a piece of their newfound fortune. Being a man of endless generosity, Abraham wanted to help them all, but Sarah turned them away. She knew if they all were given money, she and her husband would be broke, the others would spend theirs rashly and end up with nothing, and ultimately blame them. If they did not give, they would be blamed as well. "Might as well keep the cash," she was often known to say." She closed the book and handed it to Zeke, who was sitting with his mouth open and eyes glazed over.

After a speechless moment, Zeke looked at the book cover. Two men were standing, arm in arm. Zeke was on the left, though he looked older, with gray hair. The other was quite old, and there was something familiar about his face. He was stunned again when he read the author's name: Peter Smith. "What is this, Bea?"

"Peter was one of your best friends, according to the books from my time," she replied. "He wrote several memoirs as well as biographies about you." She took the book from him, set it on the table, and held his hands tightly. "Zeke, you have to know that I'm doing this for a reason! Normally, this kind of thing is strictly forbidden, but this is the only way to guarantee that my society will ever exist."

"This is about the war again, isn't it?" he asked.

"Only partially, Zeke," she replied. "But it's more than that. All I'm allowed to discuss is how you and your dad need to do what you did in order for my society to come to pass."

"Just tell me what to do and I'll do it, Bea," he moaned.

She laughed out loud. He was beginning to love that laugh. It broke down the terror in his heart and filled him with joy and contentment. He wondered if he was already in love with this woman and what that would mean. "The way you said that was like you were about to be spanked! Do you want to be spanked, Zeke?"

He blushed and turned his head. He could feel the warmth of her hand caressing his cheek and turned to face her again. She leaned over and kissed him lightly on the lips. "I really like you, Bea."

"That's a good start," she said as she kissed him again. She sat back and picked up another book and thumbed through it. "Zeke, you are going to have a long and wonderful life. A lot longer than you might imagine, in fact. I know it sounds like I'm giving you an onerous job, but nothing could be further from the truth. Let me read you something from another book. It says: "As I travel and meet new people, I am constantly in awe of the majesty of His Creation. People come from every conceivable background and culture, and yet, inside each is that undeniable spark, whether they see it or not. It is often said that you can see a person's soul if you look deeply enough into their eyes. I disagree. If you look deeply enough, you will see God looking back at you." Isn't that amazing?"

"Wow! That's really cool. Who wrote that?" he asked. She handed him the book. Zeke closed it and looked at the cover. The cover image was thousands of tiny photos of people from all over the world. The title read: "A Simple Life, Volume 4, by

Ezekiel Thompson." The tome fell out of his hands and landed on the concrete floor.

Bea leaned forward and picked it up. "Be careful with that, it's more than a thousand years old," she said and then looked up with an odd look on her face. "Oops. That just slipped out. Forget that, I am not allowed to let you know that." He only stared at her in disbelief.

"Dinner, Ms. Watson," Kally called from the French doors.

§

The rays of the early morning sun were moving across Zeke's face, so he rolled over to avoid them. He had a wonderful evening with Bea. Kally's dinner was flawless and the conversation afterward over wine with this lady of the future was warm and intimate. Zeke was beginning to understand the feelings he felt but could only wonder if those feelings might be requited. It was too early in their relationship to be concerned for such things, he told himself and tried to fade off to sleep again.

"Excuse me, Zeke," Kally said from the bedroom door. "Ms. Watson asked me to tell you that breakfast will be in forty-five minutes."

"Thank you," Zeke yawned as he sat up in bed. He looked at his watch, which showed it was 7:45 a.m. He wondered why she was in a big hurry today but quickly realized that every moment with her was better than a night's sleep. He walked toward the bathroom to prepare for his second day in Hawaii. He paused as he passed the picture window and looked out onto the formal gardens surrounding this side of the residence and thought perhaps it would be an excellent purchase, although he did not yet know the price.

As he climbed out of the shower, wrapped in his towel, Zeke heard his phone ring and rushed into the bedroom to answer it. He noticed that someone had already made his bed while he showered and thought his family should have someone like that too. All his life, his parents were on his back about keeping his room neat and organized. Such was not the mind of Zeke Thompson. He saw it was his father calling, so he pressed the connect button and said, "Hi Dad."

"Son, I'm sorry to bother you so early."

"Don't think about that, Dad. I'm already up and coming out of the shower. What's up?"

"Zeke, the FBI was here yesterday," Abe began. There was no sound on the other end of the line. "Two agents were here with a sergeant from the Chula Vista police. They said they just wanted to talk to you."

"Did you tell them where I was?"

"Yes, I told them you flew to Maui yesterday," his father replied. "That didn't seem to bother them. Are you still there?"

"Yes, Dad, I'm still in Maui. I suppose you realize this line is probably bugged."

"You really think they would do that?"

Zeke laughed. "Don't think that makes us special, Dad. They monitor everyone. After what happened at Starbucks the other day, I'm sure of it, although I'm not sure how they figured out who I am."

"Maybe they interrogated that reporter?"

"She didn't do anything wrong. They'd get the crap sued out of them for that. After all, they were spying on her, not the other way around. And all I did was point at the guy and he flipped out. If they're questioning anyone, it ought to be him."

"Calm down, son," Abe urged. "I don't think any of this is a big deal. He said you should call their office here when you get back from vacation, okay?"

"Thanks, dad," Zeke replied. "I'm sorry if I freaked out or anything. I'll talk to you later." He disconnected the call and turned to go back to the bathroom to finish up. He stopped when he noticed Bea standing in the doorway. "Hi."

She walked over to him and put her arms around his neck and kissed his lips. He wrapped his arms around her waist and kissed her again. He began to move his hands down her body. "Not now, Zeke," she said as she stepped back. She took his hands in hers. "I want to, Zeke, I really do, but the time isn't right."

"It's okay, Bea. You don't have to explain anything."

"There isn't much time. Get dressed as quickly as you can and I'll be waiting in the main room for you," she said.

"What happened to breakfast?"

"It's a surprise," she giggled as she turned and walked out of the room, closing the door behind her. Confused, and a bit frustrated, Zeke went back to the bathroom to get dressed.

When Zeke walked out of the bedroom, he found Bea pacing back and forth. Kally was wearing a bulletproof vest and ballistic helmet, and carrying a strange weapon that seemed totally unlike an automatic rifle, but equally deadly. "What's going on, Bea? This is beginning to frighten me."

She stopped pacing and turned to look at him. "There's been another change in plans, Zeke. We have to leave here right now."

"Bea, my dad told me the FBI wants to talk to me. That's no big deal, really."

"It's not the FBI, Zeke," Kally said. He turned to Bea and said, "The terminal reports ready, Ms. Watson."

Bea grabbed Zeke's hand and began to pull him toward one of the small offices around the center chamber. "Come with me, Zeke, quickly now." He followed her and Kally was less than a yard behind him, walking backward as if watching for home invaders. Bea opened the door and pulled Zeke inside. Just before Kally slammed the door closed, Zeke thought he saw shadows near several windows and heard a gunshot.

The room was painted bright white. There were no light fixtures, and yet light seemed to emanate from the ceiling and walls. There was a pedestal near one wall that held an electronic control panel of sorts. Kally walked over to it and began to tap away on a keyboard. Zeke heard a noise and turned to the door. It seemed someone was on the other side, turning the knob, but it would not open. "How long, Kally?" Bea asked.

It sounded as though someone was banging on the door or trying to kick it open. "Only a few seconds now, ma'am." A green light from the panel illuminated Kally's face and he pressed a large button. A massive guttural "whump" sound seemed to deafen Zeke. The sounds of banging stopped and he could not hear Kally's fingers on the keyboard anymore. A strange feeling of static electricity rose in the room. Zeke could feel his hair standing on end and braced for the zap of current. He looked at Bea, whose gaze was focused in another direction, so he looked there.

In the center of the wall, a small black circle appeared. It grew in size slowly at first and then quickly grew to eight feet in diameter. It was not a normal black like the paint on a wall, or even the sky on a starless night. The blackness seemed to shimmer and oscillate as if it was breathing. He looked at Bea who was smiling at him. She leaned over and kissed his cheek and then took his hand and started to move toward the black. Zeke's feet did not cooperate. She turned to him and said it would be okay, although he could not hear anything, but the movement of her lips seemed to express that. Without other options, he stepped forward with her toward the black circle. He looked back at Kally who was removing the control panel from the pedestal and falling in line behind them. Then Zeke and Bea stepped forward into the absolute black.

Zeke was totally disoriented. Bea was still standing there, holding his hand, but all else was black. He could not feel the floor under his feet or see anything but their bodies and blackness. He wondered what had happened to Kally. What had this crazy woman done to him now, he thought. After a second or a minute or an hour, a tiny white dot appeared in front of them. In the black, he had no sensation of time passing. Now the dot was growing and his sense of temporal movement returned. After a short time, the white circle was eight feet in diameter. The white circle moved forward until it was almost touching them. Bea pulled his arm to get his attention. When he looked at her, she was motioning that they needed to step into the white circle. He nodded at her and watched her feet to stay in step. He was terrified of being left alone in the black. She raised her left foot as if ready to step and he copied her and they stepped through.

There was suddenly light and sound again. After a second of nausea, he looked around his new location. It looked identical to the other white room, except the pedestal was larger and seemed more permanent. A woman in a military-style uniform was standing at the controls. She smiled at them and said, "Welcome home, Bea."

Bea pulled Zeke away from the wall just as Kally stepped into the room with the control console still under his arm. The woman said, "Good job, Kally."

Zeke looked back at the shimmering black circle on the wall. There was an audible snap, a flash of light, and it disappeared. "What's going on, Bea?"

"First things first," she replied. "Zeke, this is my grandmother, Colonel Aria Watson. Grandma, this is—"

"I feel I already know you, Ezekiel Thompson," she said as she shook his hand.

"It's a pleasure to meet you, Colonel, but please just call me Zeke," he responded.

"Sure, Zeke, and you can call me Aria," she noted. "Breakfast is waiting in the other room for everyone. Kally, I'll lock up the console so you can eat too, okay?"

"Where the heck are we, Bea?" Zeke asked.

"Don't be too disappointed," she said as she opened the door and they walked into the great room of the Hawaii house. "As you can see, we didn't go anywhere."

Zeke was in shock. Nothing made sense. Minutes ago, he heard gunfire and people trying to break down the door. Now, he was back and nothing seemed to have happened. He had thought Bea was insane, but realized her insanity was contagious because he had lost all sense of reality. He walked over to the nearest couch and sat down heavily. He held his head in his hands and rocked back and forth trying to wrestle with his confusion. Sensing his pain, Bea and Aria sat on either side of him. Aria put her arm around his back while Bea rubbed his knee and stroked his hair. After a minute, she put her lips to his ear and whispered, "You're not going crazy, Zeke. You're just confused."

It hit him like a ton of bricks. He sat up straight and said, "We traveled in time!"

"Bingo!" Aria exclaimed.

"When is this?"

"August 24, 3267," Aria reported.

He turned to Bea and said, "But why? I thought you told me I was going to be a prophet or something in my time. How can I do that here?"

Bea giggled and replied, "You are going back, silly. This was just an emergency, Zeke. Someone else was trying to change time, and we had to avoid the intended consequences."

"Why did I buy that ticket?"

"Not everything is about you, Zeke," Bea began. "There are others out there who want to stop my society from existing. We had expected an attack on your parents, but not you." A look of despair crept across his face. "Don't worry, we are protecting them."

"Zeke, we did not consider the attack on you," Aria noted. "There was an anomaly in time near the Maui house this morning. We expected it in Chula Vista. I immediately ordered Kally and Bea to extract you before Untor could act. This is all my fault. I should have surmised that he would try to distract your father from writing by killing you. If I had thought that through, this would not have occurred. Believe me, Zeke, we don't want you to learn about our time yet."

"Who is this Untor?" he asked.

Bea kissed his cheek and said, "Zeke, you have to trust me. Let's go have some breakfast and Aria and I will tell you everything we can. As soon as we get an all-clear from your time, you and I will return, okay?" He nodded and kissed her soft lips. They stood and headed for the lanai and their food.

§

The all-clear signal came shortly after they ate. Now it was 10:00 a.m. and Zeke was sitting on the lanai in his own time again. He told Bea he wanted to be left alone for a while to digest the story they told him in the other time. He felt shortchanged by the lack of specifics, but realized that too much knowledge might change his actions in this time and that would defeat the purpose of everything they were trying to do. According to this story, a man named Fola Untor had been the leader of a secret police unit that terrorized the largest society of humans in the universe. The actions of one of Bea's grandfathers caused him to be disgraced and thrown from power. He had vowed revenge on the man and planned to kill him, but had first created two back-up plans in case the murder attempt failed. His first plan was to travel to his own future, kidnap the man and then strand him on an isolated planet in the distant past. Untor thought the man would then suffer and die even if the murder attempt failed. Planning his evil acts, Untor had to learn a lot about the humans of Earth. He learned about the war and the actions of the Thompson family. That gave him another plan. If the Thompsons could be stopped, the future Bea's grandfather lived in would never exist. When Untor then went to the man and attempted to murder him, the plan failed and Untor died, but the other plans still moved forward. Ultimately, the kidnap plan failed as well, and the teams on Earth were now working to stop this only unresolved thread. When he had asked Aria whether there could be more such plans that no one knew about, she had just shrugged her shoulders.

The thing that had driven him to distraction happened when Zeke noted that they were still there, and so the plan must have failed. Aria said something about how time was fickle that way and some nonsense about multiple universes and membranes of space-time. At that point, his brain shut down for protection. He looked back at the house. The dream house was beginning to look like a prison. He yearned to run down the beach and get away from all of them, but in the back of his mind, he saw Untor waiting to kill him.

He saw the patio door open and Bea stepped out and approached him. He looked at her and wondered what she wanted now. Hours ago, he had kissed her and groped her body, and now he only wanted her to leave.

She sat and smiled at him. The twinkle in her eyes and quick smile melted his mood and he struggled to keep it. "It's okay, Zeke. I understand."

"Just tell me everything will be okay."

"Everything will be okay."

"I don't believe you."

She laughed out loud. "You're a lot like my grandfather, Dave. You're a hard nut to crack. Zeke, I want to give you a couple of things. First, let me see your phone." He handed it to her. She pulled an identical-looking phone from her bag and handed it to him. "This phone is a bit upgraded, so please don't ever take it in for maintenance or upgrade. It's from my time. If you look, you'll see Aria's and my numbers are there now. Yes, you can call us in the future with it. But don't ask me how that works, because I have no clue."

"What if it gets stolen or broken?"

"We'll know and deactivate it. The phone can tell if someone else is using it. If that happens more than once in a row, the unique components will dissolve. So don't loan this thing around. If you lose or break it, someone will come and give you a new one, okay?"

He smiled at her and said, "Thank you, Bea."

"You're welcome, Zeke," she smiled. "I really need you to trust me on this next one."

"That doesn't sound good."

She opened a small case and offered a large green pill to him. "Please swallow this."

"What is it?"

"I can't tell you."

"Are you poisoning me?"

"Never, Zeke," she scowled. "It's for your health."

"Some kind of future medicine?"

"I can't tell you that either."

"Bea, I think I'm falling in love with you," Zeke said.

"Are you saying that so you don't have to take the pill?" she laughed.

Zeke took the pill and washed it down with his glass of water. "Shit! That thing tastes disgusting. What was in it?"

"I'm falling for you too, Zeke," she said. "I have one more gift." She pulled a ring from her purse and handed it to him.

"An engagement ring, how nice."

She laughed again. He loved her laugh. "It's not an engagement ring, Zeke. Don't you remember? That's your job."

"I thought it might be different in the future."

"Sorry, some traditions go on forever," she said. "Zeke, this ring detects temporal anomalies. The stone will flash red if there is a disturbance in time. If that happens, it might mean Untor is coming back. If you see red, press down on the stone and someone will come to your aid, okay?"

"What if I'm asleep or in the shower and don't have it on?" he asked.

"It will also beep and shock you just a bit," she replied. "But please try not to take it off."

"Will it shock me if you step into that black circle again?"

"No, the electronics know when it's one of us. You'll get a green flash."

He slipped the ring on his finger and said, "Thank you, Bea."

She sighed. "I'm really sorry to tell you this, Zeke, but we all have to leave now." He looked shocked. "The activity this morning alerted the police, and it's too hot for us anymore, at least for a few days."

"Where are we going?"

"Zeke, my team and I are going back to the future," she said with tears welling in her eyes. "We have booked you a suite at the Grand Wailea for tonight. You can take the Bentley. Tomorrow, someone will pick it up there."

"I don't want to leave you, Bea."

"This is the way it is for now, Zeke. I will see you again soon, please trust me."

"And tomorrow?"

"The FBI is picking you up there at noon. They'll be holding on to you for a while. Don't worry, they've got nothing on you. Look at it as a free ride on a private plane back home to San Diego."

"What do I do now?"

"That's totally up to you, but if you like, you could check out that spiritual retreat on the island and see your best friend Peter Smith again?"

# Chapter 6

After loading his bags into the trunk of the car, Zeke looked back at the house that his parents would buy in a few short months. He wondered if he would ever see Bea Watson again. In the few days since she came into his life, his perspective on life and existence had changed completely. She had told him his talent at premonition would become his life and not the burden and terror it had been to date. He wondered if he really had traveled to the future. From what he knew about physics, that was not supposed to be possible. But if it was true these people came from the future, perhaps the knowledge of what was possible had changed? Something had happened when he stepped into the inky blackness—that was for certain. He thought for a moment about running back inside and jumping through the circle with Bea and living in the future. Now he just stared at the house, feeling lonely and heartsick.

"Excuse me, Zeke," the guard said.

"Yes, Taron?"

The guard was quite tall with a unique skin coloring, somewhere between olive and brown, and startlingly green eyes. He wore black body armor and carried some kind of rifle across his back and two odd pistols clipped to his belt. "HPD will arrive here in less than fifteen minutes, and we all should be gone before they arrive."

"I understand," Zeke sighed as he looked back at the house one last time. "Is Bea still here?"

"No, she and the others have used the portal and taken the console with them," he reported.

"How are you getting back?"

"Don't worry, Zeke, we have a safe house in San Diego. I'm catching a flight to the mainland in a few hours," Taron noted.

Zeke stuck out his hand and Taron shook it. "It's been fun, and I hope to see you again."

"You will see us all again before you know it, Zeke." He pulled a small pill bottle from a compartment on his belt and handed it to the other man. "Bea wanted to make sure you got these."

There were three more of the large green pills in the bottle. "Ugh. I thought one was all I had to take."

Taron laughed. "They are pretty disgusting, I grant you that. Take one tonight before you go to bed and the other two in the morning. Four is the magic number."

"What the heck are these for?"

Taron patted him on the shoulder. "Sorry, that's classified; but trust me, they are for your own good. Take care, Zeke."

"All the best," Zeke replied, and then climbed into the car. "By the way, can I give you a lift?"

"That's okay. I have a few friends waiting outside the gate."

"From the future?" Taron only smiled back at him. With nothing else to do, Zeke drove the Bentley down the drive, out of the gate, and headed down the road. Taron ran down the drive and pressed a button to close the gate. A black van pulled up, and he climbed into the passenger seat. The van drove away.

After driving a couple of miles, Zeke pulled the car into a convenience store parking lot and stopped. He removed the card for the retreat from his pocket and keyed the address into the GPS. Once it was set, he pulled out of the lot and followed the route guidance. He had no idea where he was going and was not really certain why he was following Bea's advice right now. He wondered if he should head back to the airport and try to fly out before the FBI caught up to him. Then he realized that was a stupid idea. He had done nothing wrong and had nothing to hide. If he ran, that would be very suspicious for an innocent man. He drove for hours and found himself traveling up the slope of Haleakala. Finally, the GPS told him to turn left on a gravel road. He followed it for a mile or so until he came upon a closed metal gate in the middle of a long stone wall. He pulled up to it and stopped. He climbed out of the car and approached the gate. There was an intercom on one of the pillars supporting the gate. He pressed the talk button and said, "Hello?"

A female voice said, "Sacred Life Tranquility Retreat, how may I help you?"

"I was hoping to learn more about this place."

"Were you referred to us, sir?"

"Yes. I met Peter Smith on the flight over and he gave me your card," Zeke replied.

"May I have your name, sir?"

"I'm Zeke Thompson. And you are?"

"Zeke, my name is Judy Vance. I'm opening the gate now. Please just follow the asphalt road until you reach the main buildings. Welcome friend. Reflect in peace." The gate began to open and Zeke rushed back to the car and drove through. He continued slowly along the winding road. To his left was a forest. Through the trees, he could see a large lake with small islands scattered about, each of which held a small wooden or stone temple. To the left was a large open field, punctuated by flower gardens and stone cottages spaced far apart. The road crested a small hill to reveal a massive stone temple, reminiscent of Roman ruins, and a long two-story wooden building that looked like a hotel. The main road ended in a parking lot in front of that building. The main building was built like a log cabin with large picture windows. He climbed out of the car and walked toward it. He stepped up on the broad veranda encircling the building and through a pair of tall glass doors. The chill of air conditioning reminded him of the midday heat on the island. There was a small counter on one side of the room. The rest of the large space was filled with seating areas. A few small groups of people sat in some of the areas while most were vacant. He stopped and looked around until he noticed a woman walking toward him. As she approached, she held out her hand, which he shook. "Hi, Zeke. I'm Judy, the one you spoke with. Please come with me." She led him to a group of four chairs in a conversation area and sat on one of them. Zeke sat opposite her.

"Judy, this is quite the place you have here," he said at last.

"Thank you, Zeke," she replied. "By the way, I've sent word to Peter and Reverend Paul, who should be joining us in a few minutes. We're all glad you came to see us."

"What kind of retreat is this place?"

"Well, first of all, we are ecumenical. We treasure all people of faith and want to give them the opportunity to reconnect to the spirit within. Are you a man of faith, Zeke?"

"Yes, I think I am."

"You don't sound so sure, Zeke, but that was not unexpected," she replied. "Ah, here they come now." She stood up and Zeke followed as two men approached them. One was definitely the man from the plane. The other was an older man with a white beard and shaved head. His face was heavily lined and he wore a long tunic and a brocaded robe. "Zeke Thompson, this is Reverend Paul Isaac, and of course you know Peter."

After everyone was introduced, Judy went back to her office while the three men sat down. "Zeke, this is a pleasant surprise," Peter said.

"I just thought I'd stop by to learn more," he replied.

"Your friend seems conflicted, Peter," the reverend said. Zeke looked surprised but said nothing.

Peter chuckled and said, "It's okay, Zeke. Reverend Paul has a knack for that sort of thing. He does it to all of us."

Paul reached forward and put his hand on Zeke's knee. "Son, you are among friends here. I can feel the turmoil within you. If you want to tell me, I will listen and not judge you. Are you in trouble with the law?"

"No!" Zeke exclaimed. "At least I don't think so."

"Zeke, you can say whatever you want or nothing at all," Peter said. "If you want me to leave you two alone, I'll do that too."

For an instant, Zeke felt trapped, as though these men would hear his tale and realize he was insane or worse. That feeling passed quickly when he remembered he would definitely be trapped tomorrow when the FBI came to collect him. All his life, he kept his notebooks a secret from anyone outside the direct family, and they had sworn never to tell anyone. But the knowledge of future events gnawed at him. His ability was a terrible curse. He knew one day he would foresee his own death and know it was inevitable. He would see his mother and father die in the days before the actual event and know he could do nothing about it. Or could he?

Zeke Thompson told them everything. He gave a detailed account of his notebooks and as many events as he could remember presaging. He told them about Bea and the people from the future, including the books that Bea had read from. He told them about the lottery ticket and the FBI and even the man from the future who was trying to kill him. He talked for hours, it seemed. When at last he finished, he sat crying in front of them. Peter gave a look of deep concern to the reverend who only smiled back at him. Zeke felt empty inside with no hope, yet somehow lighter. He felt warmth starting to grow in his body. It was a feeling he had not felt for a long time.

"Son, would you like to stay here tonight?" Paul asked.

"I'm supposed to be at a hotel so the FBI can pick me up tomorrow," he replied without looking up at them.

"Zeke, you told us the police would come at noon. Please stay with us tonight and Peter will drive you to the hotel in the morning," Paul said.

Zeke looked up to see the reverend smiling and seeming at peace with everything he had heard. "Do you think I'm crazy?" he asked.

Paul laughed out loud. It was a throaty laugh that broke down the tension in Zeke's muscles until he laughed too.

After a few seconds, Paul said, "No, Zeke, I do not think you are insane, although it would probably be better for you if you were."

"What? I don't understand."

The reverend replied, "If you are insane, then your predictions are the rants of a lunatic. You would have no fear that the lottery winnings were somehow stolen and the FBI and others would leave you alone. If you are sane, as I believe, you are in serious danger now. Can you imagine what a government would do to have advance knowledge of future events?"

"Reverend, you think he's telling the truth?" Peter asked. "Much of what Zeke said is unbelievable."

"Let us try an experiment," Paul said as he stuck out his hand. "Zeke, please take my hand for a moment, and then tell me something about me that no one knows."

Zeke shook Paul's hand and then let it drop. He thought for a moment and said, "You had an identical twin brother named Simon who died in infancy." The reverend stared at him without emotion. "This retreat is running out of funds, but it does own the house where I stayed the last two nights, which my parents will buy soon."

"Anything else? Pick something no one could possibly know."

"You're in love with Judy Vance. She's been with you for years and you've always loved her, but you're afraid she might take it wrong since you are her spiritual leader."

"That's crazy talk," Peter scoffed.

Paul smiled. "Yes, Peter, it is crazy talk, but every word of it is true, except the part about his parents buying the beach house. That hasn't happened yet, so I can't confirm it."

"Oh my God," Peter gasped.

"He works in mysterious ways," Paul smiled.

"I think I need a drink," Peter replied.

"I think we all could," Paul noted. "Zeke, give me your car keys. I'll have someone prepare a room for you. We have a lot to talk and drink about."

"Reverend, I need to call home first, if I may," Zeke replied. "I want my folks to ship my notebooks here for safekeeping, if that's okay. Once they have me in custody, they'll probably hear about those books and try to get them. I'd like to make them a gift to the retreat."

"Thank you for your faith in me," Paul smiled as the three rose and headed toward the bar.

§

Zeke woke up at seven o'clock in the soft bed at the retreat. He could not remember having slept so well. He had confessed about everything he knew and was accepted. He walked over to the bathroom and filled a glass with water. He opened the pill bottle and removed the last two pills and swallowed them. He accidentally spilled some water on the bottle lid and noticed it was dissolving. He took the lid and bottle and dropped them into the toilet where they quickly melted away. He flushed the residue away. Pretty clever to hide the evidence of future medical science, he thought. After showering, he packed his bags and headed downstairs.

A large group of people were swarming around the open room. Each wore a floor-length tunic and a small cap on their heads. He wondered what this was all about, but knew he would be leaving for his appointment with the federal police soon and would likely not find out. He walked over to the counter to see who had his car keys and found Judy Vance behind the counter. She smiled at him and her eyes lit up. "It's a great morning, Zeke!" she announced.

"It is," he replied.

"Thank you so much, Zeke. It's like a dream come true."

"I'm sorry but I don't know what you mean."

"Zeke, after you three broke up last night, Paul came to my apartment and confessed his feelings for me. I was so happy. You can't imagine how long I have loved that man. Now, I have everything I will ever need and I owe that to you," she said.

"You are very welcome, Judy. I am so happy for you both," he replied. "By the way, do you know where my car keys are?"

"I've got them," said a voice behind him. He turned to see Taron standing there with the keys in his hand.

"I certainly wasn't expecting you, Taron. I thought you flew out yesterday."

"I rescheduled. No one is staying at the house in San Diego right now, so I'm taking a short vacation. My grandfather Charlie is due to arrive next week, so I'll be back there for that."

"Do we have time for breakfast?" Zeke asked.

"Sure."

"The breakfast room is just through that opening," Judy said. "Just help yourself to anything you like."

"Thanks, Judy," Zeke replied.

"No, Zeke. Thank you," she smiled.

Zeke and Taron went through the buffet line and then found a small table by the window and sat down. A server offered juice and coffee. After he left, the two men began to enjoy their food. Zeke was relaxed and looked out the window at the broad field of grass and the large temple. All the people who had been in the lobby were making their way up the steps and into the large stone building. He took a sip of coffee and looked at his table mate. Taron looked edgy as if something was wrong and the story about vacation was a fabrication. After each bite of food, Taron would look around nervously. It suddenly struck Zeke that Taron had picked this specific table so there was a clear external view and a solid wall behind him. "Taron, what is going on here? Something's up, I can sense that."

"Where is your ring, Zeke?" the man said.

Zeke had forgotten to put it on. He reached into his pocket and pulled it out. The stone was bright red. He slipped it on his finger and could feel the tingling sensation. "Untor?" he asked. Taron nodded. "But why now and why here?"

"It's off the beaten path. The guards are not trained for an assault, only to keep vandals, burglars, and petty thieves away. There were two attempts on your parents last night after you called them. Don't worry, they are safe. I think one of my men wounded Untor, but that might be wishful thinking. As soon as you're finished eating, we need to get to the car."

"Is that any safer?"

"It looks like a regular car, but it is well protected. Are you ready, Zeke?" Taron asked.

"I have no appetite," he groaned.

"Okay, let's go. Stay low and behind me and keep your head on a swivel for anything unusual. Keep your back to a wall when you can." He opened his pocket and pulled out two small electronic devices and handed one to Zeke. "The opening is the business end, so keep that pointed away. The button on top is the trigger. Don't shoot unless you have to. We are going to go slow," the guard said. The room was empty now except for them. Taron led the way toward the door and out into the main room. It seemed deserted as well. They walked slowly forward past the furniture groupings and toward the front doors.

When they were ten feet from the door, a tall, pale man opened the door and walked in. He had shoulder length platinum blonde hair and silvery eyes. His left forearm was covered with an electronic device of some kind covered in flashing lights. He held an unusual looking weapon in his right. He was smiling broadly. "I guess this is the right place!" he shouted.

"Get out of here, Untor!" Taron snarled. "You're almost out of power and you'll be stuck in this time."

Untor laughed hysterically, brandishing his weapon at them. "You idiot! I have no intention to go back to my time. Once either Ezekiel or Dave is dead, this line of time will evaporate! I will have never been here. I will lead the Brotherhood again!" He leveled his pistol and fired. Rather than a bullet, a stream of light shot toward them. Zeke and Taron dived behind the couch and the blast shot over their heads and smashed into a wall, setting it on fire. Taron pointed his weapon at Untor and fired. The plasma ball shot past his ear and struck the glass doors, blowing them to pieces. Untor fired again. The blast hit Taron's weapon causing it to explode, injuring his right hand. He cringed in pain.

Zeke stood up and fired at Untor. The blast hit him in the left forearm. The device short-circuited and fell from his arm.

Untor fell to his knees in pain and he dropped his blaster. Taron launched himself at the enemy, knocking him to the ground. He kicked the blaster away and Zeke ran to grab it. Untor and Taron rolled around on the ground. Finally, Untor kicked him off and scrambled to his feet. He saw that Zeke had his weapon, so he turned and ran through the shattered doorway and across the field. Zeke leveled the blaster on Untor, but before he could squeeze the contact, Taron put his hand on the gun and pushed it down. "No, Zeke. It is not your legacy to be a killer."

He handed the weapon to Taron and said, "But now he'll be back and try again."

"I don't think so, Zeke. Untor will die next week when he tries to kill Dave Brewster in San Diego," Taron said.

"But I thought Dave was from the future?"

"It's a long story. We'd better get on the road. You have an appointment with the FBI, as I recall."

"What about the damages here? We can't just leave," Zeke argued.

"We'll take care of everything, don't you worry," Taron said. "We contacted the reverend earlier this morning and suggested the group session meet in the temple just in case something like this happened."

They loaded Zeke's bags into the trunk of the Bentley, and Taron drove them down the road toward the highway and the Grand Wailea Resort.

After fifteen minutes of riding shotgun, Zeke was fast asleep, dreaming about another encounter with Fola Untor.

Taron held his phone between his shoulder and ear. A woman's voice said, "Hello?"

"Bea, it's Taron. Zeke is safe and Untor is likely on his way to meet with Dave."

"Why didn't he press the stone?"

"He forgot to put it on."

"Oh boy. I hope you chastised him," she said.

"I think the encounter with Untor was all the encouragement he needed."

"What happens if Untor jumps again? We could be going through this again and again," Bea asked.

Taron chuckled. "Zeke is a good shot. He fired at Untor and hit his jump device and damaged it. I don't think Untor is jumping anymore."

"Wow! I'm impressed with Zeke's shooting. Thank him for me when he's awake."

"Tell her she's welcome," Zeke said.

Taron laughed.

Hours later, Taron dropped Zeke off at the lobby entrance to the Grand Wailea Resort. He walked across the lobby and sat on a long couch with his roller board and backpack sitting in front of him. He looked at his phone. The time was 11:50 a.m. He scrolled through his e-mail. He saw the shipping confirmation on his notebooks and smiled. He texted his father to delete all records of the shipment. He deleted the e-mail and the text message and then slipped the phone into his pocket. Zeke picked up a magazine from the table and looked through it. After a couple minutes, he heard a woman say, "May we help you, sir?"

He looked up to see one of the hotel front desk clerks standing in front of him smiling. "That's okay. The FBI is picking me up any minute now." A terrified look crossed her face and she hurried away. For a moment he felt guilty about frightening her, but realized what he had said was true. He sighed and tossed the magazine back on the table. When he looked up, he saw two men and one woman in black suits walking into the lobby. A large black SUV was waiting for them out front. Zeke immediately recognized the man he had pointed at from

Starbucks and stood up. As they approached, he said, "I've been waiting for you guys." Agents Marcus, Jackson, and Marshall introduced themselves. Then they led Zeke out to the vehicle where he and his bags were loaded, and then the truck rushed away.

§

Zeke looked out the window as the jet lifted off and headed east. He was seated toward the rear of the cabin on the FBI jet. The three agents were seated together just before the door to the cockpit. He had never flown in a private jet and was thoroughly enjoying the experience. There was no luggage check-in or security line or trudging down the gangway to stand in line with other frustrated passengers desperate to get where they were going. Agent Jackson did frisk him as a precaution, but other than that, he felt like a movie star or billionaire. Unlike those celebrities, he knew his reception back on the mainland would be less thrilling, but it was just something he had to go through in order to get on with his life. He closed his eyes, slid down into his seat and wondered if the agents had learned about his notebooks or the lottery ticket. It struck him as odd that the FBI would believe this random young man could have such abilities. They had probably already written him off as a nut. "Mr. Thompson," Agent Marshall's voice said softly.

He opened his eyes to see her sitting in front of him. The space between the seats was quite narrow and their knees were almost touching. He sat up straight and replied, "Yes?"

"I didn't mean to bother you, sir, but may I ask you a few questions?"

"Please call me Zeke. And of course you can ask me anything you want."

"And I'm Stephanie. Zeke, I want you to know that I think this is all unnecessary. Stan is a new agent and I'm sure he was staring at you and the reporter. I would have found him suspicious too," she said.

"Thank you, Stephanie. I guess you are the only one who thinks that or else I wouldn't be here."

She smiled and replied, "No, I wouldn't say that. Our section chief is a careful man who always likes to tie up all the loose ends. If anyone thought you were a threat, you'd be in handcuffs right now."

"What's going to happen to me when we land?"

"We have a place east of San Diego where we interview unique people. We heard about the auto accident. Then there was the incident with Agent Jackson. Have there been more episodes like those?" she asked.

"What do you mean?"

"Have you had other cases where you knew what was going to happen in the future?"

"I have a hunch every now and again," he admitted.

"Like picking winning lottery numbers?"

"Everyone has his or her favorite numbers, Stephanie," he replied.

"What happened to your notebooks, Zeke?" she asked.

"What notebooks do you mean?" She stared at him incredulously. He looked back at her for a moment and then replied, "I gave them to a charity."

She leaned forward and put her hands on his knees. "Zeke, you seem like a nice young man. If you play straight with us, this will all be over soon and you can get on with your life. Otherwise, this experience may be a bit unpleasant." Zeke only stared back at her. She stood up and walked back up the aisle toward the other two agents.

Perhaps if the visions had not filled his head, he would have told her that he fully intended to comply. Instead, his mouth and lips seemed disconnected from his brain. The images were stark and brutal. Stephanie was lying on a concrete floor in a pool of her own blood, gasping for breath. The other two agents sat dead near the entrance to the building with bullet holes in their foreheads, trickles of blood oozing down their faces and their pistols still in their hands. Zeke could feel the bindings on his wrists behind him. The others wore balaclavas to conceal their identities and spoke a language he did not understand. After they had bound his ankles, one man grabbed him on each arm while a third pulled a bag over his head. He felt himself being dragged away. The last thing he remembered was Stephanie's labored breathing.

# Chapter 7

The jet landed at Lindbergh International Airport at 9:30 p.m. local time. It was dark and a fine rain was falling as the plane pulled up next to a black SUV and powered down its engines. When the door was opened, Zeke and the agents filed down the gangway and hurried into the vehicle, which pulled away and headed into the city. "Where to, Agent Marcus?" the driver asked.

"The ranch, Steve."

The SUV went north on the 5 and then east on the 8, flying through Mission Valley and then heading up the hill into La Mesa. Zeke watched his city pass by and began wondering about the vision he had after Stephanie touched him. He wondered if they would believe him and what would happen to him if the vision came true. At least now he was in the hands of federal police and they were supposed to be on his side. There was no telling who would risk assaulting an FBI office to get him. "Agents, why don't we go to the main office? I think it's a lot safer," he suggested.

"That isn't protocol, Mr. Thompson," Marcus replied. "After a couple of days at the ranch, we'll know what makes you tick." The SUV descended into El Cajon and then back up as it headed toward Alpine.

"You don't understand, Agent Marcus," Zeke said. "I had a vision on the plane when Stephanie touched me."

"That's funny," the driver replied. "I have visions all the time of her touching me." The other men laughed.

"That's not funny, Steve," Stephanie exclaimed. "Tell me what happened in the dream, Zeke?"

As he told them, Stephanie became more and more nervous, while the men seemed to think it was all a joke. The SUV exited the 8 at Alpine and then drove south several miles before turning up a side road that led to a small fenced compound. A guard opened the gate and the truck pulled up to a nondescript concrete building with no markings. The agents led Zeke into the building where the door was secured. Agent Jackson led Zeke to a holding cell and locked him inside. With nothing else to do, Zeke sat on the side of the bed and wondered when the assault would come.

The agents had taken his phone but he still wore the ring. The stone was dark. In his vision, there had been multiple attackers, unlike his encounter with the killer from the future. He reasoned that Untor was not his problem this time. He remembered that Bea had told him to press on the stone if it glowed to summon help. He pressed it over and again, but nothing happened. He heard the lock turn and looked up to see Stephanie entering the cell with a bag from McDonalds and a drink cup. She locked the door and sat on the small side chair. She removed a hamburger from the bag and handed it to him. She set a container of fries on a small table and placed the drink there as well. "Please eat something, Zeke. I only have one drink, so you can have it."

"We can share if you'd like," he replied. She smiled at him. "Stephanie, I'm 90 percent sure my vision is going to come true." He took a bite of his sandwich.

She sighed at him. "I don't know, Zeke. That sounds very unlikely. Who would have the guts to take on the FBI just to get to you?"

"Give me your hand, Stephanie," he said. He held her hand for a moment and then let it drop. "You will survive the assault if you wear two ballistic vests. What happens here will cause you to reevaluate your life. You will transfer from the FBI to the CIA where you can try to track down the terrorists who attacked this place. In three years, you will meet a good friend of mine named Peter Smith. You will leave government service, marry Peter and join us at the retreat. You will have three children and name your son Ezekiel. Thank you for that." She sat silent with her mouth opening and closing as she tried to comprehend what he said.

"You're making that up!"

"Maybe I am," he replied. "But for God's sake, put on a second vest for me right now. If I'm wrong, it won't hurt you. If I'm right, at least you will be alive tomorrow."

She stood and said, "I'll be right back." She left and locked the door.

Zeke continued his dinner and realized how hungry he was. His last meal had been one-third of his breakfast before he and Taron had to flee Untor. After eating, he sat back and thought about the future. Would he really see Bea again, or would the attackers here sell him into slavery or kill him outright when one of his predictions failed. Minutes later, the door opened and Stephanie reentered. Her face was bright red and she looked very angry. "Those stupid bastards!" she shouted. "'Bring in some reinforcements, just in case,' I said. And they laughed at me. 'What harm can it do,' I said. 'We can't waste department assets on some perp's dreams,' they said. I am pissed off!"

"Are you wearing the two vests?"

She pulled open her vest to reveal a second underneath it, and then closed the top one again. "They even told me I was a stupid bitch for wearing this. Like I'm some kind of disciple of yours or something. I pray to God that nothing happens tonight, Zeke. But those bastards deserve some punishment from the brass for the way they treated me."

"Are you armed, Stephanie?" Zeke asked. She turned to show him the pistol in its holster on her hip. "Good, it's happening now." Her eyes opened wide. She was about to say something when the gunfire erupted.

"Get down on the floor, Zeke!" she shouted. He dove for the ground and she moved over to the door. It sounded like machine gun fire outside. Then there were two explosions, like grenades. They could hear the agents firing their side arms. Suddenly, it became very quiet. He could hear Stephanie's breathing from across the cell as he lay under the metal bed frame.

"Stephanie," he whispered. She looked back at him. "After they shoot you in the chest, just lay there quietly if you want to live." She glared at him as though he were speaking another language. But it was another language outside the cell. Unlike in his vision, he knew it was Spanish. His brain was stunned. He had expected Russian, Chinese, Farsi, or even Korean, but not this.

A grenade blew the door open, knocking Stephanie down to the ground. She jumped to her feet and began to fire. More shots rang out and Stephanie was hit in the chest. She fell backward and stopped moving. Four men ran into the room. Two pulled Zeke from under the bed and began to tie him up. A third went over to Stephanie and prepared to shoot her in the head. The fourth man said, *"Oye, ella no, hombre. La mujer no es culpable. Ayundalos con el profeta!"* The man put a bag over Zeke's head and cinched it around his neck. *"Vamanos!"* the fourth man said and Zeke could feel them pulling him out of the room. The last thing he heard was Stephanie's labored breathing. Zeke was pushed into the back of the vehicle and it pulled away into the night.

After several minutes, Zeke could feel a change as the vehicle pulled onto the freeway and accelerated. The voice of the fourth man said, "Senor Zeke, don't worry. We will take good care of you. Just relax." He felt a sharp jab in his arm. "This shot will help you sleep." Zeke held onto consciousness as long as he could, but after only a couple of minutes, he passed out.

§

Sarah Thompson hurried to answer the doorbell. Looking through the peephole, she saw two men wearing dark suits with badges hanging from their front pockets. When she opened the door Agents Tyrone Baker and Fred Emerson introduced themselves and were led into the living room as Abe came to join the group. "Mr. and Mrs. Thompson, we have a bit of a situation on our hands."

"What do you want now?" Abe snarled. "You are already holding our son for no reason."

Baker sighed and replied, "That is the problem, sir. We no longer have your son in custody. Our compound was assaulted last night. Four agents were killed and one was wounded. It appears the perpetrators kidnapped Ezekiel."

Sarah looked aghast and sat heavily. Abe stood trembling as he said, "Perhaps we should all sit down."

"Who would want to kidnap my boy?" Sarah asked.

"That's a very good question, Mrs. Thompson," Baker acknowledged. "Two of the assailants were also killed. They appeared to be Hispanic, but their fingerprints had been surgically removed. Why would anyone be so desperate to get their hands on your son?"

Abe and Sarah exchanged worried looks. Finally, Abe said, "Sometimes, Zeke sees things that are going to happen in the future."

Agent Emerson turned to Baker and said, "That's what Agent Marshall was saying, sir." Baker nodded.

"Who is Agent Marshall?" Sarah asked.

Baker cleared his throat and said, "Stephanie Marshall is one of my team. She is the agent who was wounded last night. She is in the hospital and expected to make a full recovery. She told us Zeke had foretold the attack but none of the other agents took him seriously. You have to admit that fortune-telling is not something serious, right?"

"And in this case?" Abe noted.

"Point taken, sir," Baker replied. "I can also tell you that Stephanie is alive today thanks to your son. He demanded that she wear two bulletproof vests. If she had not done that, she would be dead now too. When we find Zeke, I will thank him personally for that."

"So, you think the attackers are Mexicans? Why?"

"I didn't say that, Mr. Thompson. However, Agent Marshall did report hearing the assailants speaking in Spanish just before she was attacked. That could have been a deception, but there's no way to tell at this point," Baker concluded.

"Chief, I think this might be drug cartel related," Emerson said to his boss. "If this guy can foretell the future, a drug lord would know which trucks would be searched, and which of their enemies are about to attack."

"Fred, that is a lead that we can trace, but it's way too early to eliminate the other possibilities."

"Like the Russians or Chinese?" Abe asked.

"At this point, anything is possible, sir," Baker replied. "I just wanted you both to know that the FBI will use all of its resources to find and free your son. We deeply regret this incident and promise to do whatever we can to resolve this as soon as possible." The two agents stood up. "Excuse us. We don't want to waste any more of your valuable time."

Emerson pulled Zeke's cell phone from his pocket and handed it to Abe. "Mr. Thompson, this was in a locker at the compound. We also have Zeke's luggage, which I'll bring in right now. I think the phone might be fried. We were checking his contacts and it began to smell funny." He walked back to their vehicle and removed the backpack and roller board and brought them to the Thompsons. "Here you go." The two agents walked down the steps to their car and climbed in, just as a small car parked behind it. A pretty girl with short black hair and bright red lipstick got out, waved at the agents and ascended the steps. The FBI drove away.

"Can we help you?" Abe said to the young woman.

"I'm Bea Watson. Where is Zeke?"

They invited her inside and closed the door.

Sarah went to the kitchen to make coffee as Abe led Bea into the family room and they sat on the couch. "So, you're the crazy girl that Zeke has been seeing?" Abe asked.

She laughed out loud, "So that's what he's been saying behind my back! Where is he? I brought him a new phone."

"How did you know his phone was broken?" Sarah asked as she brought a tray with coffee and cookies over to the table and set it down. "We just got the phone back from the FBI a minute ago."

Bea was stunned. "Where is he? Does the FBI still have him in custody?"

"Those two men who left just as you arrived are from the FBI. They told us their place was attacked last night and that Zeke was kidnapped," Abe reported.

"Damn it! History is changing again! This was not supposed to happen," she shouted.

"Please calm down, dear," Sarah urged. "What do you mean about history changing again? Do you really believe you are from the future?"

Bea opened her purse and removed a book and started furiously paging through it. Abe could see the cover, which read: "A Simple Life," Volume 1, by Ezekiel Thompson. "Where did that book come from?" he asked.

"May I sit with you both?" Bea asked. "I swear I'm not dangerous." They split apart and Bea sat between them. She handed the book to Abe who thumbed through it and then passed it to his wife. The cover image was a family portrait taken when Zeke was only ten. "This was the first of his autobiographies. I always keep it with me. As the line of time changes, the content of the books changes too. It's confusing and complicated, I know." She took the book from Sarah and opened it to page 36 and read, "I have never been more frightened than when the cell door blew open and Stephanie was shot in the chest. I knew my turn would be next, but they took me with them. Being the guest of the cartel was a harrowing experience and I heartily recommend that no one attempt to do the same." Bea closed the book and set it on the coffee table. "I know you won't believe it, but until this morning, it was crooked FBI agents who sold Zeke to the North Koreans. I think this change might be for the best."

"Just tell us Zeke will be okay," Abe begged.

"Zeke will be okay, I promise that. Remember that he wrote this book, so that proves he will be fine."

"How is he going to escape? It seems impossible. No one even knows where he is," Sarah cried.

"My team and I are working to protect him," Bea replied.

"What about the North Koreans?" Abe asked.

"That's a great question, Mr. Thompson. Clearly, the cartel was helping the Koreans but decided to double-cross them. That was probably a fatal mistake and we'll do what we can to keep Zeke out of the cross fire."

"Why is all of this happening to my baby boy, Bea? Why?" Sarah moaned.

"Do you think the cartel is after the lottery money?" Abe asked.

"No, I don't. That money is spare change for them. They want his ability to tell the future. He could give every winning number forever, but even that isn't enough. They will try to turn him to be one of them, enabling them to beat their competitors and stay a step ahead of the law."

"And if he doesn't?"

"Don't worry about that, Mrs. Thompson," Bea said as she patted her on the knee. "The cartel still has to deal with the North Koreans, the FBI, and a certain man from my time. I guarantee that I will save Zeke."

"How can you make such a guarantee?" Sarah asked.

"Because I love him, Sarah. Because I love him."

§

Zeke woke with a terrible headache. He sat up in bed and looked around. The room was large with beautiful French-provincial furniture. One open door led to a marble covered bathroom. A wide picture window and a patio door were covered with delicate drapes. He reasoned the other door had to lead into a hallway. He stood, walked over to the door and turned the handle. Much to his surprise, the door was not locked. He pulled it open and saw his room was on a long hallway. To his left, the hall ended in a seating area. At the end of the hall on his right, a broad staircase led downward. He closed the door and walked over to the patio door and pulled it open. He stepped out onto the balcony, which was fifteen feet wide and eight feet deep. It was edged by an ornately decorated black iron railing from which flower baskets hung. There was a small table with four chairs in the middle of the balcony. He sat and surveyed the area. The house sat on a broad green lawn on a hilltop. A long driveway looped around the front of the house and then back. The road disappeared after it entered a dense forest a few hundred yards away. To the left of the house was a large ornamental vegetable garden rimmed by fruit trees. To the right, several smaller buildings sat in the warm sun. As he began to relax, he noticed several men guarding the compound. Each wore a dark gray uniform and carried a high-powered rifle. Now he knew why his door was not locked.

He heard the door to his room open and turned to see an old woman approaching him with a tray. On the tray sat a coffee pot, two cups, and a tray of pastries. The fourth man from the night before followed her in. He appeared to be wearing pajamas. The old woman smiled and set the tray down, and then quickly moved away so the other man could sit. "*Algo mas, jefe*?" she said to the man who shook his head. She turned and walked away.

When the bedroom door was closed, the man said, "Good morning, *profeta*. How are you today?"

"My name is Zeke. Why did you kidnap me?"

"Yes, we know your name, Mr. Thompson. We like to call one another by nicknames here. You are our prophet, so we will call you *profeta*. Trust me, it's better not to know anyone's real name. You stay alive longer."

"What's your nickname?"

"Outside our little family, they call me El Tigre. Here, everyone calls me boss, or *jefe*," the man said.

"Why am I here? What do you want?"

"You're kidding right? They tell me you can see the future," Tigre laughed. "That kind of thing is quite valuable to our business."

"Where are we? Is this Mexico?"

"Yes, of course."

"And you run a drug cartel?"

Tigre laughed again. "You wound me, *profeta*. I rescued you from the crooked FBI agents. You probably didn't know it, but Agent Marcus planned to turn you over to the North Koreans one hour after we saved you."

"What? That's impossible! Why would the FBI do that?"

"Not the FBI, *profeta*, just Marcus and Jackson. The Koreans were going to pay each of them a million dollars for you. You'd be on your way to a prison in Pyongyang right now if not for my men and me."

"Why should I believe you?"

Tigre grinned and pulled his phone from his pocket. He pressed a button and then said, "*Esteban, ven al quarto del profeta—gracias.*" He disconnected and set the phone down on the table. "You are going to love this," he said as he poured coffee for both of them. "Eat something, *profeta*. Elena, the old woman who brought this tray makes these pastries every day. They are very good."

Zeke sipped his coffee and bit a piece of pastry. It was delicious, full of cinnamon and nuts. Then, his mind filled with the image of Stephanie lying on the floor and the dead agents. He certainly did not feel lucky right now to be rescued by a drug lord. He considered the man across the table. Tigre seemed supremely confident and in control of his life, which Zeke admired greatly. He knew Tigre would ask for his help in trafficking drugs and attacking his enemies. He did not know how he would react when asked, or what would happen if he refused.

The door opened and closed again. A young man with short blonde hair crossed the bedroom and came out onto the balcony. "*Aqui estoy, jefe.* Good morning, Mr. Thompson, it is good to see you again." It took a fraction of a second for Zeke to realize he had seen this man before. He was the driver of the vehicle that took Zeke from the airport to the FBI ranch. Zeke had assumed he was one of those killed during the assault. Now it made sense why the attack was successful.

"Sit down, Esteban, and have some coffee," Tigre said. "You recognize him, don't you, *profeta*?"

"You were the driver."

"Zeke, you have to understand what is going on here. I've been with the FBI for ten years. You are probably thinking I'm a mole for El Tigre's business, but that is not true. This man is my brother-in-law. He is married to my sister, Evelyn," Steve explained. "When I learned that Marcus and Jackson were trying to sell you to the Koreans, I tried to report them, but no one would listen. Everyone at the Bureau knows El Tigre is related to me, so they tend not to pay attention to what I say. They can't fire me because there is nothing linking us together outside of family."

"Until now," Zeke interjected.

"Yes, until now, Zeke. I had a choice to make. If I did nothing and the Koreans got you, the balance of power in the world could change. Once the treachery was uncovered, I knew I would be blamed too, even though I tried to report it in advance. I could quit, but that wouldn't do anything for you or the world.

In the end, I decided to ask El Tigre for help. I knew that would end my FBI career, but I still think it was worth it."

"So, *jefe*, what are Steve and I supposed to do now? Run drugs or shoot your enemies?" Zeke asked.

Tigre laughed out loud. He laughed so loud and long that tears welled in his eyes. When he could finally catch his breath, he replied, "You are a funny guy, *profeta*. First of all, I would never do that to Esteban. I have many legitimate businesses here and in the United States. I'll put Esteban in charge of one of them. He'll make a good living, find a wife and have a houseful of beautiful children. Second, I would never do that to you either. That would be like buying the goose that laid golden eggs and then roasting it for dinner!"

"I didn't mean to offend you, *jefe*."

"My skin is a bit thicker than that, *profeta*. I do think it would be fair to get some reward for saving you from the North Koreans."

"If that story is true."

"We are all about to see the proof, *profeta*. Just because their friends in the FBI are dead doesn't mean the Koreans will give up on you. Once they learn where you are, they will enlist other cartels to come for you. Those thugs will be more than willing since it gives them the chance to kill me and my family." Tigre leaned toward Zeke and continued, "Let's be honest. Esteban and I are adults and can take care of ourselves. If it is my time to die, so be it. However, Zeke, what I want you to do is to keep my children safe. Once the battle is over, you are free to go."

"I'll do my best."

Tigre laughed again. "That's all any of us can do, *profeta*."

# Chapter 8

Captain Han Ji-hun stepped out of the bathroom in the hotel suite and walked toward his leader, Colonel Park Seo-Yun, who was sitting on a couch with his back to the other man. As Han came around the side of the sofa, Park set down his cell phone. He was trembling and holding back tears. Han sat on a side chair and asked, "What is wrong, Colonel?"

The older man looked up at Han and rubbed the tears out of his eyes. "I'm afraid our Dear Leader is not pleased with our failure, Ji-hun."

All the color drained out of Han's face. "Colonel, there was nothing we could do. Thompson had already been taken and the compound was overrun with agents, police, and ambulances when we arrived at the time Marcus requested! Surely, he recognizes that."

Park frowned at his friend. "Ji-hun, don't be a fool. You know it doesn't work like that. Suffice it to say that our families are now in custody until we return with the target. If we fail again, all of them will live out their lives in prison, and we will be executed."

"Now what?"

"We simply must not fail, Captain. What is the status of our search?"

"We believe that El Tigre has Mr. Thompson at his ranch outside Guanajuato. We are to fly to Guadalajara this afternoon and start meeting with the other cartels tomorrow morning," Han reported.

"I am certain we'll be able to enlist a small army within a day or two. Each of the cartels hates the others. El Tigre is probably one of the most despised of all. My biggest concern is that our group may turn on itself. Ideally, we should try to use only one cartel in this matter," Park replied.

"The incident last night makes me wonder if another cartel might want to keep Mr. Thompson for themselves. This could start a new cycle of incidents, Colonel."

"That is precisely why we must be on the raid as well. General Kim is moving a squad of elite troops to the area, just in case. If the cartel turns on us, or the raid fails, they will complete the job themselves."

"And make sure that you and I are dead," Han said.

"And our families too."

"Sir, if our Special Forces attack a home on sovereign Mexican territory, won't that be seen as an act of war?"

Park smiled. "Do you think our Dear Leader cares about that, Han? Don't be a fool. The Dear Leader wants Thompson. Nothing else matters."

"Colonel, do you think this man can really see the future?"

"No, but our opinions on this matter are irrelevant. We serve our Dear Leader. If he wants Thompson, we must bring him to Pyongyang," Park replied. He stood, walked over to the window and pulled open the drapes. It was a beautiful morning in San Diego. People were filing into Horton Plaza, and cars were pouring into the city for another day of work. "Tell me, Ji-hun, what do you think about the decadence of the Americans?"

"It is a sin that these inferior humans have so much wealth. They live only for their sexual gratification and do not care if the rest of the world starves," Han replied.

Park was not so certain, although he could never let the words out of his mouth. Everyone had a car here and the stores were full of merchandise and foods he had never seen. If the Dear Leader did not have his wife and children held as hostages, he might just seek asylum in this amazing city. "Yes, Han, I agree. This city is repugnant. I can't wait to get out of here."

Although he would never admit it, Han was also amazed by the Americans. None of the propaganda he had been fed all his life matched this place. With his parents and siblings locked up, he had little choice either. "We should have some breakfast, Colonel. It is going to be a long day."

The two men walked out of their room and closed the door behind them.

§

"What a freaking disaster!" Agent Tyrone Baker exclaimed. "One hour, just one hour was all we needed. Our containment team would have been there in twenty minutes for Christ's sake!"

"Calm down, boss," Agent Gina Preston urged. "You're going to give yourself a heart attack if you keep this up."

"And where is the hell is Agent Branson anyway? Did they kidnap him too?"

Gina cleared her throat and focused her eyes on the carpet. "Sir, we believe Steve was involved with the kidnappers. You know who his brother-in-law is, right?"

"Yeah, we all know that, but up to now, he has distanced himself from El Tigre and acted with the utmost integrity. What makes you so sure?"

"First, he's gone. Steve hasn't missed a day of work in years. Now, Thompson is kidnapped, four agents are dead, and Steve has disappeared. Second, Steve was one of only a handful of agents who knew Thompson was going to be at the ranch. Four of them died there. Stephanie was shot. That leaves you, me, and Steve. I know I can ignore you and me since we set up the sting."

"But why would he turn on us?"

"Well, there was one thing . . ." she started.

"Oh, shit, I can't wait to hear about this one."

"Steve tried to file a report that Marcus and Jackson were going to sell Thompson to the North Koreans, but it was stifled, if you know what I mean," she said, squirming in her chair.

"Didn't anyone tell him about the sting?"

"It was top secret, need to know basis only, boss. I couldn't get clearance from Washington to tell him. They were too concerned about his ties to El Tigre," she replied.

"So, the numbskulls in Washington keep him out of the loop. He doesn't want the Koreans to get their hands on Thompson, so he enlists his brother-in-law to break him out. You really want me to believe that?"

Gina opened her folio and removed a letter and handed it to Agent Baker. "This was put in my inbox after midnight last night. I found it when I got here this morning."

Baker read the letter. It was Agent Branson's resignation. It said he could not stay knowing that Ezekiel Thompson was being sold to the North Koreans, and the Bureau was not doing anything about it. At the end, he listed the names of the four agents who were behind the scheme. "Oh, boy!" he groaned at last, "the director is not going to be happy about this. If they had let him in on the sting, he would still be here, Thompson would still be here, and the four agents and the North Koreans would be in jail. Now, we've got nothing but bodies, a wounded agent, and another who is in the cartel."

"Yes, sir," she replied. "There is some good news though. We bugged the suite where the Koreans stayed last night. They are flying to Guadalajara to set up a team to take Thompson back. They believe he is at El Tigre's ranch near there. The North is also sending a military unit to Mexico in case the raid fails."

"Gina, pardon me for being skeptical, but it's hard to believe the North would launch a military attack inside Mexico to get this man. What is the big deal with him anyway?"

"Marcus said the guy might be a psychic or something," she replied.

"Come on, now! That stuff is all just hokum. That's why Marcus went to Hawaii? He wanted to pick up a fortune-teller? This is just stupid."

"It is crazy, boss. But the North Koreans are willing to pay millions for him."

"What a bizarre world!" Baker said and then began to laugh.

§

Zeke sat beneath a large shade tree behind El Tigre's home. The backyard included a massive swimming pool, two Jacuzzis, and a formal garden edged with trees. There was a swing set close by, and El Tigre's two children were playing on it. Maggie and Miguel were sweet kids. At eight, Maggie was a year older than her brother. She was blonde with blue eyes, just like her mother, who was swimming ten yards away. Miguel was not as fair as his sister, and seemed the spitting image of his father, who was laughing with some of his friends near a large outdoor grill. El Tigre had given Zeke a margarita over ice. He sat with his back against the trunk of a tree and watched this seemingly normal family at play. He closed his eyes and thought about Bea Watson. He wondered if she was looking for him, or just going about her normal workday in the future. A beautiful vision slipped quietly across his mind. She was in his arms and they were kissing. When he released her, a crowd of people began to applaud. Bea was wearing a wedding gown covered with beads and stones. She reached up to wipe her lipstick from his lips. He looked out at the crowd, but did not recognize anyone and wondered why his parents did not attend his wedding. He tried to hold onto the image of her smiling face but it faded away quickly.

He opened his eyes to see Maggie and Miguel shot dead and bleeding on the ground. Dozens of armed men were charging them from the wall at the end of the formal garden. Bullets zipped by his ears and he jumped to his feet and ran for cover. Tigre and his men were firing back with machine guns. A hand grenade landed at Zeke's feet and he threw it back toward the intruders. It exploded, blowing several men into pieces. He ran again, trying to get away from the attack. He saw Evelyn's dead body in front of him and jumped over it. He ran around the side of the house, desperate to reach the road and run away. Just as he came into the front yard, a Korean man knocked him to the ground. Before he could move, the man fired a Taser at him. The needles pushed into his chest and the shock made him shake uncontrollably. Before he slipped into unconsciousness, he heard two men laughing and speaking in Korean.

"*Oye, profeta,*" Tigre said. "Are you taking a nap already? How do you want your steak?"

It had been a dream, a nightmare really. "Medium," he said weakly.

Tigre knelt next to him. "Are you okay, man? You look like shit." Zeke dropped his head. Tigre turned to his friends and yelled, "Hey, Nacho, make his steak medium, okay?" The other man waved back. "Tell me everything, Zeke." Zeke followed orders. He told him in graphic detail about his dead wife and children, the grenade explosion, and the Koreans. "So, how many did you see, *profeta*?"

He pointed toward the wall in the distance and said, "They were coming over that wall. I saw at least fifty men with rifles and pistols. It looked like you had no more than ten men to fight them off. When I ran around the front of the house, the two Koreans were there with at least another thirty men."

"Do you know when the attack happens?"

Zeke shook his head. "Not the day, no. The sun was high, so it had to be around the middle of the day. When I saw the Korean's face, I had the impression that he is currently on a flight from San Diego to Guadalajara with the other man. I also felt they hadn't hired anyone yet. So maybe as soon as a couple days from now."

"You see, Zeke, you are already repaying me for rescuing you. I will make sure I have at least one hundred men here by tomorrow morning and three hundred the day after that. My army will scare those bastards away, don't worry," Tigre replied.

"The Koreans won't give up, *jefe*," Zeke noted. "I felt the terror in that man. His family is being held hostage until they return with me."

"You want me to turn you over to them?"

"I didn't say that. I just feel terrible for his family."

"I feel the same way, *profeta*, but we can't save the world," Tigre replied. "Or maybe you can."

"Don't give me that much credit, *jefe*," Zeke laughed.

Tigre stood up and offered his hand to Zeke. "Come on, let's eat. Maybe you can tell our futures while we dine. I really want to know what Maggie and Miguel will be like as adults."

"I honestly hope I can tell you that, *jefe*," Zeke said as he climbed to his feet.

Tigre put his mouth near Zeke's ear. "*Profeta*, let's not share any visions of death and destruction with my wife and kids. I don't want to freak them out."

"Of course, *jefe*, I would never do that. Have you thought about sending them out of the country until this blows over?"

"I think about that every day, *profeta*. Whenever I ask Evelyn, she tells me no. She says we are a family and a family stays together, till death us do part."

"You have a great family, *jefe*," Zeke said.

"Thank you. That means a lot coming from you, Zeke." The two walked back toward the house.

Several hundred yards away and unseen by anyone in El Tigre's compound, Fola Untor spied on them with his binoculars. After the two men stepped into the house and closed the door, Untor shimmied back down the tree and considered his situation. In four days, his other target would go to the coffee shop and meet Watson, initiating a series of events that would lead to his disgrace. He pulled a small tablet device from his backpack and pressed a series of contacts. The screen flashed green and Untor smiled. There were no other travelers within range of the device. He had already failed to kill Thompson twice, each time foiled by other travelers. This time would be different. He had a nagging feeling in his gut that his stranding Brewster on Solander would somehow fail. Untor had planned to travel even further into the future to find out until Thompson's lucky shot disabled the time sequencer on his power pack. He had managed to patch it, but its power supply would not last much longer. He needed another two days here until the Koreans arrived. Their assault on the compound would give him cover to sneak in and kill Thompson. His power pack should still have enough energy to jump him to San Diego, if his calculations were correct. If he could kill Thompson here, that trip would not be necessary, although the thought of blasting Brewster out of existence would salve his ego and secure his revenge. He put the binoculars and tablet into his backpack and set it on the passenger seat of his rented Jeep and then drove off.

§

The sun was beginning to set as the Aero Mexico flight touched down in Guadalajara. Han and Park filed off the plane and headed to the baggage claim area. From the end of the line of people moving up the gangway, Bea Watson kept her eyes on the Koreans. She was beginning to doubt her decision to come here alone. Kally had begged her to take him along, but she did not want to risk his life as well. When the passengers arrived at the baggage claim, she walked over to a row of chairs and sat down. She pulled out her copy of "A Simple Life, Volume One" and opened it to the bookmarked page. The words were the same as she showed Abe and Sarah. She smiled, knowing that the future had not been changed yet. She paged through the tome for a few pages and did not find any mention of the North Koreans. That was another good sign. She heard a commotion and looked up. Several police officers were confronting the Koreans. They showed their South Korean passports and argued with the officers. A crowd of people formed around them, wondering what would happen next. Bea lost sight of the men in the crowd and considered going over there to find out what was happening.

It became deathly quiet. Bea looked to her left to see a tall, dark-skinned man walking into the terminal, followed by four other men. The leader had a big smile on his face, but his companions looked stern and unhappy. As the leader approached the crowd, the people moved away quickly, many even leaving their luggage behind. In the center of the thinning crowd, the police were still arguing with the Koreans. The leader said something she did not understand and the officers stopped talking and turned to face him. Even from this distance, Bea could tell the men were trembling. Han and Park were confused by this turn of events. The leader said a few more words to the police. They smiled at the man, bowed and hurried away.

The leader walked up to the Koreans and offered his hand. *"Buenos tardes*, gentlemen! I am El Tiburon." After they shook hands, he continued, "I had a call from your Dear Leader and he requested that I give you a hand. Unfortunately, the FBI notified our government that you were traveling with forged passports."

"You talked to our Dear Leader?" Park gasped.

"Mr. Kim is a very gracious man," Tiburon said. "When he explained the situation, I offered to help you get Thompson." He laughed. "I owe El Tigre a bullet to the head, and the money your government will pay me to help is fair. Show my men your bags and we'll leave. I'm sure more soldiers will arrive very soon, so we need to hurry."

Bea watched them as they grabbed their bags, exited the terminal, and climbed into two large white SUVs. They drove off. Within a minute, twenty soldiers wearing black uniforms and balaclavas rushed into the terminal carrying automatic weapons. The policemen came to talk to them and they started to argue. Bea rose slowly, grabbed her bag and headed toward the taxi stand.

El Tiburon opened a bottle of whisky and poured into two glasses and then handed one to Park. "Welcome to Mexico, Colonel Park," he said as he touched his glass to the other. He swallowed the whisky and refilled his glass. "Tomorrow we will plan the details of the assault, which we'll execute the following day at noon. How does that sound?"

Park sipped his drink. "Your plan is fine. Mr. Tiburon, I still cannot believe that our Dear Leader spoke to you. You must be a very powerful man."

"I do all right. I will have some men keep an eye on the compound. Mr. Kim believes this Thompson fellow can see the future. Do you think that is true?"

"Mr. Tiburon, I would never question anything from our Dear Leader."

Tiburon laughed again. "I'm sure that is a safe answer, Park. But this is Mexico, not North Korea." The Korean just stared at him. "Frankly, it seems like a load of bullshit to me. But who am I to argue with a man who will pay me fifty million dollars for a one-hour job?"

"Fifty million?" Park gasped. "For a fortune-teller?"

"I thought the same thing, Mr. Park, but business is business. If we're lucky enough to get rid of El Tigre too, that will give me control of half of the drug traffic and prostitution in Mexico. That's what I'm really after. Mr. Kim must have a lot of confidence in you, Park," Tiburon said.

"I doubt our Dear Leader knows who I am, sir."

"Yes, he does, Park. He mentioned you by name."

"The Dear Leader mentioned my name? What did he say?"

Tiburon downed the rest of his whisky and replied, "He said that Park is in charge of this operation and I need to do as you say."

"He really said that?" Park asked.

Tiburon nodded and said, "And then he said that if we fail or if Thompson is killed by accident, I am to execute you and your friend, Han." Park stared at him in disbelief. "Come on, Park, I won't let you come to harm. This is Mexico! If the plan fails, it will probably be my fault. How could I kill you for something I did?" What he didn't bother to tell Park was that he would receive five million if the plan failed and he sent the heads of the Koreans back.

# Chapter 9

Zeke groaned as he climbed out of bed. It had been a long evening with too many drinks. He walked out onto the balcony and looked out on the compound. Two large trucks had arrived and several dozen more armed men were sitting on the ground listening to El Tigre update them on the situation. All evening, Tigre tried to get Zeke to tell his children's future. Every time Zeke would think about them, all he could see was their bullet-riddled bodies. He would look away and find himself staring at Evelyn. He saw her hanging from one of the trees in front of the house, which was ablaze. Then he pictured a tall, dark-skinned man slitting her throat from ear to ear. Zeke was startled by someone yelling, "*Profeta!*" He looked down and noticed that Tigre was motioning for him to join them. He rushed back into his room and pulled on his clothes and then headed downstairs.

As he was about to walk out the door, Evelyn saw him and said, "I need to talk to you later, Zeke. It's important."

"I'll be right back," he told her as he stepped out onto the broad veranda and down the steps and toward the group of men.

When he arrived at Tigre's side, Tigre put his arm around Zeke's shoulder. "*Este hombre es el profeta,*" he said. The men applauded. "Look at him closely and memorize his face. Your job is to keep this man alive and well. His job is to protect my children and let us know when the attack will come. What news do you have, *profeta*?"

Zeke had not thought about the attack since he sat under the tree yesterday. His mind was a blank, but images began to flash across his mind and he spoke, "The attack will come tomorrow at noon. There will be one hundred and twenty men. Half will storm the rear wall to draw all of you from the front of the house. The others will then attack the uncovered front entrance and try to surround you."

"How do you know it's at noon, *profeta*?" Steve asked.

"The leader of the others knows that the rest of your reinforcements can't get here until mid-afternoon. He can't get any more men either, so they attack at noon," he replied.

"How did you know that?" Tigre asked. "I just found out about the arrival delay fifteen minutes ago. Who did you talk to?"

"*Jefe*, you know I don't have a phone and all of your lines are tapped. These images are just coming to me now."

Tigre looked dumbfounded. He stared at Zeke but said, "Esteban, you know the details now. Start making preparations while I go chat with *el profeta*." Tigre grabbed Zeke's arm and pulled him back toward the house. Once inside, Tigre called his wife and the three of them walked down a staircase into the basement. At one end of the open room was a heavy metal door. He pulled it open and the three of them walked inside. "Sit down, Zeke." After they sat, Tigre held his wife's hand and looked at her lovingly. He kissed her on the cheek and then turned to Zeke. "This is our safe room, Zeke. Tomorrow at 11:00 a.m., I want you, Evelyn, and the kids to lock yourselves in here. You'll be safe here. There is a satellite phone over there. Once things cool down, one of my men will come for you all. There is enough food, air, and water for three months, if necessary. You got all of that?"

"I can't do that, *jefe*," Zeke replied.

"What the hell are you talking about, Zeke? You do what I say if you want to stay alive."

"Please listen to me, Tigre," Zeke begged. "All last night, I kept having images of Evelyn and the children dead. Not once did I see how they could survive."

"Oh, no," Evelyn groaned.

"They are just dreams, darling. Zeke doesn't know what he's talking about. Tell her you made it up, Zeke!" Tigre bellowed.

"No, I won't do that. You told me my job was to protect Miguel and Maggie. If I do what you ask, they will both die tomorrow, along with you and your wife!"

"So, what do you want me to do, *profeta*? Are you going to surrender to the Koreans? Will that save my family?"

"I don't think that matters anymore. The Koreans will take me to Pyongyang where I will likely be executed when I don't give their leader the fortune he wants to hear. But the men who will attack tomorrow want you dead. Their leader wants your territory."

"Who is this man? Who is their leader?"

Zeke thought for a moment and then said, "I think they call him the shark."

"El Tiburon?" Tigre laughed. "That old man doesn't have the balls to attack me."

"That's what I see, *jefe*," Zeke answered. "Please send your family away. That is their only chance."

"I'm not leaving," Evelyn said.

"Listen to her! Where could I send them if she agreed anyway, *profeta*? Tiburon or my other enemies will find them wherever they are."

"I have friends in Hawaii who can help," Zeke said as he pulled the card for the Sacred Life Tranquility Retreat from his pocket and handed it to Tigre.

"You want them to go to a retreat? How can they be safe there?"

"I'm not going!" Evelyn exclaimed.

Zeke stood up and walked over to the door and closed it. He turned back to the couple and said, "*Jefe*, you have traitors in your group. Tiburon knows about this safe room. After the attack starts, half of your men will change sides. Your friend Nacho will kill you himself."

"I don't believe you," Tigre scoffed. Evelyn had started sobbing softly.

"I don't care if you believe me or not. You'll believe it when he shoots you in the back, but then it will be too late."

"Jaime, I don't want our babies to die," Evelyn cried.

"After the battle is over and the children are dead and the Koreans leave with me, Tiburon's men will rape Evelyn and then hang her from one of the trees in front of the house," Zeke reported. He turned to the woman and whispered, "I'm sorry."

"What are we supposed to do?" Tigre moaned.

"I have a plan, but only you, Evelyn, and Steve can know anything about it," Zeke announced.

"I'm not leaving my husband alone to die, Zeke," Evelyn said.

"Don't worry, Evelyn, he's going with you," Zeke replied.

"What?" Tigre exclaimed.

§

"I think we should delay the attack," Colonel Park said. "You heard what your man said, Tiburon. They have more than one hundred men there. It will turn into a battle of attrition lasting long enough for the authorities to intercede."

Tiburon sat back and chewed on the end of his cigar. He studied the fear in the eyes of the two Koreans. His own men sat quiet and expressionless. "Mr. Park, please leave the situation up to me. The longer we wait, the more time El Tigre has to amass his army. In a week, he could have five thousand men there. There is no way I can compete with that!"

"Sir, you have to know the likelihood of Mr. Thompson being killed is much higher when the two sides are evenly matched. We need an overwhelming strike to insure that he is alive when we take him to our Dear Leader," Han argued.

Tiburon put his cigar into an ashtray and looked at one of his men. "Paco, send the men back to finalize the assault plan."

Paco was short and very thin with black eyes and a dark complexion. He had a scar across his right cheek from a previous encounter with El Tigre's men. He stood and said, "Okay, *compadres*, you heard the boss. Get out." The other four men stood and quickly filed out of the room. Paco followed them to the door and closed it after the last man left, and then turned the lock. He walked back to the table and sat next to his mentor and best friend.

El Tiburon leaned across the table and said, "You see, my friends, we have some of our men inside El Tigre's army. They are getting detailed defensive instructions right now and will know where every man is stationed. I even know where Tigre's safe room is and have a copy of the key."

Park looked startled. He blinked for several seconds before he could speak. "How many of your men are in his army?"

Tiburon looked over at Paco, who said, "Forty. When El Tigre sent out his desperate call for support, those men volunteered immediately." He chuckled and continued, "He would have been better served by only having his loyal troops there. Now they will all die."

"Is there any chance Tigre knows of this deception?" Han asked.

"Could some of his men be in your contingent?" Park queried.

Paco stared back at his boss. Tiburon sat back and replied, "No one can be certain of these things until the lead starts to fly. I think it is doubtful he knows about the spies. If he did, his men would have killed them already. As far as Tigre having men in my group, he probably does. If I were you, I wouldn't let any of them stand behind you. If they turn to shoot you, at least you will have a chance to defend yourself."

"None of the revelations are very comforting, Tiburon," Colonel Park noted.

"War is a messy business, my friends. Let's go to my ranch. We are having a carne asada in honor of our new friendship," Tiburon said as he headed for the door.

Two blocks away from El Tiburon's office, Fola Untor pulled his headset off and then walked over to the window and disengaged the suction device on his listening pod. He set it on the table and walked over to the hotel bed where he sat. He pulled a small cube from his pocket and set it on the bed. He pressed the top of the cube and said, "Tomorrow at noon, Ezekiel Thompson dies at my hand. When I see his head explode, this misbegotten timeline should end. I never will have been to Earth 47 nor had the misfortune to meet Dave Brewster. If by some chance, this attempt fails; my transiting sleeve will have just enough power to jump me to San Diego for my meeting with Dave." He chuckled to himself. "In an odd way, it would be better if I did not kill Thompson. That young man never did anything to me. Dave Brewster is the enemy. Is it better to sacrifice this planet, or just to run Dave over in the parking lot?" He thought about the collapse of the Society of Humanity. As leader of the Brotherhood, he had directed and carried out innumerable assassinations. The good of the many had to take priority over one man's life, or even one planet's history. "No, my plan is solid. Both men must die to insure the survival of the Society. Now is not the time to be softhearted and weak. If I let one of these men live, I would not be worthy of my job. My next narration will occur after the assassination attempt tomorrow. Untor out." He pressed the top of the cube to stop the recording. He stood up and walked over to the mini refrigerator and removed a Dos Equis beer. He took off the bottle top and took a long drink. He stepped over to the window and looked out on central Guanajuato. It was going to be a sultry night, he thought. As he watched the sun dipping toward the horizon, he heard a faint chirping sound. When he realized what it was, he ran over to his backpack and began rummaging through it. He found the offending device, his small tablet, removed it and began to tap on the screen. The screen turned red. He gasped and sat on the bed. "Oh, shit! There's another traveler close by."

Bea Watson sat under an umbrella at a sidewalk cafe across the street from Untor's hotel room. She too had been listening in on the conversation in El Tiburon's office, but did not know what else to do. She had no way to find Zeke or El Tigre's ranch. She did know the Koreans were with El Tiburon and planned to follow them to the ranch tomorrow. She pulled the book out of her purse and thumbed through it again. The pages that told of Zeke's escape from the ranch were blurry and unreadable. Bea had never seen that before and stared at the pages. Was her past changing before her eyes? She put the book back in her bag and tried to calm down. Now was not the time to lose her head. Untor was in town, and he likely knew another traveler was here as well, although she had never met him or seen his picture. He was from the Zu race, so he would stand out in a crowd here, being over six feet tall with platinum blonde hair and light blue eyes. She scanned the area, but did not see anyone unusual. The future of the Earth was in the balance. Ezekiel Thompson was the key to insuring the eventual arrival of the Kalideans, and now there was a Mexican gang, North Koreans, and even a time traveler, all here to stop him from becoming the man he was destined to be. Bea felt weak and alone. She thought about calling Kally for support, but did not want to risk another life. She considered crying, but decided instead to order a glass of wine. As she looked for the waiter, a man's voice said, "Excuse me, miss, are you American?" She turned to see Fola Untor standing two feet away from her, smiling.

"*No, senor,*" she said. "*No hablo ingles.*" She could feel her body starting to sweat and her breathing was rapid and shallow.

Untor sat down at her table. "I know who you are. You're a traveler, aren't you?"

"*No intiendo, senor,*" she squeaked.

"Cut the crap, sister," he barked. "You look a lot like a Pa, but you're pretty short. Do you have a disease or something?"

"I'm just a tourist on vacation, pal. Why don't you leave me alone?" she said.

"If you want me to leave, just tell me who you are and why you are here," he demanded. "I have a blaster in my hand and will use it."

"I'm Ensign Beatrice Watt of the Society Temporal Command. I am learning the trade and on an expeditionary mission. Who the hell are you?"

"None of your damned business," he replied. "What year is it where you're from?"

"It's April 3185," she said. Her eyes widened and she smiled. "What a minute, I've seen your picture. You're Fola Untor, Supreme Leader of the Brotherhood, aren't you?"

"There aren't any pictures of me," he replied.

"That's what you think, sir. The Temporal Command knows what everyone who is trained for traveling looks like. That's how we keep from track of each other. It is an honor to meet you," she said as she extended her hand.

He did not shake her hand. "How do I know you're telling the truth?"

"Sir, you are welcome to discuss my position with any of the senior leaders in the Temporal Command when you return to our time," she noted.

"I will do that, Ms. Watt," he replied. "How much longer will you be here?"

"Can you believe it; my boss wants me to be immersed in this time for two weeks. Ugh. Everything is so primitive here, and most of the people stink."

"Ms. Watt, this is a different time. These people will live seventy or eighty years. Life is hard and short. I fully understand your boss's intention. The universe is a big place. There are all kinds of life-forms out there. We must remember our roots."

"Sir, I appreciate your thoughts, but our roots are in another galaxy," she replied.

"Okay, Ms. Watt, I'll leave you now. Please do not mention that you met me, and stay away from me while I'm in this time."

"Yes, sir! I meant no disrespect." Untor rose and smiled slightly at her, and then walked across the street and into his hotel.

Bea ordered her wine and drank it while sitting and trembling for several minutes. She had a second glass of wine and waited for it to be quite dark before she walked across the street and returned to her room. As soon as she was inside, she put her intruder alert module on the door and barricaded it with a bureau. She sat on the bed with a blaster in her hand. "Where the hell are you Zeke?" she whispered. After several more hours, she fell asleep.

# Chapter 10

The line of black vans followed the white SUV down the highway. El Tiburon sat in the front passenger seat with his elbow resting on the open window frame. Paco drove and kept an eye on the vans behind him. From time to time, he glanced at the two Koreans in the back seat. He thought they looked too nervous and considered mentioning that to El Tiburon until he realized that their families were probably being held in a labor camp to insure their loyalty and success on this mission. The vehicle turned right onto a gravel road and proceeded up a slight incline toward the top of the hill that stood between them and El Tigre's ranch. Half of the vans followed while the others continued on the main road. The stand of trees began halfway up the hill. The SUV continued through the dappled sunlight of the tree-shaded road. The sun was almost at zenith now. "*Aqui, Paco,*" Tiburon said. Paco pulled over and stopped the vehicle just before the top of the hill.

"Why are we stopping?" Colonel Park asked.

Tiburon unbuckled his seatbelt and turned to face the two men. "As soon as we crest this hill, El Tigre's men will be able to see us. We have to wait for the others to attack the rear and draw his men behind the house. Then we attack."

"How long do we wait?" Han asked.

"As long as it takes, my friend," Tiburon laughed. "When the gunfire starts, we wait two or three minutes, and then we go."

Park was examining his pistols and only nodded in response.

"I have a bad feeling about this, Colonel," Han admitted.

"No choice now, Ji-hun. If we do not take Thompson back to our Dear Leader, our lives and those of our families are over," Park replied.

Two hundred yards away and high up in a tall tree, Fola Untor sat with his blaster rifle pointed at the SUV. He examined the vans, but could see little through the dark window tinting. He swiveled around to look on the ranch. At least fifty armed men had staked out positions in front of the house. From his vantage point, he had a limited view of the back of the house, but knew an equal number were in position there. Suddenly, he became very nervous. He had enough power pods for his rifle to take on an even larger army, but knew he could not survive the hail of bullets if they spotted his location. He looked at his transiting sleeve. The power readout said ten percent. The jump to San Diego would take at least half of that. Without a minimum of fifty percent, he knew he could not risk a temporal jump. He thought about leaving this place. If he killed Dave Brewster, this attempt was totally unnecessary, maybe. He wondered whether Divine Providence would give that same role to another. That line of thought became too difficult to control, so he pushed it out of his mind. He had thought this plan out clearly and now was not the time to second-guess it. If it was Dave's fate to destroy the Society of Humanity, all of his attempts would fail, but that would not be his fault. "They are just two men out of trillions," he whispered. "People die every day."

He pointed his rifle at the house and looked through the scope. He was shocked to see Zeke Thompson standing outside talking to another man. Zeke was unarmed, but appeared to be wearing a ballistic jacket. Untor had been convinced that El Tigre would hide him and his own family in a safe room somewhere in the house. His plan was to wait until the Mexicans passed

Zeke over to the Koreans for his attack. If those three could be separated from the group for even a few seconds, he could kill the Koreans and Zeke and press the launch button on his sleeve. It would be simple if he had that moment to act.

Zeke looked at his watch, which showed 12:04 p.m. He looked nervously at Steve and said, "It should start any second. Is everything in place?"

Steve smiled and replied, "Don't worry, Zeke, I've taken care of everything." He looked around and then led Zeke to an open spot where no others could overhear him. "Zeke, why are you even here? This whole thing is about kidnapping you. You realize that, don't you?"

"Steve, this is where I need to be. I want them to see me and come after me. They have to know I'm here."

"Zeke, I really don't understand, but that's okay. I want to thank you again for helping my family. Frankly, I'm amazed that Tigre went for it."

Zeke smiled and patted him on the arm. "For most of us, the thought of our death is an abstraction, Steve. That's why Tigre told me he could face his own death but couldn't live with anything happening to his family. I told him of two different futures, which were the only ones I could see. Either everybody dies here, or we make a big change."

"It certainly was a big change," Steve agreed.

"Steve, I want you to join them after this."

"You mean, if I survive."

"You will, Steve. You and I will meet again," Zeke replied.

"God willing, Zeke." Steve pulled a balaclava out of its pouch and pulled the mask over his face. "Stay out of the line of fire. I'd hate to have given up my job at the FBI just so you can get killed here." He turned and ran toward his men, ordering them to put on their own face masks. The masks were Zeke's idea. If the men's faces were concealed, the attackers would not know which of the men were Tiburon's moles. If anyone pulled off their balaclava, Steve and the top lieutenants in El Tigre's army would kill them. Only Nacho had not been let in on the plan. Steve had known he was a traitor for months, but it was Zeke's vision that finally convinced El Tigre.

At exactly 12:15 p.m., the gunfire began. Nacho led the group behind the house, and radioed Steve to let him know what was happening. Dozens of men were breaching the wall while others laid down cover fire. Steve slipped around to the rear to monitor activity. He smiled when he saw Nacho take off his mask. Steve shot him three times in the back and then returned to the front just as the SUV and vans droved out into the open. The doors opened and dozens of men rushed out and attacked. Steve dived behind a barricade and squatted next to Zeke, who was out of breath and sweating. "I told you to get out of here, Zeke."

"I guess it's too late to take your advice now," Zeke said through a forced smile. "You know what to do now."

"Zeke, this is insane! Why don't you come with us?" he asked. Bullets bounced off the low wall and zinged over their heads.

"They'll just keep killing people until they have me, Steve. Now order the retreat!"

Steve patted Zeke on the head and pulled his radio from its clip. He pressed the talk button and shouted, "Retreat!" He rushed out from behind the barricade and toward an open side gate some fifty yards away. Zeke could see many other men running toward other escape routes under withering fire. He smiled when he noticed that Steve had left his machine gun on the ground next to him. Zeke pulled back the lever and stood up and started firing. Several men fell to the ground and soon the rest turned their attention to him. Zeke fell to the ground as hundreds of rounds blasted into the low wall. Zeke threw the weapon over the wall and sat quietly. The gunfire stopped. He could hear his breathing and the chatter among the soldiers nearby. "They won't kill me," he said out loud. "I'm the one they want." He heard a click and turned to see El Tiburon standing at the end of the wall with his pistols trained on him.

"Mr. Thompson, I presume?" he asked. Zeke only nodded. "Are you armed?" He shook his head. "Okay, stand up and come with me. Move very slowly unless you want to die."

Zeke stood and put his hands on top of his head and walked toward the man. He glanced around and saw sixty or more men watching him, including two Orientals. The North Koreans, he thought. A very thin man said, "Take off the vest, Senor Thompson." He complied. "Now lean on the wall so I can check you for weapons." After he was frisked, Paco said, "He's clean, *patron*."

The big man laughed. "Before I turn you over to the Koreans, let me ask you something. Where is my dear friend El Tigre?"

"I have no idea," Zeke replied.

Tiburon walked up to him and slapped his across the face, causing Zeke to fall to the ground. "Be careful with your attitude, Zeke. I could kill you, you know."

Colonel Park interjected, "Tiburon, that was not part of the deal."

Tiburon pointed his pistols at the two Koreans. "I could kill you both as well." Park and Han backed away.

Tiburon laughed again and pulled a cigar from his pocket and chewed on it. "Don't worry, my friends, I won't kill you. I just want Zeke to understand that I am a very serious man." He turned back to Zeke who had climbed to his feet and was rubbing his cheek. "Now, once again, where is El Tigre?"

Zeke lowered his head and said, "Mr. Tiburon, I honestly do not know where he is. I saw him earlier today, but not for several hours. Please sir, you must know that he kidnapped me. I am his prisoner here. He is almost as important a man as you, sir."

"What about the safe room, patron?" Paco asked.

Tiburon considered that idea for a moment and replied, "That is a possibility, old friend. The only other option is that he ran away like a coward dog. I never imagined him to be that." He turned to the Koreans and said, "Mr. Park, you may take Zeke now. Your flight will leave the Guadalajara airport in five hours. Please take my car. One of my men will pick it up later."

Park and Han bowed deeply. "Mr. Tiburon, you have been generous with your hospitality and honest in your word. Once the flight enters international airspace with Mr. Thompson safely inside, the money will be deposited into the account you requested."

"Adios, my friends," Tiburon replied as Zeke was led down the lawn toward the white SUV. Tiburon turned to Paco and motioned for him to lead them to the safe room. "Finally, I will have my revenge on Jaime Ortiz Sanchez."

Zeke and Park sat in the back while Han drove down the hill, away from the scene of the massacre. Halfway down, Park said something in Korean and Han pulled over and stopped. "Mr. Thompson, you should know you are going on a magical adventure. You will be working directly with our Dear Leader. With you to help guide him, the future of my country is indeed bright."

"I doubt it. The first time I disagree with Kim, I'll be stuck in front of a wall and shot."

"Don't disagree with him," Han mentioned.

"If I tell him an unfortunate truth, he'll shoot me because he doesn't like it. If I make up a story to make him happy, he'll shoot me when it turns out to be a lie," Zeke noted.

"You have to have faith that our Dear Leader will be fair," Park said.

Zeke chuckled and then replied, "Now all three of us are living in Fantasyland."

El Tiburon took ten of his best men down the staircase into the basement of the ranch. He told them to stand back with their guns ready in case El Tigre came out firing. The rest of the men were outside, putting the bodies of the dead into one of the trucks. They all knew the Judicial Police would arrive soon, once they were certain the shooting was over.

Tiburon walked over to the metal door and knocked on it, saying, "Yoo hoo, is there anyone home?" His men laughed. He turned to the men and said, "Okay, I'm going to unlock and open the door. I will be behind the door in case he attacks so I don't have to worry about one of you shooting me too. Try not to kill the woman. I would like to give her a special treat." He smiled and the men chuckled in agreement. He put the secret key into the lock and turned it. Everyone could hear the tumblers click. He smiled, turned the handle and pulled the door open.

The opening door closed the contact, detonating the first bomb, which exploded out the door in a ball of fire, incinerating everyone in the basement before they could react. A series of explosions rocked the house and blew debris and shards of glass out onto the men outside who ran for cover. The other buildings on the ranch exploded one after another until nothing was left but piles of burning debris and dozens more dead men. The few left alive looked on the scene in horror, uncertain what to do now.

The Koreans heard the blasts and raced the SUV back up the hill so they could see what happened. Dark clouds of black smoke rose into the sky over the ruined ranch. About two dozen men were standing on the lawn looking back at the carnage. After a minute, they headed away, trying to disappear into the woods. Han turned the SUV around and headed down the hill. At the point where the woods ended, a tall, pale man was standing in the road, leveling a rifle on them. "What do I do, Colonel?" Han asked.

"Run him down, Han! This vehicle is armored."

Untor pressed the trigger and a blast of white light shot toward them. It slammed into the front of the vehicle and exploded. The SUV rolled four times and landed back on its tires. Han was dead. One of the pistons from the engine had been launched by the blast and was lodged in his chest. Park pulled his pistol and jumped out of the vehicle and began to fire on the man. Untor fired again, blasting Park into hundreds of tiny pieces. Untor walked to the door that Park had left open and smiled at Zeke. "Come on out, Zeke. Let's talk," Untor said.

"You're just going to shoot me, so why should I bother?" he replied.

"I'm giving you the chance to stay alive a bit longer, Zeke. Maybe God will intervene and save you."

Zeke unbuckled his seatbelt and slid across the seat. Untor backed away. Zeke climbed out and stood before the other man. "You've got all the cards, Untor. What do you want to talk about?"

"You're the guy who knows the future, right?" Zeke only shrugged his shoulders. "What is my future, Ezekiel Thompson?"

"You are going to die very soon," Zeke said.

"You're going to kill me? With what?"

"I didn't say that. When you try to kill Dave Brewster, you will die instead."

"That's good to know. That proves that killing you is a good idea. Once you die, your planet will stay in blissful isolation forever. The Kalideans will never arrive, and I will be Supreme Leader of the Brotherhood again," Untor replied. "Maybe Dave will live, but he will never come to Earth Prime, and that is all I need."

Zeke frowned and said, "So, as soon as you shoot me, you will have never been here to shoot me. Is that how it works?"

"Time travel is a confusing thing, Zeke. I have to admit I get lost in the paradoxes from time to time. But your statement is true. I will have power again. Dave will be an accountant for the rest of his life. And you will be dead."

"And if you don't kill me?"

Untor laughed. "I hardly see that as an option, Zeke."

A flash of white light shot through the air and struck Untor's rifle, cutting it in half. It turned white hot instantly and Untor screamed and tossed it to the ground. His clothes were singed and he was clenching his burned hands tightly. Bea Watson walked up to Untor with her blaster pointed at his head. "It looks like a viable option to me, Fola."

"You damned bitch! I should have killed you at the restaurant yesterday. I knew you were a fraud," he screamed.

"Give me one good reason not to end this now, Fola," she replied, her weapon a foot from his forehead. Before she could react, he used a knuckle to press a flashing red button on his transiting sleeve. A blast of white light knocked her to the ground. Untor was gone.

Zeke rushed to her and knelt on the ground by her side and pulled her into his arms. "Are you okay, Bea? What just happened?"

She smiled, kissed his cheek, and replied, "I'll be okay in a couple of minutes. Untor used that thing on his arm to send him back to San Diego."

"Rence Rialto will shoot him dead there in two days," Zeke said.

"Yeah, I know. Help me up to my feet, Zeke."

When they were standing, Zeke said, "Can you hear the sirens?"

She nodded and said, "And the helicopters too. The police will be here soon. I hope they have enough body bags. Zeke, we have to leave."

"I know that, but how? I don't have any ID or a passport. You're from the future."

She pulled her phone from her pocket and pressed a button. "Kally, I've got Zeke. I need an emergency wormhole to his bedroom. We are going to have hundreds of police here in a minute." She listened for a moment and then clicked the disconnect button. She held the phone straight out in front of her.

"What's going on, Bea?"

"Just wait a second and you'll see for yourself," she answered. She took his hand and held it. The first police vehicles were just turning off the main highway and heading toward them. The intersection was less than three miles away, so they would arrive soon. A black dot appeared to float in front of them. It was about the size of a quarter and shimmered in its blackness. It grew suddenly until it was seven feet in diameter. It hung there silently like an apparition. Zeke could feel the power of the thing.

After another few seconds, the blackness faded until they could see his bedroom through the large circle. "What the hell is that?"

Bea bent down and picked up Untor's rifle, handing one piece to Zeke. "We don't have time to talk now and we can't leave this evidence behind," she said. "Watch my feet. We will start on the left foot and just step through. Now, Zeke!" They stepped through the window and were now in his bedroom again. He turned to see the Mexican countryside and the exploded SUV. The circle shrank quickly until it had disappeared altogether. Zeke felt suddenly woozy and Bea helped him to sit on his bed. She sat next to him and held him up. "Zeke, that was a spatial wormhole that Kally projected. They take some getting used to."

"No kidding. I thought I was going to throw up."

"Are you okay, now?"

"Yeah, I feel a lot better now."

Bea took his head in her hands and kissed his lips. "This part of the adventure is now officially over."

"What happens now?"

"Can I stay for dinner?"

"*Mi casa es su casa,*" he replied.

She kissed him again. "Zeke, after this, it will be a while until I see you again."

"But I will see you again, right?"

She laughed. "You're the prophet, not me, Zeke. What do you think?"

In his mind, he saw her standing next to him. A thin veil covered her face. He was wearing a tuxedo. To his right, a pastor stood smiling. To the left, a crowd of people were seated and watching them. He had a ring in his hand and slipped it on her finger. "Yes, I will see you again, Bea Watson."

"Good," she said. "But I think two other people want to see you more right now."

"Huh?"

She pointed toward the bedroom door, where Abe and Sarah stood in tears.

# Chapter 11

Zeke woke and sat up on the bed, looking around at his surroundings. The room was small, but comfortable, certainly larger than his bedroom back home, but by inn standards, it was not much to look at. He walked over to the window and pulled aside the curtains to look down on the small city square across the street. Only a few cars moved past at this early hour. He could smell bacon frying at the small cafe two doors down through the open window, and his mouth began to water. He turned back to the small bathroom and turned on the hot water. Zeke sat on the toilet lid while the water heated up. He had been gone from home for six weeks already. After the events in Mexico, he lived in constant fear that others would come looking for him, so he vowed to travel around, never staying in one town for more than a few days. He pulled off his pajamas and stepped into the soothing heat of the shower.

After finishing dressing, he walked over to the small table and opened his laptop. Bea had told him that his phone would provide hi-speed Internet access, and she had not been kidding. He hoped this phone from the future would also be untraceable, but he still kept on the move. He scanned through the contact list on the phone until he reached Bea's number. He sighed and thought about calling her. He set the device down and logged into his blog, which he had named "What's Next by Zeke." He pressed the button to start a new post and then sat and stared at the blank spot on the screen. Every day, he had posted something new, but never bothered to find out later if his predictions had come true. Seven thousand people were now following his blog, but he never tried to know who they were or if they were really reading or just cross-linking to their own blogs. He typed:

"Wednesday, November 12, 2014. Dow Jones Industrials will be up 110 points today so get your buy orders in early. Severe thunderstorms will flare across northern Mississippi and Alabama in the afternoon. A few tornado sightings will occur but no appreciable damage. Looking further out, a major earthquake and tsunami is coming, but the location is not yet clear. An airliner is going to crash this week, but casualties will be low. That's it for right now. Zeke."

He pressed the post button and closed his laptop. He picked up his phone and sent a text to his father: "Dad, lottery money to arrive today. Don't spend it all in one place, and don't forget the Maui house. Love, Zeke." He stared at the screen. He had been in this inn already for five days. That was too long. Someone would find him here if he did not get out. A grumble in his stomach broke his concentration. He pressed the phone into his pocket and left the room in search of breakfast.

Ten minutes later, he was sitting at his favorite booth at Bert's Diner. Where he sat, his back was to the wall and he had a clear view of the street outside. He had sat like this in different cities every day for the last six weeks, scanning for more North Koreans who would spirit him away. Now, he realized that he had spent too much time in this town. If they were looking for him, they would find him soon if he did not get out. His server, a pretty young blonde, set his omelet and sausage in front of him. "So, Zeke, how are you today?"

"I'm good, Sally, how about you?"

"As well as can be expected since I'm at work," she replied. "What do you do for a living, Zeke?"

He considered this young woman with the long hair in a tight ponytail and no makeup. He figured she was between eighteen and twenty-two by her perfect complexion. A few freckles dotted her face and her large hazel eyes pulled him in. "I'm a blogger."

"Is there any money in that?"

"Probably less than serving tables," he chuckled. "But I'm just starting."

She sat next to him and pushed him further into the booth. She leaned close to him and whispered, "Zeke, there have been some men looking for you."

He pulled his head back and stared back in shock. "Who? Were they Asians?"

"No. One was black and the other white. They said they were from the CIA. They showed me your picture and asked if I'd seen you. Of course, I said no."

"Sally, I appreciate what you did, but you should have told them the truth. I don't want you to get in trouble. If they really are from the CIA, you could be arrested," he replied.

"Are you in some kind of trouble, Zeke? What did you do?" she asked, her face only an inch from his.

"I didn't do anything, Sally," he answered.

"Well, well, well," a man's voice said.

They both turned to see two men standing by the booth. Zeke had been so focused on Sally's words and face that he had not noticed them come in. Sally turned bright red and mouthed the words "I'm sorry" to Zeke. "Can I help you gentlemen?" Zeke asked.

"Mr. Thompson, I'm Agent Langley and this is Agent Stanford. We're with the Central Intelligence Agency," the black agent said. "Can we talk to you for a minute?" Zeke nodded and the two men sat on the opposite side of the booth. "Miss, could you please get us a couple cups of coffee?" Sally rose quickly and retreated for the counter.

"What do you want to talk about? I'm in a hurry," Zeke said.

"Let's be frank, Mr. Thompson," Stanford said. "First of all, you're not going anywhere unless we let you go."

"Chill a bit, Max," Langley interjected. "Mr. Thompson, may I call you Zeke?" He nodded. "Zeke, we know what's been going on. We know that some of our agents attempted to sell you to the North Koreans. We know a drug cartel killed those agents and took you to Mexico. We also know that the Koreans hired a second cartel to get you, and most everyone died in the attempt."

"We also know about the traffic accident near your parent's house and the lottery numbers," Stanford added.

"That was my father's ticket and I had nothing to do with that," Zeke lied.

"Zeke, we don't care about the money," Langley replied. "We've been following your blog too. Do you know that your prediction accuracy is almost one hundred percent?"

"No. I don't bother checking that out. Obviously, I've been too busy trying not to be kidnapped or arrested again to worry about my accuracy!"

"Zeke, you're missing my point," Langley noted. "You are in a dangerous predicament right now. If we know all of this, don't you think everyone else knows it too?"

"Like the North Koreans," Zeke said.

"Yes, them and others too," Stanford replied. "Zeke, now that the North Korean story is out, governments all over the world will be after you. But that's the least of your problems. There are mobs, gangs, organized crime, warlords, and everyone else, not to mention every stock picker and gambler. Knowing the future is a valuable commodity, Mr. Thompson."

Sally came up to the table and set down the two coffees along with a plate of pastries. "It's on the house, gentlemen. Bert is honored to support the United States." She smiled and walked away.

"That's why I ran away," Zeke said. "I screwed up by staying here too long. If I had left two days ago, you still wouldn't know where I am."

"How long can you keep this up, Zeke?" Langley asked. "You honestly want to move from hotel to hotel every couple of days until you die of old age? That's not a life, Zeke."

"What else can I do?"

"Come with us, Zeke," Langley replied. "You can live anywhere you want and the US Government will protect you."

"And what do I have to do for this generosity?"

Langley and Stanford exchanged a wry smile. "Just keep us in the loop for anything major. We don't want stock tips or the ten-day weather forecast. But if something big is about to happen, you could save many lives."

Zeke watched the two men for any deception, but saw nothing. He glanced out the front windows to see four black SUVs and two Highway Patrol cars parked in front of the cafe. "Well, it doesn't look like I have much choice. I have been freaking out that the North Koreans would come for me again. Can I at least eat my breakfast first?"

Ten minutes later, the two men flanked Zeke as he exited the restaurant. Zeke had winked at Sally and given her a twenty-dollar bill with his phone number on it as a tip. Langley led him toward the second SUV. Its right side passenger door was open, as if waiting for him. For a moment he wondered if this was another trap. He hadn't asked the men for their badges and regretted his shortsightedness. They arrived at the open door, and Zeke could see his backpack on the seat. He was about to climb in when a screeching sound made him freeze in place. Four more black SUVs raced around the corner toward the cafe.

Armed men piled out of the cars next to them. Stanford pushed Zeke to the ground just as gunfire erupted.

The front passenger in the lead attack vehicle had extended some kind of weapon out the window. There was a poof of smoke and a missile or projectile of some sort shot through the air and exploded into the lead Highway Patrol car, which flew through the air and smashed into a storefront. "Keep your head down, Zeke!" Stanford shouted. Bullets zinged by Zeke's head and he hugged the sidewalk with all of his strength. Suddenly, Stanford was not on top of him anymore. "I'm hit!" Stanford shouted. Zeke could see the trail of blood pouring out of the man's chest. "Get out of here, Zeke. Save yourself," the man pleaded and then blacked out.

Zeke grabbed his backpack from the vehicle, pulled it over his shoulders and began to crawl down the sidewalk away from the action. He glanced to his right as he crawled past the cafe door. He could see Sally coiled up in the fetal position at the back of the shop. He reached into his pocket and pulled out his phone. He tried to remember what Bea had done to get them rescued in Mexico, but his mind was a blank. A man's voice shouted, "There he is!" Zeke turned his head to see an Asian man rushing toward him. He jumped to his feet and began to run. The man chasing him could be another CIA agent or perhaps a North Korean. All Zeke knew is that he did not want to find out. He ran around a corner and kept going. "Stop Mr. Thompson!" shouted a voice behind him. "I don't want to kill you!" Zeke's phone vibrated. He looked at the screen and saw a red light flashing. Some kind of nozzle had also come from an opening in the top. Zeke pointed the phone behind him and pressed the red light. A flash of white light shot from the phone, and the recoil knocked Zeke to the ground.

He hurried to his feet and noticed the Asian man lying in the street groaning in pain. Five other men came around the corner and were closing in on him. He wondered if he should shoot again. When he looked at his phone, the nozzle was gone and a green light was flashing. It was now or never. The men would be on him in seconds. He pressed the light. A huge ball of white light exploded where he had been standing, knocking all the men to the ground. Zeke was gone.

Zeke's head was throbbing and his limbs tingled. He remembered pressing the green button, but then blacked out. The sidewalk felt strange. He forced his eyes open and saw a full moon and stars. How long had he been out, he wondered. He felt around his body and realized he was laying in the sand on a beach somewhere, but how? As his eyes became accustomed to the darkness, he could see the waves slowly rolling up onto the beach. There were a few residences a few hundred yards up the beach, but where could he be? After a minute, he tried to stand up, but his head disagreed and he fell back into the sand. Now there were sounds, the sounds of people coming in his direction. He thought about crawling out into the water. Several people came over a low rise and were walking right toward him. He looked at his phone for help, but it seemed dead. Zeke could now tell they were holding weapons of some kind with lights mounted on them. Soon, he was surrounded by at least fifty people wearing black uniforms and balaclavas pointing rifles at him. "I'm not armed," he said.

"Zeke, is that you?" Bea's voice said.

"Bea?"

One of the people rushed to his side. Bea pulled off her face mask and put her arms around him. "What in hell are you doing here, Zeke?" she asked as she kissed his lips.

§

Zeke, Kally, and Bea were sitting at the breakfast table in the Maui house. Each had a cup of coffee, and a plate of pastries sat in the center of the table. Zeke told them of the events of the day. Bea immediately began flipping through "A Simple Life." The exact story was there in print, even though it had been completely different the last time she had looked. "What did I say about the events there, Bea?" Zeke asked.

"It's not really clear. You said you did not know who the good or bad guys were," she reported. "What does your intuition tell you, Zeke?"

"I'm not sure," he replied. "At this point, I'm not sure there are any good guys. Is this the future again?"

"Yes, but I'm not exactly sure how that happened," Kally replied. "Your phone doesn't have the power to do what it did."

"Can I stay here? Things are crazy back in my time right now," Zeke said.

Kally and Bea exchanged worried glances. "No, that's too big a risk, Zeke."

"Maybe a day or two would be okay," Bea suggested.

"But we have a new problem, Bea," Kally countered.

She sighed heavily. "Yeah, I know. Zeke, people in your time saw what you did with the phone. That kind of technology would be a very dangerous weapon in your primitive time."

"Primitive?"

"Don't take offense, Zeke," Kally interjected. "But if anyone from your time thinks this kind of technology is possible, or gets their hands on a sample, the balance of power would change forever. Time will change, maybe irreparably."

"So when I go back, I'll use a regular phone," he agreed.

"The good news is the attackers were undoubtedly Black Ops," Bea began. "There won't be any news coverage of the incident at all. Everyone will deny everything. But their governments will now be intrigued by what happened."

"It did happen, so what can I do now?"

"Just like them, Zeke, you deny everything," Kally replied. "They have no evidence to prove anything. As long as you keep denying everything, nothing else should happen."

"Should. You said nothing else should happen," Zeke noted.

"We can't control the future, Zeke. You might be able to see it, but you cannot control it either," Kally replied.

"We can't just let Zeke be a sitting duck, Kally!" Bea argued. He nodded and walked out of the room.

"Did you piss him off or something?" Zeke asked.

"He'll be right back. We do have some things that might help."

"Bea, remember when you asked me to look into the future to see if we would meet again?"

"Yes. Is this what you saw?"

"No. Do you think that's important?"

"The future is infinitely variable, Zeke. The attack you just lived through was not in the book a few days ago when I last looked. Somebody changed a decision and made that happen."

Zeke looked down. "It's just that the earlier vision made me very happy."

She flashed her smile at him and said, "Do you want to tell me about it?"

Zeke coughed and muttered, "Not just yet."

She laughed softly and squeezed his hand. "Well, just sit back and think about the future again. If the same image comes again, then it's still a real possibility."

Zeke sat back and closed his eyes. He cleared his mind and thought of his future. A gauzy image formed in the front of his mind and quickly cleared. He was kissing Bea's lips. A crowd of people were applauding. A man's voice said, "Ladies and gentlemen, I present Mr. and Mrs. Ezekiel Thompson." He took her hand and led her up the aisle.

His eyes shot open when Kally walked back into the room. He held a pistol-like device in one hand and a plastic container with multiple compartments in the other. Bea was carefully watching Zeke's expression for a clue to his vision. Kally said, "Okay, Zeke, this is going to hurt." He opened a compartment and removed a green slug and snapped it into the gun.

"What the hell is this?" Zeke balked.

"It's okay, Zeke, trust us," Bea replied.

Kally grabbed the top of Zeke's head so firmly that he could not move. He felt the gun pressed to the back of his skull. "Please don't shoot me!" Zeke begged. Kally pressed the contact and the green slug was shot into Zeke's skull. Waves of agony rolled across his brain and he thought he would vomit, pass out, or both. Kally released his head and Zeke dropped his face onto the tabletop and groaned.

Through partially opened eyes, Zeke saw Kally load a red slug into the gun. He grabbed Zeke's head again and fired. Pain and shock almost knocked him out. Zeke felt his consciousness slipping away. He had traveled to the future twice on a mission to save the future of mankind, only to be murdered by a man claiming to be his friend. He forced one eye open and saw Kally shoot Bea in the back of the head as well. She flinched and clawed at the table. After a minute, she sat back as normal and sipped her coffee.

After several minutes of pain and anger, the pain abated. Zeke felt almost normal again, except for the holes where the slugs had penetrated his head. He sat back and looked at the two watching him. "What the hell was that?" He touched the back of his head and looked at his bloody fingertips.

Kally touched his hand and said, "I'm really sorry about that, Zeke, but it couldn't be helped. I'll let Bea tell you about it." He stood up and collected the gun and case and walked out of the room.

"Zeke, I'm sorry too," she said, "but you know we can't send you back with any new devices that could be copied. The risks to the future are too great."

"What did he shoot into my brain, Bea?"

"This is very radical technology, Zeke. It is used only by our top spies and certain time travelers. The green device is like a beacon. No matter where or when you are located, we can see you. If your stress level is extremely high, it will allow us to pull you away from danger." She winked at him and continued, "But don't worry, making love doesn't generate that high of a stress level, so we won't be yanking you out of anyone's bed." He blushed. She giggled.

"So I'm like an endangered species with a radio collar."

"Exactly! But you are more than endangered, Zeke. You are the only one like you we've ever encountered."

"What about the red bullet, and why did he shoot you too?"

"The red device is a thought tether. Your cerebral cortex and mine are now linked. You can't have a phone to call me, but now all you have to do is think of me and we can communicate," she said.

"You can read my mind?"

She laughed. "Even our technology isn't that good, Zeke!"

"I just thought."

"Wait a minute, what do you have to hide from me, Zeke Thompson?" she asked through a giggle.

"I love you, Bea," he thought with his mouth tightly closed and his eyes averted.

She stood and walked next to him, taking his head in her hands. She kissed his lips lightly and looked at him sweetly. She thought, "I love you too, Zeke." She kissed him again.

# Chapter 12

Zeke fell asleep with Bea's arms wrapped around him and their bodies pressed together. He was blissfully happy and hoped to enjoy her company more when they awoke. Zeke woke wearing pajamas and in his own bed, back in his family home. He got up and looked out the window. Two black SUVs were parked in front of the house. He thought about climbing out a back window, but realized the drapes would be open and the agents would outrun him easily. "I hope these are the good guys," he said to himself. He stepped into his slippers and headed downstairs, stopping halfway down. He could hear hushed voices in the family room. He thought, "Bea, how did I get home?"

Her voice said, "Kally and I took you there when you were sound asleep. Sorry for the bad surprise, but it would be difficult for you to explain disappearing from the planet."

He thought, "I know you're right, but I would love to wake up in bed with you one day."

She giggled and said, "Hopefully that time will come soon, my love. Bye."

He went down the last steps and walked through the short hallway to the family room. His parents were sitting with a strange man and woman, who stood when he arrived. "Mr. Thompson, it's a pleasure to meet you," the woman said extending her hand. "I'm Natalie Anderson from the White House, and this is Director Anthony Marshall of the CIA."

"It's good to meet you, son," Marshall said. Zeke shook their hands and sat on the couch between his parents. "First of all, I want to apologize for the problem in Idaho. We had no information about the other group that attacked. We lost some good men yesterday."

"Mr. Marshall, how are Agents Langley and Stanford?" Zeke asked.

"Thank you for caring, Zeke. Langley was shot but will recover. I'm afraid Stanford died at the scene."

"I'm sorry to hear that," Zeke replied.

"Who were the men who attacked them?" Zeke asked.

Marshall and Anderson exchanged worried looks. "I'm afraid it's too early to tell. All of them were either killed in the firefight or escaped. We have theories, but no evidence we can share with the public," Anderson replied.

"One man was Kang Min-ho. He was a North Korean spy," Zeke said.

"How on earth do you know that?" Anderson cried.

"Natalie, think about what you're asking," Marshall replied. "Zeke, that brings up an interesting question. We examined Mr. Kang's body. It seemed like all of his cells exploded at one time. How did that happen?"

"I have no idea. What happens now?" Zeke asked.

"Son, the government has helped us buy that house in Maui you mentioned," Abe Thompson said. "They are going to provide security for us."

"And we're just locked up there forever?"

"Don't look at it that way, Zeke," Sarah replied. "This will all blow over soon."

"How?"

Director Marshall said, "Son, may I call you Zeke?" He nodded. "Thank you and you can call me Tony. There are two good options in my mind. One, you can give a few erroneous predictions that are well publicized. Others will see you are nothing but a fraud, and pass off your earlier predictions as lucky guesses."

"I am not a fraud, Mr. Marshall," Zeke growled.

"That's not what the director meant, Zeke," Anderson interjected. "Zeke, please call me Nat. You and I will probably be spending lots of time together soon. That idea is just to discourage foreign governments from trying to kidnap you, but if you don't like it, that's fine. The other option is to stop altogether for a while. In a few weeks, you'll be old news."

"But I can help people," Zeke countered. "If I say nothing, I'll be allowing bad shit to happen."

"Zeke, we want you to help people, please believe me," Tony said. "But it might be better if it was a little under the table to keep the press and others from broadcasting it and making you an even bigger target."

"Zeke, do you want to be a celebrity?" Natalie asked. "You will lose all privacy and have big security concerns for the rest of your life. And most celebrities are actors, models, and athletes. They have their moment in the sun and fade away. You can see the future! That skill may last forever. Is that what you want?"

He sat back and considered what was happening. "What do you think, Mom and Dad? Are you willing to be stuck in the Maui house for months while my headlines cool off?"

"Oh boy!" Sarah exclaimed. "You can't imagine how many distant relatives and friends of friends have been hounding us since we won the lottery. That doorbell and our phones ring all day long. First they talk to Abe and everyone loves him. Then I take the phone and tell them to drop dead and they all hate me. It's not their money, but I'm the bitch who won't give it all to them."

Abe chuckled softly and said, "Zeke, my boy, if we can get a little peace and quiet and get away from the damned freeloaders, it will be a blessing from God. You said I should write a book, and all I do is answer the door, smile, and get your mother."

Zeke stood up and extended his hand to the director. "Tony, Nat, it looks like you have yourselves a deal."

"You won't regret it, son," Marshall said as he shook Zeke's hand, but Zeke already did.

§

The Thompsons sat in the back of the black SUV as it traveled north toward the Coronado Bay Bridge. Natalie Anderson sat in the front passenger seat. Director Marshall told them a crew would pack up and move all their possessions to the new house immediately. For security reasons, they had to leave the only home Zeke had ever known within minutes of agreeing to the deal. Abe's and Sarah's cell phones had been confiscated and new secure government phones had been given to everyone. Zeke told Tony that he lost his phone in the gunfight in Idaho. The truth would have been too hard to believe. The SUVs took the off-ramp and began to rise over the city on the long graceful arch that is the Coronado Bay Bridge. Zeke could hear worried tones from the driver who was speaking to the other cars in the group. He thought another driver mentioned a rocket attack from a helicopter. They descended into the city of Coronado without incident.

"Zeke, can you hear me?" Bea's voice said in his mind.

"Yes, is something wrong?" he thought back.

There was an agonizingly long pause. Finally, she said, "Maybe."

"That's not very reassuring, Bea."

"Zeke, I was just leading a discussion group on your first book, and twenty pages became illegible in each book. Something's changing and I don't know what to do."

"First of all, just relax. It could be a good change."

"God, I hope so. Please be careful. Bye."

The line of SUVs passed through the gates to the North Island Naval Station. Military police officers saluted as they moved past. They moved quickly through the base and out onto the tarmac of the airfield. The vehicles pulled to a stop near two small jets. "This is our ride," Natalie said as she opened the door and stepped out. The Thompsons followed her.

Director Marshall had already climbed out of a second vehicle and stood talking to two men in black suits. As they approached him, he turned and shook their hands again, saying, "The front jet is my ride back to Washington. The other will take you to the commercial airport on Maui where a car will be waiting for you. Have a safe trip." He turned and walked to the plane, then quickly stepped up the gangway and disappeared.

"Let's go," Natalie said as she turned to the other plane. The Thompsons followed right behind her and up the gangway. One of the men in black suits followed them and closed the door.

Zeke was not surprised that this jet was almost identical to the one he took back from Maui with the FBI agents. He only hoped this experience would end better. Everyone sat down and buckled their seatbelts, except the man in the suit, who opened the cockpit door, said something, and then closed it again. He sat in the front seat and buckled himself in. The jet powered up and moved over to the runway. The pilot pushed the throttles and the plane surged ahead, took off into the late morning San Diego sky and headed west.

Zeke sat looking out the window for a long time. He could hear his parents talking excitedly about Hawaii. He remembered going there on vacation years ago, when he and Rachel were much younger. He tried to recall if he was ten or twelve at the time, but gave up. After about an hour airborne, Zeke noticed his folks had stopped talking. He looked over and saw them sleeping. He envied them for that. He always had a hard time sleeping on airplanes. He put his head against the side of the fuselage and looked at the clouds below. A few more hours and I'll be officially at our Maui house, he thought and smiled. A movement ahead caught his eye. The man in the front row seemed to have removed something from his pocket and put it over his face. "What's going on?" he wondered out loud. Suddenly, severe weariness overtook him. He struggled to stay awake. He tried to call out to Bea, but in less than the second it took to say her name, he had passed out.

§

Zeke woke with a crushing headache. Every muscle in his body felt drained and he struggled to open his eyes. When he did, he saw iron bars, and realized he had been kidnapped again. Through the bars and across a narrow corridor, there was another cell where Abe Thompson sat holding his head in his hands. "Dad!"

The other man stood slowly, as though trudging through deep snow. Zeke forced his body to get up. When he first stood, the pain was so great that he buckled, grabbed his temples with both hands, and groaned audibly. "Take it easy, Zeke. Go slow," he father called out to him.

Zeke trudged over to the bars and rested his body against them. "What do you think happened?"

"I don't think the crew of that damned plane works for our government."

"Dad, it could have been our government. I don't trust anyone anymore. I am so sorry I got you both into this. Where is Mom?"

"She and that Anderson woman are in two cells further down the corridor. Your mother says Natalie looks like she's been severely beaten," Abe reported.

"Definitely not our government then," Zeke acknowledged.

"Son, I'm worried. Anyone who could commandeer an official government jet has many connections in Washington. No ordinary criminal could have arranged this."

"Let me see what I can do to help," Zeke said as he shuffled back to the cot and sat down. He closed his eyes and thought of Bea. "Bea, we're in trouble."

"Hold on for a second, Zeke. We're trying to triangulate your location and time stamp. Sit tight," she thought back.

Zeke stood again and walked over to the bars. His headache was abating and he was feeling almost normal again. "How are you feeling, Dad? I'm getting better already."

"Not too bad now," Abe replied. "Sarah, how do you feel?"

A voice down the corridor said, "I feel okay, honey, but Natalie still looks unconscious. Something's happening now, Abe. I feel an electric current running through my body. What do you think that is?"

"What the hell is that?" Abe gasped. A small black circle hung in the air between his and Zeke's cells.

"Don't worry, Dad. I think it's the cavalry coming to help us." The circle swelled to seven feet in diameter and floated in absolute quiet. Everyone could feel the energy. A foot appeared stepping out of the circle. Then a man stepped through. He was dressed in black with a balaclava obscuring his face. He carried strange-looking pistols in each hand, and crouched down a few feet away from the circle. A woman stepped through, dressed the same as the man. She carried one pistol and a small tablet.

"Are we clear?" she asked the man.

"All clear so far," he replied.

Bea Watson pulled off her face mask and moved over to Zeke, kissing him softly through the bars. "One rescue per your order, Zeke."

"Bea?" Abe gasped. "What's going on here? What is that black thing?"

"No time for questions, sir," the man said. "Bea, we have only a couple minutes."

"Cut open the locks, Kally," she replied.

"Wait," Zeke interjected. Kally turned to face him. "Natalie and I have to stay. We need to be here for the events to unfold as they need to. Just take my parents somewhere safe."

"Are you sure, Zeke?" Bea asked. "I don't want anything to happen to you."

"This is the way it has to be, Bea. I don't really know why, but something in the back of my head is telling me to stay."

"Don't be a fool, son," Abe said. "Come with us."

"It will be okay, Dad. At some point, people need to realize there are consequences for trying to know their future. Cut them out, Bea." Kally used one of his pistols to cut the locks on the cells holding Sarah and Abe.

Meanwhile, Bea tapped new coordinates on her tablet. The black circle glistened and began to change. The blackness faded away and was replaced by a bedroom in the Maui house. "Okay, Zeke, I've set the transit portal for the current time at the Maui house. Ten agents are outside, but the inside is empty. Your folks should have time to step through," Bea reported. She turned to Abe and Sarah and said, "You need to step through this circle and then you'll be in Hawaii. Stepping through it might make you nauseous or tired, so I set the end point to the bedroom. When you talk to the guards, tell them you just woke up there and have no idea how you got there."

"What is that thing?" Sarah asked.

"It's better that you don't know, Sarah," Bea noted.

"We're running out of time, Bea!"

"I know, Kally. Abe, take your wife's hand and just step through. It will be okay." Abe turned to his son and thought about saying something, but did not. He took Sarah's hand and they stepped through the circle. When Bea saw them safely walking on the other side, she pressed more keys on the tablet. The Maui house faded back into the inky blackness. "We're clear, Kally." Kally looked at Zeke, saluted and walked into nothingness. Bea kissed Zeke again and smiled, but she was filled with concern and Zeke could tell.

"It will be okay, Bea," he whispered. She stroked his cheek with her hand, turned and walked through the circle. Zeke heard a key turning a lock and the black circle was still hovering there. There was the sound of a door creaking open as the circle shrank. It disappeared in a flash as voices speaking in Spanish approached. The voices began to shout and rushed forward.

Two men stopped at Zeke's cell and pointed their rifles at him. "Where are the others?" the older of the two men demanded.

"I don't know," Zeke lied. "I just woke up." He shook the bars of his cell to show he was still locked inside. "They left me here. Why would they leave me here?"

"Rafael, unlock the cells. We need to take these two to *El Presidente* before they disappear too," the older man said.

"Si, Antonio," Rafael replied.

Zeke and Natalie were handcuffed and led out of the jail. Natalie did look awful. She had a welt on her forehead, a black eye and split lip. Her clothing was torn by long gashes that looked like she had been whipped, and she limped. "What did they do to you?" Zeke whispered.

"You don't want to know," she replied. "I'm so sorry about this, Zeke."

"You two be quiet. You can talk when *El Presidente* says you can speak," Antonio barked.

They followed the guards out of the jail building. The air was hot and humid. The area appeared to be surrounded by a heavy forest or jungle. Several short buildings sat on a large lawn crisscrossed with asphalt roads. Small groups of soldiers appeared to patrol the area. They wore battle gear with camouflage uniforms, ballistic helmets and carried automatic rifles. Where the lawn gave way to the trees, a twelve-foot fence was topped by a coil of razor wire. They walked along a curving road for some time. Zeke could see that Natalie was having a difficult time keeping up, so he stood on her weak side so she could lean against him for support. As they continued along the road, a large white structure began to appear around the bend. The closer they approached, the more the building looked like the White House. That struck Zeke as very peculiar that a foreign president would model one of his residences on the United States. Zeke could feel his clothes becoming soaked in sweat in the blistering heat. The guards led them up a few steps, across the portico and through the front doors, where a blast of air conditioning was very welcomed. The guards led them through a few rooms and then down a long corridor. Antonio stopped and tapped on a door, then opened it. They moved into a large reception room where four assistants were typing on their keyboards. A single large male guard stood by a second door. He smiled as the group approached and opened another door for them to pass through.

The room they were now in was a replica of the Oval Office. It looked remarkably correct in even the smallest details, except the large, Hispanic man sitting at the Resolute desk was not the president of the United States. He stood up and frowned. "Where are the others?"

"Their cells were cut open, *Presidente*. My men are checking the grounds, but no one has seen any sign of them yet," Antonio reported.

"What happened to your parents, Mr. Thompson?" *Presidente* asked.

"I don't know, sir. When I woke up from the anesthetic, I was alone in my cell. What happened, sir? Why did you risk an international incident to kidnap my family?"

"Why would they run away and leave their precious son behind?"

"I do not know that either, sir. What good could they have served you anyway?" Zeke asked.

"Hostages always help, Mr. Thompson," *Presidente* noted. "But I have forgotten my manners. I am Tomas Gutierrez Martinez, President of San Tomas. Antonio, please remove their handcuffs. There is no chance they will escape." The guard did as he was told. "Please sit down," Tomas said pointing to a long couch in the center of the room. "You two guards can return to your posts, and let me know when the Thompsons are located."

"*Si, Presidente,*" Antonio replied and led the other man toward the door.

"Antonio, please ask Dr. Sanchez Gomez to join us," Tomas said. The guards saluted and left the room.

"Mr. President, with all due respect, we demand that you turn us over to our Ambassador," Natalie said.

Tomas laughed. "You are in no position to demand anything, Ms. Anderson, or would you prefer another discussion with my men."

"Leave her alone," Zeke fumed. "You do not have the right to kidnap and assault US citizens."

The president laughed again. "Listen to me, boy, I am the law in my country. You show respect and help me out and you will live a decent life. Otherwise . . . " He drew his finger across his neck to simulate slitting a throat. There was a soft knock and a door opened. A slight man with gray hair and steely blue eyes stepped in. He bowed stiffly to his president and then sat on an armchair between the two couches. "Zeke, this is my friend, Doctor Angel Sanchez Gomez. He is going to try to understand your gift. If we can isolate the genes that gave you clairvoyance, we might be able to give others the same ability."

"You're going to dissect me?" Zeke asked.

"No!" the doctor exclaimed. "We will take some DNA samples and examine them. I will run you through a number of psychological examinations to find out what makes you tick, nothing more."

"Plus, I require that you assist me as well," the president said. "We will discuss certain matters of State, and you will advise me. If there are any threats to me or my government, you will warn me."

"What about Ms. Anderson?" Zeke asked.

"Hmm. That is a good question, Zeke," Tomas replied. "We had hoped she would be a CIA covert operative. She would be worth a lot of money then, but it seems she is just a paper-pusher from the White House. That makes the situation tenuous, don't you see."

"That means they are going to kill me and bury me in the jungle, Zeke," Nat said.

"I did not say that!" Tomas shouted. "But the jungle is a dangerous place."

"Mr. President," Nat began, "you said this country was called San Tomas, but I am not aware of any country by that name. Where are we?"

Tomas frowned and his face contorted as if he were going to scream at them. "Please, *El Presidente*, let me answer the question," Angel said. Tomas' face calmed and he nodded at the other man. "Miss Anderson, as you are aware, vast amounts of South America are claimed by various states that invest nothing in those regions and ignore the needs of the people. Those people are treated like second-class citizens with virtually no civil or legal rights. *El Presidente* is the voice and the hope of those people. San Tomas includes under-managed regions of Venezuela, Colombia, Peru, and Brazil. We are building our infrastructure and plan to declare independence in the coming months."

Tomas stood and began to pace around the room. "No longer will our people be left to struggle to survive. No longer will their voices be ignored in colonialist bastions like Caracas, Bogota, Lima, and Brasilia! Finally the needs of these people, my people, will matter and be fulfilled! That is the promise of San Tomas!" Angel jumped to his feet and began to applaud.

While the two exulted in their joy, Nat leaned over and whispered in Zeke's ear, "He is a warlord and drug dealer." Zeke stared at her odd response.

When the two men were seated again, Zeke asked, "What can I do for you, *El Presidente*?"

Tomas laughed and slapped Zeke on the knee. "That's better, my friend. I am making a televised speech in a few minutes. I want you to tell me the future so I can tell my people and the bastards in the capitals!" Zeke reached across the open space and touched the arm of the president for a moment, and then sat back with his eyes closed. After a minute, his eyes opened very wide. "Tell me the future, Zeke!"

"I don't think you want to know."

"Of course I want to know. Tell me if you do not wish to go back to your cell."

"*El Presidente*, you will be dead very soon," Zeke squeaked.

The color drained out of Tomas's face. "There has to be another possibility." Zeke shook his head. The president's face changed to one of hatred and anger. He jumped to his feet and walked behind his desk. He opened a drawer and removed a golden pistol and walked back to the couch and pressed it against Zeke's forehead. "Tell me another possibility if you want to live."

Zeke thought and wondered why Bea hadn't yanked him out yet. He was certainly frightened enough. An idea glowed in his mind. "Sir, if you leave in the next few minutes, you can escape." After the words escaped his lips, Zeke wondered if what he said was true.

Tomas pulled the pistol away and stuck it under his belt in the back. "Zeke, perhaps you have been under too much stress with the abduction and abandonment by your own family. Let us pass this off as a dreadful error on your part."

"Thank you, *El Presidente*," Zeke said, noticing his body and voice were both trembling.

Tomas pulled Zeke to his feet and pulled his face within inches of his. "Zeke, during the speech today, I am going to make opening remarks about the great future of San Tomas. I will tell my people about your incredible gift. After that, I want you to speak. You will tell them how wonderful the future will be, with beautiful cities full of happy people, all with good jobs and nice houses. You will tell them how the great resources of this country will bring a new dawn for San Tomas, and you will tell them that was your vision."

"What if I forget something, sir?" Zeke asked.

"It will be on a teleprompter, Zeke. Just read the words."

"And if I don't?"

Tomas pointed at Natalie. "My men will rape that woman for many hours. Then they will slit her throat, cut her into pieces and leave her remains in the jungle for the animals to eat."

"I will do what you say, *El Presidente*," Zeke squeaked.

Tomas patted him on the cheek and said, "That's a good boy."

The group went back outside and across the compound to a place near the fence. A sound stage was set up so Tomas could sit on a tattered chair with his back to the jungle. He pulled off his shirt and tie and then he donned a camouflage shirt and military cap. One artist worked on *El Presidente's* make-up, while another took off Zeke's shirt and gave him a clean camouflaged one to wear. Antonio stood ten yards away, holding Natalie by the arm with a pistol in his hand, waiting for an order from Tomas if Zeke screwed up.

When the director signaled that everything was ready, Tomas smiled at the camera. The clapboard sounded and he said, "Good day, fellow citizens of San Tomas. As your president, I wanted to give you wonderful news about our future!" There was a popping sound and a bullet flew through the area and slammed into *El Presidente's* forehead, causing his head to explode, and then he fell back to the ground.

Machine gun fire erupted. The soldiers fell into formation and fired back at the attackers. Zeke dropped to the ground. He looked up and saw Natalie jam her hands into Antonio's chin. As he fell backward, she took the gun from his hand and shot him dead. She crouched down to examine the battlefield. She hurried over to Zeke and pulled him to his feet. "We've got to get out of here now!" she screamed and took off. Zeke followed behind her.

They arrived at the fence where she pulled something from her belt and cut several links in the fence and pushed it open. She climbed through and Zeke followed her again. The sounds of the battle were getting further away but still she ran. They ran across a shallow stream and up a hillside and into deep jungle. "Keep up, Zeke!" she shouted. They ran for another ten minutes and then stopped near a fallen tree. "Wow! What a rush!" she exclaimed.

Zeke was panting for air and his legs ached. When he could speak he asked, "What was happening back there? Do you think it was a rescue mission for us?"

She grabbed his head and pressed her lips to his. "That's for agreeing to lie for me, Zeke. You saved my life, but no, it was no rescue mission. I doubt anyone knows where we are. A rescuer also wouldn't kill Tomas unless they found negotiation was useless. They wouldn't even know who he was. God knows I've never heard of him."

"You are a spy, aren't you?"

"Used to be, Zeke. I've been just a White House staffer for three years now. I had more than enough time as a spook."

"Do you have a way to get us rescued?"

"Zeke, I'm not a spy anymore. Nobody knows where we are. We have to find civilization so we can make a call," she said. "I've been meaning to ask you something. Where the hell did your parents go?"

"It's complicated."

She frowned. "Now, you're the spy, is that it?"

"There's too much risk if I say any more, Nat. The future is at stake already."

"You're a funny guy, Zeke," she replied. "But in case you hadn't noticed, we are lost *somewhere* in the Amazon rainforest. The nearest town could be hundreds of miles away. We could wander around for years and never find anything or anybody. There are jaguars and deadly snakes everywhere. We also have no food or water. The rivers are fresh, but there are so many microbes living in them, we'd be better off dying of thirst. If we don't find shelter in forty-eight hours, we will likely die here. Is that risky enough for you?"

"There might be a way," Zeke noted. "But you'd have to promise never to tell anyone or ask me anything about it ever. I won't risk the future of the world for our lives."

"Anything else I have to do to save my skin?"

"Wear a blindfold and forget everything."

She kissed his cheek. "You drive a hard bargain. Seeing as I'd like to live, do whatever you have to do." She ripped a strip of fabric from her blouse and tied it around her own eyes. "Okay, I'm blind as a bat." Zeke waved his hand in front of her face to see if she noticed. Satisfied, he sat back and thought about Bea. "You're awfully quiet over there, Zeke."

"Just shut up and relax," he replied.

"Always the gentlemen," she laughed. "Whoa, what's going on? I feel static electricity coursing through me."

"Don't take off the blindfold and don't talk," Zeke said. He picked her up in his arms. "Just relax, it's almost over."

"I trust you, Zeke." Suddenly, a wave of nausea swept her. "Zeke, put me down, I think I'm going to throw up." He set her down and she felt softness under her. "What the hell? Can I take off the blindfold now?"

"Just a moment," Zeke replied. Ten seconds later, he said, "Okay, now take it off."

She pulled it off her face and looked around. She was sitting on a couch in the Maui house. Abe was sitting on an armchair a few feet away. She could hear Sarah puttering around in the kitchen. She stared at Abe and then at Zeke. "What the hell just happened?"

"You promised not to ask," he replied.

"But this isn't possible," she gasped.

"Do you want to go back to the jungle?" Zeke asked.

She shook her head vigorously. "No, no, no. This is perfect, and I promise I won't ask, but it's killing me."

"How about a nice glass of white wine?" Abe asked. She nodded and smiled.

# Chapter 13

Zeke was startled awake when a man's voice said, "Good morning, Zeke." He opened his eyes to see CIA Director Anthony Marshall standing at the foot of his bed.

"What are you doing in my room, Tony?"

"We're having a meltdown in the White House over your second kidnapping by a drug cartel from federal custody. Everyone is embarrassed and pointing fingers at one another. Congress is demanding hearings and investigations into federal employee corruption and everyone's job up to the attorney general is in danger."

"That doesn't explain why you are here in my bedroom," Zeke complained.

"I'm sorry, Zeke. The attorney general and the president are waiting to hear your side of the story, especially the facts about the kidnapping and how you and Ms. Anderson escaped."

"What did Nat tell you?"

Tony sighed and sat on an armchair next to the bed. "Not enough, I'm afraid. She has already been asked to resign for refusing to testify."

"That's a mistake, Tony. If not for her, I'd be dead already and you'd have more yolk on your face," Zeke said. "And I bet she told you everything she knew."

"I agree, but the White House wants more. She told us the plane's crew was involved."

"Absolutely, I saw the agent in the cabin slipping something over his face just before I passed out. I think it was a gasmask," Zeke interjected.

"Natalie must not have seen that. Thanks for that bit of information. She told us about Tomas Gutierrez Martinez and his White House in the Amazon rainforest. She said you saved her life twice, thank you for that as well," Tony noted.

"She made up for that."

"Yes, she enabled you to escape the gunfight. We're still working with our partners in those countries to find out exactly where that place was." Tony sat quietly staring at Zeke for any sign of emotion. "She said you blindfolded her and told her not to look, and then suddenly you were both back here. How did that happen?"

"Sorry Tony, I won't answer that," Zeke said flatly.

"Do you want our protection or not, son?"

Zeke laughed out loud and then climbed out of bed and stood in front of the other man. "Protection! This is about protection! For whom? The FBI protected me and I was kidnapped and almost sold to the North Koreans. The CIA protected me and I found myself in a South American jungle with a gold pistol pressed against my forehead by a madman. If that is what you call protection, trust me, I don't want any."

"You have a point, Zeke."

"You're damned right I have a point, Tony!" Zeke exclaimed. He face softened and he smiled at the CIA director. "You know Tony, this really *is* about protection. Not my protection but yours and the rest of the leadership in Washington. Did Nat tell you about my prediction for Tomas Gutierrez?" Tony shook his head making Zeke smile even more. "I told him he would die very soon unless he ran away quickly. That's when he pressed his pistol against my head. He told me to lie or his men would rape and kill Nat, so I agreed. Twenty minutes later, a bullet flew through his forehead and blew his brains out. That's why he wanted me and why you want me too. He didn't listen and I wonder if you will if you don't like the answer."

"Okay, Zeke. Just tell me what you want me to tell Washington," Tony sighed.

"Tony, please tell them I am happy to help, but I have a few conditions. First and most obviously, you need to do a better job of protecting me."

"Of course."

Zeke frowned in disbelief. "Try at least, okay? The second condition is that Natalie cannot lose her job. If she wants to leave, that's fine. I can always use someone to help me here. Third, unlike Tomas Gutierrez, I expect you to believe what I have to say. He didn't and you know what happened. Fourth, protecting my parents is your top priority. I know lots of folks would love to kidnap them to use them as leverage against me. In a way, that is exactly what you are doing by guarding this place."

"I don't think that's exactly fair, Zeke."

"Finally and most adamantly, those around me will experience unexplainable things, like when Nat and I were suddenly here and not in the Amazon jungle. Don't ask about that. As long as things work out for the best, leave well enough alone."

Tony stood and shook Zeke's hand. "Son, I will relay your conditions. I have to say that last one might be a deal breaker, but I will try." Zeke stood silently as if in a trance for a full minute. "Zeke, are you okay?"

Zeke gasped for breathe, and then said, "Here is a sample of how I can help you guys to sweeten the deal. One of the president's planes has severe structural weakness and if not fixed, it will fail in the next fifty hours of flying time. I don't know if the president will be on board when that happens, but it's not worth the risk. Check them both and you'll find out."

Tony stared back incredulously for several seconds. Finally, he smiled and replied, "Okay, I've have the Air Force check it out. Thanks, I guess." He turned around and walked out of the room.

§

After preparing for his day, Zeke walked into the kitchen and prepared a cup of coffee. His parents were sitting silently at the small breakfast table. After adding half and half and sweetener to his drink, Zeke sat with them. "Good morning. You two are awfully quiet today."

Abe sighed and replied, "We're sorry about that man going into your room."

"Don't even think about it."

"I can't help but think about it, Zeke," Sarah said. "Ever since the accident at the barber shop, it feels like our lives are spinning out of control. We almost died the last time. If it wasn't for your friends from the future, we wouldn't have made it."

"What can we do about it now?" Zeke asked.

Abe looked around and leaned toward Zeke and whispered, "We think this house might be bugged. Do you think your friend Bea might be able to change things so that woman was never killed?"

Zeke sat back in shock. "Is that what you really want?" Abe and Sarah looked at each other but said nothing.

"No, that is not an option," Bea said as she walked in from the other room. The Thompsons were stunned by her sudden appearance. "Also, the house is not bugged."

"Bea, what are you doing here?" Zeke asked.

She kissed Zeke on the forehead, sat next to him, and took a sip from his coffee. "I'm sorry for the shock, but since you are living my ancient history, I knew this conversation was going to occur."

"Please Bea," Sarah urged, "this is no life for my family. We live in virtual isolation and are constantly in fear of our lives."

"I promise that you will all be okay," Bea said. "Please remember that all of this happened a long time ago from my perspective. Zeke wrote all about this in his "A Simple Life" autobiographic series. This is a frightening time for sure. But it will calm down before long. Once Zeke makes a few more predictions for the US government, they will realize what they have and make sure you are all safe."

"Bea, I don't think I want to be a government agent all my life," Zeke said.

She kissed him softly. "Don't worry, you won't be. This is just a phase and you will go on to do wonderful things. Abe, you'll write stories that will capture the consciousness of the planet. All of you will have long and happy lives."

"Don't bullshit us," Sarah quipped. "You could be making that up just to keep us here. Zeke told us when he's gone to your future, he's just been here at this house and things don't seem that different. Maybe you're a spy too?"

Bea sat back with a stunned expression, but it quickly melted and she laughed. "Wow! You three are a tough crowd! Let me try to work something out. Just give me a few minutes." She stood and walked out of the room.

"Was that really necessary, dear?" Abe asked. "She seems like a nice girl and she saved our bacon yesterday."

"Mom is right that I've never seen anything other than this house in the future," Zeke noted.

"That may be true, but I don't think our government has the technology to zip us from the Amazon rainforest to this house by stepping through a black circle," Abe replied.

"As far as we know," Sarah said. "Who knows what sort of stuff they keep under wraps?"

"I trust Bea," Zeke said. "If she says she is from the future, I believe her."

"Ah. Thank you Zeke," Bea said from the doorway. "It's all set. Let's go."

"Where are we going?" Sarah asked.

"To the future, of course!" Bea exclaimed. "You doubted my story, so I now have approval to show you three a few things, but you'll have to promise not to tell anyone else. Come on, we're wasting time!" She turned and walked out of the room with the Thompsons following her.

Bea led them into the same small room where Zeke had stepped through the black circle for the first time. The circle had already formed and hovered there on the wall, pulsing with energy but totally featureless. While Bea explained the procedure to his parents, Zeke considered this incredible thing. It struck him that it looked like something he had seen on television. He turned to her and asked, "Is this thing a black hole?"

"Not precisely, but that's a great guess. There is an infinitely-dense singularity formed by a solar collapse inside a black hole. This is just a portal between places or times or both," she explained. "Since you've done this before, why don't you take your mother and I'll take Abe?"

"What about the console?"

"Don't worry, Zeke, I'll take it. You two go first."

"Bea, when we stepped through the portal in the rainforest, we could see the other side. Why is this one just black?" Abe asked.

"Another great question," she replied. "The two locations in that trip were in the same time and not far apart. Now, we're stepping through more than a thousand years. Large distances in space, time, or both make the other side invisible. Go ahead, Zeke."

"I'm afraid," Sarah noted.

"Don't worry, Mom, I'll be with you the whole time. Just hold my hand," Zeke replied. They stepped through.

"Now it's you and me, Abe," she smiled. She grabbed the console and held it under her arm and took his hand with her free one. "It will only take a second, less actually." They stepped through. There was a crackle of electricity and the circle disappeared.

"This is disappointing," Sarah said. "We're back in the same place, so what's the big deal."

"Hello, I'm Aria Watson, Bea's grandmother," said the woman standing behind the console. "Zeke, please move away from the portal."

"It's good to see you again, Aria," Zeke said. "This is my mother, Sarah." Bea and Abe appeared through the portal. "And that's my father, Abe."

"It's nice to meet you both. Your son is quite a hero to us," Aria replied. "Please go on into the main room, and I'll join you soon."

Bea and the Thompsons walked into the living room, which seemed identical to the one they left moments ago. "So, this is the future, huh?" Sarah quipped.

"It doesn't look any different to me either," Abe noted.

Aria walked out of the small room and closed the door behind her. "I know this place looks familiar, but there is a good reason for that. Since it's your responsibility, why don't you tell them, Bea?"

"This home is a historical monument belonging to the Ezekiel Thompson College of Science and Prophecy," she began. "I am a professor of prophecy and languages and director of the museum that owns this place. But as you note, it doesn't look much different from the twenty-first century, and we pride ourselves for that. Let's go see something else that does look different. Follow me." She walked to the front door, opened it and stepped into the midday sun.

In the center of what had been the large sloping lawn was a concrete circular slab about sixty feet in diameter. Sitting in the center was a vehicle of some sort. It was sixty feet long and ten feet wide and sat on several struts. The front was a glass cone and windows lined the rest of the fuselage on both sides. A door was open and a gangway reached down to the ground. At the back of the vehicle were three large nozzles that looked as if they came from a rocket of some kind. Bea walked to the top of the gangway and motioned the others to join her inside.

When the Thompsons entered the vehicle, they saw there were ten rows of seats, two seats on either side of a wide aisle. The seats were plush with a three-point harness for security. Three more seats were located at the power console up front. Bea sat down in the first row of passenger seats and demonstrated how to buckle the restraints. "Okay, everyone sit down and buckle in."

"What kind of game is this, Bea?" Sarah asked.

"Sarah, this is no game," Bea noted. "You wanted to know that you and your family will be safe. I said I know that because I'm from the future. You doubted that, so now here we are in the future. You're going on the ride of your life that will prove I was telling the truth. Hopefully, you will go back to your time and stop worrying so much." Sarah said nothing, but sat next to Bea and buckled herself in.

Aria checked everyone's restraints for safety and then sat at the pilot's seat and buckled herself in. She pressed a button and the gangway folded away and the door closed and sealed itself. She put a small headset on and said, "Shuttle ZT5 is ready for takeoff for the mainland. Do I have clearance? Roger that." She moved some levers and keyed commands into the console. The engines came to life, but their sound was soft, like a low rumble. "Here we go, gang!"

The shuttle floated up into the air. Within seconds, it was several hundred feet over the surface. The Pacific Ocean glistened in the afternoon sunlight. The ship turned silently. "The acceleration can be a bit disconcerting," Bea said. The shuttle shot away to the east at high speed. Maui disappeared within seconds. The Big Island was visible for five seconds on the right and then nothing but the deep blue of the ocean.

"How fast are we going, Aria?" Abe asked.

"We're heading up to five thousand miles per hour. We'll cruise at that speed for twenty minutes and begin our deceleration."

"Wow!" Abe replied.

Zeke watched the world zip past in stunned silence. He would see a bank of clouds in the distance. The shuttle would reach them in seconds and leave them far behind almost instantly. He looked to his left and saw his mother and Bea chatting happily. "It's all real," he thought to himself as he closed his eyes and dozed off.

§

"Zeke, we're here," Bea whispered in his ear. He opened his eyes and noticed the shuttle had landed on a concrete circle in the center of an expanse of grass. Bea unbuckled his restraint and led him out the door and down the gangway where Aria was waiting with Sarah and Abe. Bea took his arm and said, "I envy you, Zeke. You can fall asleep just about anywhere. Did you dream about anything?"

"Nothing good," he replied as they joined the others. Aria turned and began to walk toward a large sandstone building with a portico across the entire front supported by columns. "Where are we, Bea?"

"This is the campus of the Ezekiel Thompson College of Science and Prophecy," she replied. She pointed toward the portico and asked, "Can you read what it says up there?"

"Science knows, but prophecy believes," Zeke read. "Is all of this real? Sometimes I think I'll wake up back in that barber chair before all of this began to happen."

"Oh, it's real all right," Aria laughed. She stopped and pointed to her right. Sitting inside a gated fence was the Thompson home. It was no longer on a neighborhood street, but sat on a field of grass surrounded by flower beds. "Don't worry, it's not the original. Frankly, we've been traveling to your time gathering data for this school. Perhaps we can take a tour later, and you can tell me where we made mistakes."

The group climbed the stone steps and walked through the massive doors. The foyer was circular and one hundred feet in diameter. Sets of double doors leading deeper into the building were at each key compass point. The open walls were covered by pictures of people. Aria led them to the largest, which was a painting of Zeke and Peter Smith. They were standing in the

Oval Office with a third man between them. Zeke assumed that man was a future president. Peter looked quite old, with thin white hair and a deeply wrinkled brow. Zeke's hair was graying, but appeared much younger than Smith. "What is this picture about, Aria?"

Bea said, "According to your book, 'A Simple Life' Volume 7, you and Peter met with President Lancaster just after he was reelected. He is best remembered for trying to stop the decline of democracy in the West that eventually led to The War."

"The war?" Abe asked.

"Don't worry," Aria interrupted. "Lancaster did a great job and delayed it for more than one hundred years."

"What happened during the war?" Abe pressed.

"I'm sorry, Abe, but we're really not authorized to discuss anything else," Aria replied. "Let me check, and I'll let you know what else I can tell you." Abe nodded but did not look happy.

"Aria, I still don't understand how science and fortune-telling can be related," Zeke said.

Aria grinned and replied, "Well, I certainly can't tell you that, Zeke. You are the one who gets to figure that out."

"Okay, I suppose that's fair. So, what do we do now?"

"I think the tour is at an end," she replied. "Now you've seen the future and not just the same room. I'll fly us back to Hawaii and then it's back to your time."

# Chapter 14

Things had begun to slow down since the Thompsons had visited the future. Activities in the Maui house focused on writing and enjoying the sunshine and the nearby beach. Abe Thompson discovered a knack for turning phrases and weaving tales that had long been dormant during his business career. Each time he shared his work with his son, Zeke was impressed by Abe's hidden talent. Today was Sunday, and the plan for the day was football.

Zeke and his father sat on the couch opposite the flat-screen television. The commentators were talking about the prospects for the day and which athletes would play or were still injured. Sarah walked in from the kitchen with a bowl of guacamole and another full of tortilla chips. She set them down on the coffee table and turned to leave the room, just as a breaking news alert caught her attention.

"It has just been reported that Air Force One has crashed in the Ohio countryside. At this time, we have no details on the crash or even whether the president was on board at the time. Repeating this urgent bulletin, Air Force One has crashed. We will provide further reports as they become available."

The Thompsons were in shock. All the color had drained out of Zeke's face and trickles of sweat rolled down his brow. "Oh my God, Zeke!" Sarah cried.

"Maybe President Nelson wasn't on board," Abe noted. Zeke stared at the screen, unable to say a word. "Zeke, was he on board?"

"I don't know," Zeke squeaked.

§

Vice President Andrew Lake sat at the head of the conference table in the situation room at the White House. The secretary of defense and the directors of the FBI and CIA sat on either side of him. "What do we know, Carl?" Lake asked.

Carl Madison, director of the FBI replied, "Ben is in a medically induced coma at Walter Reed, Andy. Everyone else on board died on impact. The NTSB will be on the ground within two hours, and the Army has already cordoned off the crash site."

"Is Ben expected to survive?" Tony Marshall, director of the CIA asked.

"It's too early to tell, Tony," Carl replied. He looked at Tony for a moment and then turned his attention to the vice president, saying, "With all due respect to Tony, why is he here, Andy?"

"That was my idea, Carl," interjected Frank Albright, secretary of defense. "Tony came to Andy and me a few days ago talking about structural problems with Air Force One. When this happened, that conversation clicked in my mind."

"Frank, please excuse me for asking, but did your people check out the planes?" Carl asked.

The door opened and Attorney General Cynthia Travers entered, sat down and asked, "What did I miss?"

"Tony was just about to tell us about the prior warning on Air Force One," Carl noted.

"It was in my report," Tony began. "I met with a man named Ezekiel Thompson from California. He claims to have some capability to foresee future events."

Cindy stifled a laugh and replied, "Yes, I remember that now. Why did you go personally, Tony? I would have thought any agent would do to debunk this mumbo-jumbo."

Tony frowned at his boss. "In my report, I noted that foreign agents from North Korea and South America have both attempted to kidnap Mr. Thompson. The North Koreans actually tried twice! At first, they bribed some FBI agents to get their hands on him. Somehow, a Mexican drug lord got to him first. Then the North Koreans paid a second drug lord to get him from the first, leading to a massive gun battle where the Koreans and many others were killed. Then you authorized Carl to put him in a safe house in Hawaii. On the flight from North Island NAS to Maui, co-opted CIA agents kidnapped him and took him to South America where he was held by another drug dealer."

"So, you want us to believe that this Thompson fellow actually can see the future?" Cindy quizzed. "You really believe his stories?"

"I don't know, but this young man is drawing a lot of attention," Tony replied and then turned to the secretary of defense. "Frank, could you please answer Carl's last question? Did your people check out the planes?"

"I don't care for the tone of your insinuation, Tony," Frank bristled. "If I received the report, it was checked," Frank lied.

"I'm sorry, Mr. Secretary," Tony replied. He turned to the vice president and said, "I'm not sure if I have any other answers, sir."

Andy stood up and looked at the small group in the room, sizing them up for his brainstorm. "Let's look at this logically, folks. The only clue we have to this tragedy is the Thompson fellow, who is already known to attract attention from North Korea and multiple drug cartels. We have to wait for their report, but if the NTSB blames the crash on structural problems, there can only be a few possibilities." He smiled and waited while his words sank in. "The first possibility is that Frank lied and never told his people to check the planes. Second, he told them and his people screwed up big time. Both of those options require us to believe Thompson is a prophet, like Moses from the Old Testament. Frankly, I think that is unlikely." He walked over to a small refrigerator and withdrew a bottle of water. He twisted off the cap and took a long drink. "Fortunately, there are other possibilities that don't require precognition. Tony just told us there were crooked agents in both the CIA and FBI. I think Thompson is managing them to make us look bad."

Tony looked back in utter disbelief. "Mr. Vice President, Zeke Thompson is a very young man. I hardly see how he could have perpetrated all of this."

"Don't be naive, Tony!" Andy shouted. "Our country has many enemies. What better weapon to lead their spies than the last person anyone would ever consider? I'll bet he has people inside DOD who damaged that plane just before the fateful takeoff. Thompson has been the victim so far, making him the last person to suspect. It's the perfect cover."

The FBI director said, "Your idea has some merit, Andy, but I doubt we have anything concrete to charge Thompson with at this time."

"I don't care, Carl," the vice president scowled. "Thompson is a menace to this great country. Every minute he is free, he is likely planning the next attack. We have to lock him up and find out who his handlers and black agents are."

"With all due respect, Mr. Vice President, we cannot ignore the law," Cindy said.

"Listen to the four of you whine like babies," the vice president replied. "Our dear friend, the president of the United States is on life-support across town. The American people don't even know if he is still alive. And we can't tell them if he will recover. Our enemies do not care about any of us. They will use these moments of weakness to strike again and again." He looked at his watch. "I am riding over to Walter Reed with Alice in ten minutes. What do you want me to tell her and her children?" He sighed heavily and finished, "Carl, do the right thing. Arrest Thompson and put him somewhere no one can find him until this gets straightened out." He turned and walked out of the room, closing the door behind him.

Cindy said, "Carl, arrest Thompson as soon as possible and turn him over to Tony. Tony, find a place to keep Thompson away from everyone for a while. Now, please leave. I need to speak to the secretary for a moment." Carl and Tony stood and walked silently out of the room and closed the door.

"What is it, Cindy?" Frank asked.

"You son of a bitch! You didn't tell your men to check those planes, did you?" she fumed.

"How dare you make such an accusation?" he screamed.

She stood up and pointed at the secretary, saying, "I'm going to get to the bottom of this mess, Frank, and you'd better hope there are fresh maintenance reports or it's going to be your head." He started to reply, but she turned and walked away.

§

Zeke was handcuffed and shackled to the jump seats in a C-17 Globemaster Air Force cargo jet. Across the open interior, four military police watched over him. His face was bruised, his left eye blackened and his clothes torn. It had been early morning on the third day after he returned from the future when the soldiers arrived at the door along with two FBI agents. Now, six hours later, he was away from his family, and that was all he knew. His parents had tried to reason with the agents, but they were ignored. Agent Paul Rubens warned them that if they made the arrest public, their home would be seized and their lottery winnings confiscated as part of an international espionage plot. He then ordered the security detail to keep the Thompsons in their home, disconnect their phone and Internet service and take their mobile phones. The last image Zeke had in his mind of his parents was his mother crying and Abe trying futilely to calm her down.

Their vehicles drove from the Maui house to the Kahului Airport, where the military jet was parked on a pad far from the terminal. The FBI agents took Zeke on board the airplane and requested the soldiers wait a few minutes outside. The cockpit crew was ordered to prepare for travel but not leave the cockpit. Agent Mark Summers chained Zeke's feet together and then connected the shackles to the metal jump seats, and then pushed Zeke down. "Listen, you son of a bitch," Summers had begun, "we know you are the lead agent in the plan to assassinate President Nelson. It will go easier for you if you just confess right now."

"I didn't do anything!" Zeke protested.

Summers backhanded him across the face. "Don't you lie to us, punk!" He punched Zeke in the stomach, making him double over."

"That's enough, Mark," Agent Rubens said, inserting himself between the two men. "Listen, Zeke, you seem like a reasonable guy. Just tell us the truth and everything will be okay."

"All I did was tell Director Marshall that one of the Air Force One jets had structural problems. He said he would get it checked out."

"How did you know about the problems?" Paul asked.

Zeke looked worried. He knew no one here would believe him. "Sometimes I see stuff before it happens."

Paul slugged Zeke on the other side of his face, knocking him down on the seat. "You are nothing but a worthless pile of shit! We were told you would make up some stupid story like this. ESP is bullshit! The only way you knew is because you and your pals did it." He clapped Agent Summers on the shoulder and said, "Let's get out of here, Mark. The CIA knows how to get the truth out of trash like this." The two men walked away, opened the door of the plane, and climbed out. Zeke pulled himself up to a sitting position and spat blood onto the floor of the plane. His left eye was swelling closed quickly.

Minutes later, the four soldiers climbed on board. Sergeant Mike Singleton hurried over to a cabinet and withdrew a first aid kid and then treated Zeke's injuries. "Those assholes did this to you?" he said to Zeke.

"Let him die, Mike!" one of the other soldiers said as he strapped in. "He tried to kill the president!"

"No, I didn't," Zeke moaned softly.

"Were you involved?" Mike whispered. Zeke shook his head.

§

Zeke shuddered at the memory of the assault. He could also sense that the plane was losing altitude. Wherever they were headed, they were almost there. Singleton unbuckled his restraint and walked over and sat next to Zeke. "We're landing in a little bit at Elmendorf Air Force Base in Alaska. The CIA will meet this flight and our orders are to hand you over to them, okay?" Zeke nodded. "Mr. Thompson, if you were involved in the crash of the president's plane, I hope they kill you slowly. If you are innocent, I apologize for all of this."

"Thank you," Zeke said. The soldier went back to his seat and buckled his restraints.

§

The convoy of black vehicles snaked through the Alaskan wilderness for hours. The lights of Anchorage had long faded away. Zeke was in the fourth car in the convoy. Two agents sat up front and one next to him. All were heavily armed and appeared not to be very happy with this task. No one asked about his injuries or spoke to him at all. It was very dark outside now, with only a few oncoming headlights from time to time. He thought about his trip to the FBI ranch outside San Diego and wondered if more North Koreans might be waiting at his new home. "When can I call my parents or a lawyer?" he asked. The agent seated next to him flashed a frown and turned away without speaking.

The convoy slowed and turned left onto a gravel road, which led up a gradual hill. The ride was rough and Zeke bounced and rocked back and forth. His handcuffs were cutting into his wrists and his face was still aching. Twenty minutes later, the SUV stopped. The agent next to him pulled a sack over Zeke's head and cinched it around his neck. Then the vehicles continued. Zeke was panting and sweating inside the bag. He had always been claustrophobic and this was not helping, but he knew better than to bring that up. The FBI agents had been too eager to punch him, and they were technically law enforcement. These men were spies and lived by different rules.

The vehicle stopped. Zeke could feel the frigid air as the man next to him opened his door and climbed out. Zeke's door opened and he felt someone unbuckling his seatbelt. A man's voice said, "We'll help you out, Mr. Thompson, but don't try anything stupid." As he stepped out, he could feel the crunch of snow under his feet, which immediately brought the sensation of the sand on Maui to his mind. He wished he was there now. A man held each of his arms and led him forward. They stopped and he could hear a door being opened. They moved forward and Zeke felt warm air touching his body. He was inside. They continued for several feet and stopped for another door. After another few seconds, they stopped again and turned him to the right. He stepped forward and felt the room moving downward. Was this an elevator? When the doors opened, they went forward, waiting for another door and then continued for a ways. Finally, a door was opened and Zeke and the men entered. The agent who had been sitting next to him on the vehicle pulled the sack off his head. The second removed Zeke's handcuffs. They were in a small cell, not that different from the one at the San Diego FBI ranch. A man and a woman entered the room. The man set a tray of food down on a small table. The woman sat on the small chair. Everyone but Zeke and the woman left the room and the door locked shut.

"Please, Zeke, have a seat," she smiled. "I am Attorney General Travers, but please call me Cindy."

Zeke sat on the metal cot and said, "I've seen you on television."

"Mr. Thompson, let's cut to the chase," she began. "Were you involved in the crash of Air Force One?"

"No, ma'am!" he exclaimed. "All I did was warn Director Marshall that it might happen."

"You expect us to believe you are clairvoyant?"

"I don't expect anyone to believe me, Cindy, but I saw what I saw."

"Do you know what really happened?"

"Yes I do. While I was on the flight here, I could see everything that happened in incredible detail. Don't ask me why this kind of thing happens, but it was like a movie in my mind," Zeke reported.

"Why did the plane crash?"

"Tony reported my vision to the vice president and the defense secretary. The secretary ignored it because he doesn't believe in my gift."

"Why didn't the vice president ask for the inspection?" she asked.

"He trusted the secretary to do his job. Cindy, you would want the president and vice president to trust you, wouldn't you?"

She smiled and touched his knee with her hand. "Let me ask the questions today, okay?"

"I'm sorry."

"Do you know the status of President Nelson and whether he will survive?" Cindy asked.

"He is in a medically-induced coma at Walter Reed. His doctors think he has less than a fifty percent chance for recovery."

"How do you know these things, Zeke? None of that has been reported anywhere."

"The images just come to me, Cindy. I don't ask for them. They just pop in."

"If the president dies, that will be a black day for the country," Cindy sighed.

"You don't know the half of it!" Zeke exclaimed.

"What do you mean by that?"

"Cindy, you know that Vice President Lake has always been more hawkish than President Nelson, right?"

"That was when he was a blow-hard senator, Zeke. I think Ben has softened his corners."

Zeke half-smiled and said, "With all due respect, that is crazy and you know it. Lake would love nothing better than an excuse to attack America's enemies. Secretary Albright is his strongest supporter and advocate. If the president dies or has to resign, Lake's fantasies will come true. He can strike anywhere in the world with impunity by saying he is going after those who hurt the president. The people will support him once they learn the president's condition. More than half the Congress will chomp at the bit to fight. Escalation is almost inevitable."

"You have any more good news, Zeke?" she cringed.

"The only people who know for a fact that I told Tony about the crash are you, me, Secretary Albright, VP Lake, and Tony. Others heard second hand, but that small group has evidence, either as an eyewitness or from Tony's report. Albright and Lake will take care of each other. Tony, you and I will be collateral damage if we try to stop them."

Cindy stood and began to pace back and forth. "Zeke, you have to know that my bullshit monitor is flashing like crazy right now. Most likely, you are just making this up. But if, and I emphasize *if*, your nutty story is true, what can we do?"

"Attorney General, we have to hope that the president recovers quickly before any of this can happen."

"Frankly, Zeke, I don't feel very hopeful right now. What do you think is going to happen?"

"I wish I knew for sure," he noted. "I know there is a future where the president comes back, but I'm not sure I know how to get there." Zeke thought about Bea and the green pills she had given him. Maybe future medicine could help?

"Zeke, try not to be too miserable here," she replied as she knocked on the door. "I'll see what I can do to get the best doctors in the world on the case. Good luck." The door opened and she walked out. The lock turned. Zeke took a sip of water and bit into the sandwich on his tray.

# Chapter 15

The following morning, the national press released a statement from the White House stating that unknown agents tampered with the president's plane, causing it to break apart during a flight from Washington, D.C. to Seattle. Fifty people on board died, and President Benjamin Nelson was the sole survivor. The president was in critical condition and the medical staff was unsure of his odds of survival. It was also reported that a single unnamed person was being held as a person of interest in the case. Vice President Andrew Lake had assumed the duties of president during Nelson's recovery. By noon tens of thousands of well-wishers had placed flowers on the gates of the White House and near the two barricades that blocked the roads leading to the crash site. The vice president scheduled a speech on all major networks for that evening to share more information.

The Maui house was on lockdown. Even though Zeke had not been specifically named as the person of interest, the FBI cordoned off the house and added another twenty agents to the security team. Abe and Sarah were restricted to the inside of their home until further notice. At noon in Hawaii, the Internet exploded with the story of a Washington insider who leaked Zeke's name as the man being held. The leak also provided the names of his family members and their addresses and suggested that Zeke was the leader of a sleeper cell of terrorists aligned either with Russia or Al Qaeda. The FBI immediately took Zeke's sister, Rachel, into protective custody.

Although Zeke had no access to news or interaction with anyone, he knew everything. He sat on the chair in his cell with his head in his hands. "This can't be happening!" he moaned out loud. He looked up and said, "God, why are you doing this to me? Why did you give me this stupid defect?" His head hung down, and he began to cry, feeling totally alone and helpless while his family suffered. He thought about his notebooks and smiled. Seeing the future had been his life. Up to this moment, it seemed like a game and just an odd coincidence that some things came true. Now he knew there was a purpose and even though the near term looked dismal, he had a job to do that might save the world. Bea's words about the war slipped across his consciousness. Everything he might do was a delaying tactic, putting off the destruction until the Kalideans were ready to help.

"Zeke, can you hear me?" a voice in his mind said.

"Bea, is that you?" he thought.

"Yes, Zeke, it's me," she replied. "I wish I could be there with you now, darling, but things have to take their course. I hope you can understand that."

"I understand, Bea. Do you think it will work out?"

She laughed and the sound of her laugh warmed him to the core. "Zeke, if there was no chance of success, I wouldn't be talking to you right now, would I?"

"I guess you're right," he thought back. "Bea, I have had several visions about the next few days, and most of them end with me being executed or shot in the back trying to escape. The few where the president survives aren't much better."

"What I'm about to say won't make matters any better," she began. "Earlier this morning, I scanned the volumes of your book. From the point in Volume 1 where you talk about this incident until the end of the last volume, all the pages are illegible. That means the next days are still in doubt."

He chuckled and replied, "You're right, that doesn't make it any better. But I suppose that was to be expected. We all make decisions every minute and any one of them can change our future."

"Zeke, do you trust me?" she asked.

"Of course I do," he answered. "Haven't I proven that yet?"

"Zeke, I'll see you in a couple of days. You have to promise to do what I will tell you then, okay?"

"I suppose that depends on what you'll tell me."

"Zeke, that's not good enough. I love you and would never do anything to hurt you. But what I may ask you to do might be unpleasant. Please promise you'll do those things."

The image of their wedding drifted in front of his eyes. He could smell her perfume and taste her lips and hear the applause of the audience. "I promise I'll do whatever you ask, Bea."

"Someone's headed your way. I'll see you soon."

The lock in his door clicked and two men in dark suits came in and locked the door behind them. The first agent said, "Mr. Thompson, I am Agent Carter. Agent Montgomery and I are here to take your statement. He pulled a small recorder from his jacket pocket, pressed a button, and set the device on the table. A red light began to glow. Who is your superior, Mr. Thompson?"

"I'm sorry but I don't understand."

"Who ordered you to disable Air Force One?" Agent Montgomery repeated.

"I had nothing to do with that," Zeke replied. "I only—" Before he could finish, Carter slapped him across the face.

"I don't think you realize what's going on here, Mr. Thompson," Carter said. "In this compound, you have no rights. There will be no Miranda Warning and you can't have an attorney." He pulled his pistol and pressed it to Zeke's forehead.

"If we kill you, no one outside the firm will know or even find your corpse. Now, who is your superior?"

"I swear to God that I didn't—". Carter pistol whipped him across the temple. Zeke fell over and prayed to pass out. Carter put his pistol in its holster and pulled Zeke up to a sitting position and slapped his cheeks to keep him conscious.

"Let me try, Carter," Montgomery said. Carter walked over and stood by the doorway while the other agent sat on the chair across from Zeke, whose nose was bleeding and right eye was swelling shut. "Mr. Thompson, let us assume you're telling us the truth for a moment." Zeke nodded warily. "Why did Air Force One go down?"

"The Air Force screwed up and didn't inspect that plane for two years. There were hidden cracks in the beams that secure the wings to the fuselage. Several bolts were also cracked. During that flight, they hit unexpectedly rough turbulence and all the cracks let go. The left wing fell off; the plane tumbled out of control and crashed."

"How the hell do you know all of that?" Carter shouted from the door. Montgomery motioned for him to be quiet.

"Mr. Thompson, can you see the future?" Montgomery asked.

Zeke nodded slightly and said, "Sometimes."

"This is a joke!" Carter shouted.

"Be quiet, Sam!" Montgomery exclaimed. "Mr. Thompson, the details you gave about how the plane crashed seem to match what we have learned, although the source of the defects is still in doubt."

"Don't tell that sack of shit anything!" Carter complained.

"If you can tell the future, Mr. Thompson, what is going to happen to you now?" Montgomery asked.

"You two are going to cuff me, put a sack over my head and load me into another vehicle. One of you will inject me with a sedative, and you'll drop me off at a remote airfield where a plane will move me to Washington, D.C., for more interrogation," Zeke said calmly.

"There's a freaking mole inside telling this guy everything!" Carter screamed

"What is the name of the person inside the government giving you this information, Mr. Thompson?" Montgomery asked.

"No one is giving me any information about anything, Agent Montgomery," Zeke replied.

"Why should I believe you?"

"Would you two like to know about your future?" Zeke asked.

"Are you shitting me?" Carter fumed.

"Go ahead, Mr. Thompson," Montgomery said.

"As fair warning, your future will change depending on whether I tell you or not," Zeke said. The two men stared back in disbelief. "Should I continue?" They nodded. "Okay. After your experience with me, the agency will separate you two so you won't leak to the press what you've learned. Carter will be assigned to a covert operation in Pakistan. If he goes, he will die in the first two weeks in an IED blast. If he quits, he'll start a security business, get married, and have five children. Montgomery, they will permanently assign you here with almost nothing to do. After a few years you'll either join Carter in his new company, or if he decided to go to Pakistan, you'll start it yourself."

Carter and Montgomery exchanged worried glances. After a long silence, Montgomery said, "Wow! Either you have a very active imagination or some serious connections in Washington, Moscow, or Beijing."

Zeke forced a weak smile. "Guys, I'm a young kid just out of college and I live with my parents. Does that sound like the definition of a superspy to you?"

"Come on, Bill, this guy is obviously making this shit up," Carter complained. "We have a job to do."

Montgomery flashed a look of contempt at his partner and then focused on Zeke again. "Sam is right, Zeke. Stand up so I can handcuff you." Zeke stood and the other cuffed his wrists together behind his back. Carter walked forward and slid the bag over Zeke's head and cinched it around his neck. "Okay, Zeke, now we're going to walk you out of here. Don't try anything stupid, okay?"

"Don't worry, Agent Montgomery," Zeke replied.

Carter grabbed Zeke's right arm while Montgomery held the left. "Bill, I have the feeling you are starting to have compassion for this traitor."

"Sam, do you always have to be such an asshole?" Montgomery asked. The other man laughed as they walked out of the cell with their prisoner. "If what Thompson says is true, I wonder what you'll think when you get the orders to Pakistan?"

"This man can't tell the future," Carter scoffed. "If asked to serve in Pakistan, I'm happy to go."

"Really?" Montgomery quipped. "If there is a chance you'll be dead in a couple of weeks, you'd still go."

"Shut up, Bill. I'll cross that bridge when I get to it."

§

The president of the United States lay quietly in the hospital bed while a number of machines monitored his condition.

Doctor Hampton stood at the end of the bed reviewing his patient's status chart on a tablet. Nurses were on both sides of the bed checking the president's wound dressings. On the opposite side of the room, the vice president and secretary of defense sat waiting on a couch. It was early afternoon in the nation's capital and the view out the windows showed an overcast sky. Lake leaned over to Albright and whispered, "Is Thompson on his way?"

"Yes, Andy. I received word an hour ago that his flight is now airborne," Albright whispered back.

"Frank, I want to meet him."

"I'm not sure that's wise, sir."

"Why not?"

"Plausible deniability for one thing," Albright replied. "Until a linkage can be found between Thompson and foreign agents, he is toxic to us. Imagine if the press found out we detained and beat the crap out of a lawful citizen because he had a hunch?"

"Figure out a way, Frank," Lake said. "You know as well as I do that our country has many enemies, all of whom would love to take down Air Force One. It's just a matter of time before Thompson cracks."

"I hope you're right, Andy," Albright noted. His mind was still reeling from the crash. He knew he ignored the CIA director's report that there might be structural damage to the plane, but who in their right mind believes in fortune-tellers? Yet, there had been the tiniest mote of a doubt in his mind, and since the crash it had begun to grow. If Thompson was truly clairvoyant and the fact he ignored the warning was leaked, his career and future were over. Now he had no choice but to see this through to the end, and somehow make sure Thompson did not live to tell his side of the story. Frank Albright needed time to think.

"Excuse me, gentlemen," the doctor said. The nurses had left the room and Hampton was standing three feet in front of them. Lake and Albright stood up.

"How is he doing, doctor?" the vice president asked.

"The president is recovering quite well," Hampton said. "I am very pleased with his progress."

"When do you think he will be ready to resume his duties?" Albright asked. He noticed the odd look Lake gave him after the question.

"It's much too early to make any guesses about that," Hampton replied. "He has sustained major injuries to several organs and bones and needs time to heal. It is possible we may end the induced coma soon, though."

"Is that wise?" the vice president asked. Both Albright and Hampton looked shocked at the question. "Please let me rephrase that. All of us and the American people want Ben to recover as quickly as possible. If he is better able to heal while in the coma, wouldn't it benefit all of us to leave him in the coma until he is stronger?"

A light bulb flashed in the secretary of defense's head as he realized that Andy wanted time too. "I agree with the vice president," Albright said. "We want Ben to heal as quickly as possible. Neither Andy nor I are doctors, so we will leave the decisions to you."

Hampton considered the two officials in front of him. As one of the top surgeons in the country, he was well accustomed to dealing with the idiosyncrasies of the rich and famous. "Well, it is very true that every case like this is different. Some patients need to stay in comas for months before it is safe to revive them, but at some point all patients need to take an active role in their recovery. Please be assured that no one medical professional is going to make decisions in a vacuum. I have a teleconference in three days with a team of doctors to review the president's case. Perhaps after that, we can come to a decision."

"That seems a wise choice," Lake replied. "What is your personal opinion at this time?"

"Well, Mr. Vice President, if we make a decision in three days and begin the protocol to end the coma immediately, it will still be a week or so before the president is up and about."

"A week or two?" Albright probed.

Hampton frowned. "That is hard to say, sir. A week, maybe ten days is a better estimate. And remember that is only if the team agrees it is time."

"We appreciate your time, Doctor Hampton," Lake said, extending his hand. Hampton shook their hands and left the room. The two men walked over to the bedside and looked down on the president. "It would seem we are of one mind, Frank."

"I'm not sure what you mean, Mr. Vice President."

Lake frowned at the other man. "Don't play coy with me, Frank. I've known you too long for that. We need more time before Ben resumes his duties, and there is the situation with Tony's report to deal with. Shit, both of us ignored it, and look where we are now."

"You think that Thompson fellow really sees the future?"

"That's why I want to meet him, Frank," Andy replied. "Personally, I think fortune-telling is just nonsense, but then I wonder what would happen if the NTSB report shows no signs of foul play?"

"You and I can deal with Tony," Frank said. "Another case of plausible deniability."

"But that only works if Thompson isn't around to tell his side of the story."

"Is that a problem, Andy?"

The vice president looked at his old friend and wondered about his loyalty and motivation. "No, that is not a problem, unless Ben decides to wake up before we deal with Thompson. That's part of the reason we need more time."

"What's the other part?"

"I can't believe you asked me that, Frank!" the vice president replied. "I thought you were smarter than that when I recommended you for DOD. First, the odds Thompson is a true clairvoyant are like one in infinity, so we have to focus on real options. Regardless of the condition of the jet, someone tried to take it down and Thompson is connected to them. Who do you think would do that?"

"Al Qaeda, Russia, China, North Korea for starters," Frank answered.

"We have the cell phones and computers from the Thompson family and are looking for linkages to any of them or another group we don't know about yet. The NSA is pulling together their phone records and Internet traffic to look for something there too. Tomorrow morning, Thompson will be in the DIA secure site a few blocks from here, where we will confront him with any evidence we have found. If we find any direct connections, or if Thompson cracks, we need to launch a preemptive strike immediately to punish the perpetrators for this."

"And it all needs to happen before Ben wakes up," Frank noted.

Lake looked down at the president and scowled. "Yes, that's right. Ben is a great American, but too much of a dove when it comes to our enemies. He always wants to negotiate everything. If we find that China is responsible, he'd want to ask the UN for sanctions or suggest a summit meeting or some other meaningless contrition. If they did this to Ben, we will act."

"And what if Thompson just guessed about the plane?"

"Frank, we both know he has to die either way. No loose ends, right?" Lake said.

"Shit, do you think Ben can hear what we're saying?" Frank asked, stunned that the thought just occurred to him.

"He's in a freaking coma, Frank! Don't be ridiculous. Let's get back to the White House." The two men walked out and past the three Secret Service agents, one of whom walked into the president's room to resume his post.

# Chapter 16

The vice president was despondent and could feel the icy grip of terror rising up in his stomach. He spent the entire morning in a conference room receiving updates from the NTSB, NSA, CIA, and FBI. The secretary of defense sat to his left with his head in his hands. He had not made eye contact with anyone else in the room for at least an hour. Andy thought he could see the beginning of a smirk on CIA Director Anthony Marshall's face. "God, I hate that son of a bitch," he thought. The door opened and the attorney general and secretary of state barged in. "What's the meaning of this, Cindy?" Lake asked. "Your presence was not requested for this briefing."

"You see what I mean, Cathy," Cindy said to Secretary of State Catherine Sylvester. "Our presence is not required."

"We're not idiots, Andy," Cathy began. "We know you are considering taking military or covert actions against foreign entities. You need my input for that."

"You will be informed before any decisions are made," Andy lied.

"Also, you have taken a detainee from my site in Alaska and given custody to the DIA," Cindy argued. "No one asked my opinion on that matter."

Frank Albright looked up and replied, "The vice president was within his rights to reassign this man to us." Everyone noticed how red Frank's eyes were and the strain on his face.

Tony stood up and said, "If I may speak, we were just about to present the conclusions to our meeting. If State and Justice want to listen, I have no problem with that."

The vice president scowled at the CIA director and then his face softened to a generous smile. "Please join us, ladies. Go ahead, Tony. We might as well get this over."

The representative from the NTSB stood and cleared his throat. "To be clear, our investigation is still ongoing; however, at this time we have found no evidence of deliberate tampering to the beams and bolts that failed, leading to the crash of Air Force One. There were signs of fatigue throughout the fuselage, and we have sent a request to the Air Force and Secret Service for maintenance and inspection records."

"But that is only a preliminary report, correct?" Andy asked.

"Yes, Mr. Vice President," the man replied. He sat and the representative of the NSA stood.

"I concur with my colleague that our report is preliminary as well," she said. "Our review included records from all four members of the Thompson family, and the scope included telephone records, Internet activity, e-mails, and text messages. There were only a couple of anomalies discovered to date. The elder Thompson, Abraham, has recently been searching for information on North Korea and China. The searches seem to be generic and focused on sites like Wikipedia and even the CIA World Factbook. All e-mail traffic was examined and no encoded or otherwise questionable information has been found."

The FBI representative raised his hand and then stood up. "If I may, the Bureau has some information in that regard."

"Go ahead, Agent Morgan," Andy said.

"Thank you, sir. Our review of the computer hard drives of the Thompson family revealed an outline and the first couple chapters of a novel being written by Abraham Thompson. It seems to be an anti-war, pro-diplomacy story which begins with discussions of conditions in China and North Korea," the agent replied.

"Thank you. Anything else from the NSA?" Andy asked.

The FBI agent sat and the woman said, "Yes, Mr. Vice President. Each member of the Thompson family had a mobile phone. According to reports from their service provider, Ezekiel had a new phone which replaced one we confiscated when the FBI arrested him the first time. It seems odd that there was a period of several weeks when he did not have a mobile phone at all. During that period, the records from the carrier report that both Abraham and Sarah received texts and calls from the number of the disconnected phone."

"Perhaps he got a new phone from a different supplier," Cindy speculated.

"That is possible, but doubtful," the NSA woman said. "No service provider shows that number being active, until the current device was activated."

"Could he have had a satellite phone from a foreign country?" Frank asked. "Or perhaps a military tactical phone?"

"Without the actual device, it is impossible to tell. The current device is a standard Apple iPhone," the woman reported. "That's all we have, ladies and gentlemen." She sat down.

"Thank you," Andy said. "I look forward to your final reports in the coming days. Anything else from you, Agent Morgan?"

The FBI agent stood and thought for a moment and then said, "Just to be clear, I am a lawman and have been for my whole career. Notwithstanding the preliminary reports, I have to tell you alarms are blasting away inside my head."

"It would seem we are of an accord, Agent Morgan," the vice president said. "Please continue."

"Thank you, sir. Let us ignore the rumors about Ezekiel Thompson. Some people say he can see the future but there is no factual evidence of that. We can sit here and believe that man is a prophet and fall on our knees in front of him, but that would be a fool's errand. First, Thompson IDs an undercover FBI agent in a coffee shop. Then, we take custody of him in San Diego, and it turns out those agents were selling him to the North Koreans. But before they could sell, a Mexican drug lord rescues him. His henchmen were careful only to kill the four agents involved. Next, the North Koreans enlist a second cartel to get Thompson, and there's this giant gunfight where one drug lord and dozens of men are killed along with the two Koreans. Somehow, Thompson escapes Mexico and ends up in Hawaii where we capture him again. Then he predicts the Air Force One crash. In my professional opinion, all of that cannot be coincidental. Ezekiel Thompson is neck-deep in something, and the last thing we can afford to do is let him go."

"I don't think any of us are saying Thompson is a prophet or totally innocent," Cindy replied. "That's why we took him into custody. We need to learn where he gets his information. But the law is the law. Unless we have evidence to support holding him, we will have to let him go sometime."

"What do you want me to do, Cindy?" Andy asked.

"You can keep Thompson at the DIA site, but I want the FBI to be in charge of him. He is a US citizen and we need to give him his rights and access to counsel," she replied.

"I need at least three days of access to Thompson before he gets a lawyer," the vice president said. "During those days, the CIA will be responsible for his custody. That will give us time to interview him and to get updated reports from everyone else. After three days, if we don't have any new evidence, I'll give him to you, Cindy. Then you can decide whether to hold him, charge him, or let him go. That's it, everyone, thank you." The vice president stood and walked out of the room.

"Madam Attorney General, may I speak?" Agent Morgan asked.

"Speak your mind, Stan," she smiled.

"There are a couple situations I want you to be aware of," he began. "First, a news reporter in San Diego named Shannon Thorpe has been writing stories about terrible working conditions and safety violations at the offshore operations of major American multinationals, including Reliant Industries, the company that used to employ Abraham Thompson."

"That hardly seems newsworthy, Stan. Reliant employs hundreds of thousands of people."

"Her first story discussed inadequate fire protection at several factories in Brazil, including a new Reliant building," he said.

"What's your point, Stan?" she complained.

"That story was published four weeks ago. Last night, a fire broke out in that plant, leveling it. The fire spread to several nearby buildings, igniting propane cylinders and causing several tanks of chlorine gas to burst. The fires are still burning at this time, and the death toll is in the thousands."

"Oh my God," the attorney general gasped.

"Three days ago, Frederick Drake, the CEO of Reliant, gave a press conference calling Thorpe's article total rubbish and stating that all Reliant facilities meet local guidelines. This morning, Ms. Thorpe had a new article in the San Diego Union-Tribune attributing her story to a premonition by Ezekiel Thompson," the agent concluded.

"Cindy, isn't Reliant one of the vice president's biggest supporters?" the secretary of state asked. She nodded her head.

"Anything else, Stan?" Cindy muttered.

"Within forty-eight to seventy-two hours, every news agency in the world is going to want to meet Ezekiel Thompson. It wouldn't surprise me if the Pope or Dalai Lama wants an interview with him either. And there is one other thing." The two women stared back and Cindy nodded. "The Mexican government is following up on their request to provide permanent residence status to Jaime Ortiz Sanchez and his family."

"Remind me again why we would do that for a drug lord, Stan?" Cindy asked.

"It was their deal with El Tigre to get rid of the other cartel leader, El Tiburon, and dismantle the cartels in that part of the country. Ortiz and his family are already in Hawaii at the Sacred Life Tranquility Retreat. Apparently, Ezekiel Thompson convinced Ortiz to put his family above the business and get out. The Mexican government is also asking for no charges to be filed against Agent Branson, since he is Ortiz's brother-in-law," he stated.

Cindy sighed and shook her head. "I can't imagine how things could get any worse than this. Stan, just send the papers to my office and I'll sign them this afternoon."

§

As the aircraft carrying Zeke approached its destination, the shades on all the windows were closed and his wrists were cuffed to the arms of the seat so he could not peek outside. He had been in the CIA compound in Alaska, so he knew he could be anywhere in the world, but assumed he was still in the United States. Upon landing, he was hooded again and led off the plane and into another SUV. The traffic sounds were loud, so he assumed he was in a large city and secretly hoped it was San Diego again, although the flight was much longer than what he assumed it would be to his hometown. When the vehicle stopped, he was led through two sets of doors and then placed in this cell with no window, and only a small panel in the door for the guards to check on him and deliver meals. There were small cameras in each corner where the walls met the ceiling. He fought the urge to call out to Bea, as her accidental appearance in his cell would be very problematic for both of them. The guards had taken all of his personal effects, and now he thought how angry Taron would be that he was not wearing the ring anymore. But he still had those two devices in his skull. No one had bothered to x-ray his head, yet.

The lock in the door turned and FBI Special Agent Stephanie Marshall walked in. The door locked behind her. "Hi, Zeke, it's good to see you again."

"I'm glad to see you up and around," he smiled. "The last time I saw you, you had just been shot."

"I remember that night very well," she said as she sat on the small side chair. "Thank you, Zeke. I owe you my life."

"You know everything we say is being recorded, right?"

"Of course I know that, Zeke," she laughed. "I'm still an agent after all. But I wanted to tell you that I am moving to the CIA as you predicted."

"Maybe you made that choice after what I told you," he noted.

"Perhaps, but you were right. That night in San Diego made me reevaluate my goals. I heard what one of the men who took you said. He told the other man not to shoot me because I wasn't guilty. I guess you were right about that too. With all of that in my mind, it makes sense that I'm only half-heartedly looking forward to the CIA. Does that make sense?"

"That's probably my fault too," he acknowledged. "If I hadn't told you about Peter . . ."

"What else can you tell me about him?" she asked.

"Not much, to be honest. It was someone else who told me Peter would be my best friend for life, but I've only spoken to him a couple of times. But if you're going to marry him, he must be a wonderful guy."

She laughed again. "Zeke, you're either a prophet or a nut case. I haven't made up my mind yet. Now stand up. My last FBI and first CIA assignment is to take you to an interrogation room."

He stood warily and looked down. "Okay, I guess. But so far those interrogations have been hard on my face."

She clicked the cuffs around his wrists and said, "Don't worry, Zeke. I'll be there the whole time and report any physical acts personally. Besides, you have a special guest interrogator."

"Gee, I'm honored."

"You should be. He's the vice president of the United States." Zeke looked stunned as Stephanie led him out of the cell and down the corridor and into an elevator car. When the doors opened, the wall across from the elevator was lined with windows, and the skyline of Washington, D.C. filled the view. The Capitol and Washington monuments were less than a mile away past rows of houses and businesses. Stephanie led him down the corridor and then they turned down a second hallway to a door where two Secret Service agents stood guard. She approached them and they checked the security of Zeke's cuffs. "Okay, Zeke. These guys will take you now. I'll be in the room next door on the other side of a one-way mirror. Good luck." She walked further down the hallway and stepped through the next door on that side of the hall. The two agents led Zeke into the room. One wall was a mirror. There was a small conference table and four chairs. The vice president sat quietly at one end of the table. The agents cuffed Zeke to restraints on a chair that was bolted to the floor and then left.

"It's an honor to meet you sir," Zeke said.

The man half-smiled at Zeke and turned to face the mirror. "This is a private session, guys, so I'm going to mute the microphones. You can still watch in case something untoward happens." He pressed a button and then turned to look at Zeke. "Mr. Thompson, let's cut to the chase. Are you a terrorist or sympathizer?"

"No, sir!" Zeke exclaimed.

"What did you or your agents do to the president's plane?"

"I did nothing and I have no agents, sir. I had an image move across my mind and I told the CIA director about it. Didn't anyone check it out?"

The vice president laughed out loud, stood up and moved to a different chair where his back would be to the mirror. "You must think I'm a freaking idiot, Zeke. Is that what you think?"

"No, sir. I am only telling you what I saw. That's it."

"I have a theory about you, Zeke. Do you want to hear it?"

"I'm not certain I do, sir."

"I think you're a very bad guy, Zeke. You killed the North Koreans because you did not want to be a stooge to their leader, or because they wouldn't pay you enough. You killed El Tiburon because he was threatening your friend's business," Andy said.

"You think El Tigre is my friend?"

"Look at the facts, son; he broke you out of an FBI facility in San Diego and took you to his ranch in Mexico. Do you expect me to believe a complete stranger did that?"

"His brother-in-law couldn't allow those agents to sell me to the Koreans, and he convinced his brother-in-law to help."

"How much was El Tigre paying you to help him plan his business?" the vice president asked.

"Nothing. He never paid me a dime," Zeke replied.

"Personally, I think you're a foreign spy, Zeke," Andy stated. "I'm just not certain if you work for the Russians, Chinese, or Iranians."

"I am not a spy."

"You know, I think I just made up my mind, Zeke. I am almost positive you work for Iran. Russia and China aren't stupid enough to down Air Force One. Once the truth got out, they'd be kicked off the Security Council and every normal nation would cut diplomatic relations. The Iranians could not care less about international opinion. How could you support those bastards, Zeke? They support terrorism around the world. What kind of monster are you?"

"Mr. Vice President, I am not an Iranian spy!" Zeke exclaimed.

"You know, son, you are on my shit list for the fire in Brazil too. I can't imagine how evil you must be to kill all those people just to besmirch patriotic companies like Reliant. Once the evidence of your handiwork is discovered, you will pay with your life."

"The fire happened?"

"Oh, don't play games with me, Zeke. You can play the part of an innocent until the lethal injection moves through your bloodstream. That day is coming real soon, Zeke. There will be revenge for the president and the slain Brazilians, I swear it," Andy growled. His frown disappeared and he smiled and stood up. He turned to smile at the agents through the mirror and then patted Zeke on the shoulder. He pressed the button on the table and said, "Zeke and I are finished. You can take him back to his cell." He looked at Zeke and smiled, saying, "Thank you for meeting with me, Mr. Thompson." He walked out of the room.

§

"Good afternoon, my name is Fred Drake, and I am the CEO of Reliant Industries," a man in a perfectly-tailored suit began. He was standing at a podium in front of a group of reporters summoned to hear the corporate side of the events in Brazil. Television cameras captured every word and broadcast them across the world. Tens of millions of people sat in front of their television screens watching the event that preempted normal programming on most networks. Shannon Thorpe, the reporter who broke the initial story, sat in the front row taking notes. Drake pulled at his collar at the sight of her, and he wondered what her motivation had been. "First and foremost, we regret the loss of life and damage that occurred due to the fire in our facility in Campinas, Brazil. While it is true that our safety measures met or exceeded all local guidelines, clearly they were not sufficient, and Reliant Industries is committed to quickly and efficiently handling all injury and loss claims. Reliant is a long-term partner in Brazil and we look forward to many years of safe operation that will be mutually beneficial to our company and the people of that great country. I can take a few questions now."

Abe and Sarah Thompson watched from the living room of the Maui house. Outside each window, an armed guard protected them and kept them here. "What a jerk!" Abe exclaimed. "He knew damned well that the local standards were inadequate. He just wanted to save the bucks by not installing sprinklers."

"Calm down, sweetheart," Sarah replied. "At least he doesn't want to talk to you anymore." Abe looked back at her quizzically.

A reporter asked, "Mr. Drake, was your management team in Campinas aware that propane and chlorine tanks were nearby?"

Drake replied, "No. We had no knowledge of the existence of those hazards."

A second reporter said, "Isn't it true that the article published by the San Diego Union Tribune just last month noted the existence of those hazards?"

"I'm sorry, but I can't read every article in every publication," Drake answered. "If that information had been sent to me, of course I would have reacted."

A third reporter said, "Just four days ago, it was reported that you called that same article, written by Ms. Thorpe rubbish. Is that true?"

"Squirm, you bastard," Abe said to his television.

"I do not recall such a comment," Drake said. "But I think we are all missing the most important point. This was a terrible tragedy. Reliant lost employees, and many other innocents perished due to the inadequate protection of chlorine gas tanks. Some have claimed that sabotage may have led to the tank ruptures, and the fire only concealed the evidence."

Shannon Thorpe asked, "Mr. Drake can you share any specific information on this purported act of sabotage?"

He shook his head and said, "I'm sorry, but I do not have any details at this time. Agents from the US Government have been in contact with executives at Reliant and noted that the circumstances around the chlorine storage and ruptures seem inconsistent with damage from either a fire or impact by shrapnel, as would occur when the propane tanks exploded."

Shannon asked, "Does the government believe this was corporate sabotage, or are other nations or entities involved?"

Drake chuckled softly, "I really cannot go down this line of questions, Shannon. I have probably already said too much. One thing we all know is that certain groups and nations have a desire to cause damage to the reputation of the United States and her citizens and corporations. Although the NTSB has not made its final report, I know that all of us are reeling from the crash of Air Force One. There may be no connection between these events, but from what I understand, all leads are being examined and a person or persons of interest are currently in custody."

"Who is in custody, Mr. Drake," another reporter asked.

Drake smiled and said, "You might want to confer with Ms. Thorpe on that matter. I think that's it for tonight. Thank you for your time and attention. Goodbye." Drake walked off the stage and disappeared. The reporters were buzzing for a moment until the feed was cut and an announcer closed the special report.

Abe clicked the off button on the remote and tossed it aside, saying, "Shit, they're trying to blame all of this on Zeke!"

"Is that who he meant?" Sarah gasped.

"Who else does Thorpe know that is in custody?"

A woman's voice said, "He's right." They turned to see Bea Watson standing behind the couch.

"You shouldn't be here, Bea," Abe warned. "There are cops everywhere, and they're probably listening in right now."

"No, the house is clear," she replied. "Taron swept it before I stepped through. But listen, I only have a few minutes. I want you both to come to the future with me right now."

"Are you nuts?" Abe exclaimed. "If the police find us gone, they'll think we're terrorists. Then they'll take it out on Zeke."

Bea walked around the couch and sat between the Thompsons. She took their hands in hers. "Things are happening too fast," she started. "My future is starting to slip away. Vice

President Lake is much more unstable than our models predicted."

"What in the world are you talking about?" Sarah asked.

"Sarah, the past affects the future and the future affects the past," she said. "In the past that I studied in school, President Ben Nelson was not seriously injured in the crash. Air Force One did not lose a wing and tumble to the ground. It started to lose lift and the pilot made an emergency landing in a cornfield. No one died. Something changed that but I don't know what or why. In the past that I learned, President Nelson put the crash behind him and completed two terms where he focused on negotiation and teaming up with other world leaders."

"But that still didn't stop the war," Abe noted.

"No, but it delayed it. You and your son delayed it too, and ultimately a great future awaits the survivors of the war. But Lake isn't Nelson. He is convinced that a foreign regime is responsible for the crash and the accident in Brazil. He is going to act before the president can recover because he knows Nelson won't attack. If that happens, the war will begin now, hundreds of years before the Kalideans discover Earth. If things keep going as they are, they will discover a dead planet with no life and only the rubble of destroyed cities."

"But the president will recover, even if the first attack has occurred," Sarah said.

"Perhaps you are right, Sarah. But Lake is ready now to kill Zeke even though he has no evidence of any wrongdoing. Once the missiles start to land, I think Lake will assassinate Nelson in order to keep power and fulfill his blood lust."

"Bea, what good will our escape do?" Abe asked. "Once your future disappears, won't we just be back here?"

"We have to force the vice president's hand," Bea replied. "With you gone, Lake will be certain that all of you are spies and he'll kill Zeke."

"What?" Sarah asked.

"Don't worry, I won't let Zeke die, but they have to believe they killed him. I know this is a lot to absorb, but you have to trust me," Bea replied. "Once Lake believes Zeke can't tell his version, he will move to attack. I am hoping that gives Zeke and me the chance to save the president's life and end the madness."

"That sounds insane to me," Abe noted.

Bea looked at her watch, picked up the remote and turned on the television. "This is what I'm talking about," she said, pointing to the screen.

A newscaster said, "This is a news alert from Washington, D.C., where Vice President Andrew Lake will now make a statement to the country."

The image changed to the White House where Lake stood at a podium looking through a stack of note cards. He looked up at the camera and said, "My fellow Americans, I come to you this evening to update you on the facts we have regarding the crash of Air Force One and the condition of our beloved president, Ben Nelson. We should all be heartened to know that Ben is improving, although his progress is slow. I respectfully ask that your families say a prayer for his speedy recovery. I met with a team of physicians today, and they have decided to not to begin the protocol to end the induced coma Ben has been under. They will consider his condition again next week and decide what to do then. I must tell you I was heartbroken when I received this bad news."

"He's lying," Bea whispered. "He is delaying the protocol to buy himself more time." The Thompsons stared at her.

"Federal law enforcement agencies are tracking down agents believed to have influenced both the crash of Air Force One and the horrific gas attacks in Brazil. There is some evidence that both disasters were planned and executed acts of terror," Lake continued. "We have one person in custody here in Washington at this time. Although he has not been forthcoming, I am confident we will find his connection to either Al Qaeda or the Iranian government in the coming hours or days."

"More lies," Bea said. "I can't believe he's just making that up on live television." Abe and Sarah were too stunned by the vice president's words to react to Bea.

"I call on the perpetrators of these cowardly acts to admit their guilt!" Lake shouted. "Those responsible will rue the day they chose to attack the United States of America!" He turned and walked away.

"He is crazy loco, I'll give you that, Bea," Abe said. "So, if we go with you, won't he just launch nukes anyway? How does that help?"

"He is making this stuff up. He knows that the facts will come to light in a matter of days, so he is tempted to act now and hope the war distracts attention from his lies. But he is still planning carefully and trying to figure out a way to get rid of the president and bury the facts," she said. "With the right push, he'll stop planning and just react. That gives us a chance to save the president and Zeke. Believe me, the vice president is crazy, and if we let him do it his way, all of your family will be dead along with the president, and the war will begin. Think about who he is blaming, Iran and Al Qaeda. Those two are the only ones likely to accept blame even though they didn't do anything. This country is their devil, and they'll take any chance to claim credit for damaging it."

Someone was knocking on the front door. "It's now or never," Bea said. "They're here to take you into custody." Abe and Sarah followed Bea into a small den where a black circle hung on the wall. Bea took their hands and they stepped through. A flash of light lit up the interior of the house and the circle was gone. Seeing the flash, the men unlocked the front door and searched the now-empty house.

# Chapter 17

The secretary of defense and vice president sat on a couch in the Oval Office. A television nearby showed a live video feed from the streets of Tehran where officials were praising their spies for their work in downing the president's plane. A sea of citizens held banners in the air and chanted "Death to America." The scene switched to other cities where similar gatherings were being held. After a few minutes, the vice president turned off the set and turned to Albright, saying, "Frank, this video is priceless. I doubt Hollywood could have done better."

"Andy, this is for propaganda purposes," Albright replied. "Their UN ambassador has strenuously denied all allegations and demanded an apology from our ambassador."

Andy smiled and leaned back, "You know what? I could not care less what they want. Frank, this is more than we could have hoped for. Even if they publicly deny it now, there are hours of video where they bragged about it! Checkmate!"

"What are you going to do, Andy?"

"I'm going to bomb them back into the Stone Age!" the vice president exclaimed.

"Sir, it is possible that the Air Force did not adequately maintain that jet?" Frank squeaked.

Andy laughed out loud. "You think I still care about that! That's yesterday's news, Frank. Now, Iran is taking credit for attacking the United States president. That's an act of war, buddy."

"I'm not certain that would be wise, sir," Frank said. "You know the Russians and Chinese support Tehran. We don't want a global war over this, do we?"

"I'll leave that to Cathy to fix," Andy said calmly. "With this video evidence and pictures of millions of joyous Iranians dancing over the attack, they will have no choice but to let us do what we must."

There was a knock at the door and one of the president's assistants came into the Oval Office. "Excuse me, Mr. Vice President, FBI Agent Stan Morgan is here with a video that the FBI director thinks you need to see right away."

"Send him in, Jill," Andy said. The woman walked out and the agent walked in. "What have you got, Stan?"

He held up a DVD in his hand and said, "Mr. Vice President, this video came from a security camera in the hangar where the Air Force One jets are maintained. May I play it for you?" The vice president nodded and Stan slipped the disk into the player.

Stan pushed the play button and the screen filled with a view of an Air Force One jet sitting inside the hangar. Stan began, "This video was taken two days before the crash. As you know, security around those planes is very high. You can see the timestamp showing it was 0900 hours and the maintenance crew is just entering the hangar after having their IDs verified and scanning them for foreign objects."

"Seems very normal," Andy noted.

"Yes, it does," Stan said as he pressed the pause button. "You will note that a total of twelve men have entered the hangar. Ten are mechanics and the other two are security. Most of the video is standard, but now let me fast forward to 1145 hours," Stan replied as he accelerated through the feed. "Now it is break time. You can see the men sitting down in the rest area drinking coffee or soda and chatting." He froze the frame and walked up to the television and counted them out loud. "Twelve, right?"

"What's your point, Stan?" the vice president complained.

"Oh my God!" Frank blurted.

"What the hell is wrong with you?"

"The secretary sees it too," Stan continued. He pointed to an open access panel on the wing of the jet. A man's head was visible. "Thirteen."

"There was another man?" Andy gasped.

"Yes, sir," Stan answered. "I'm just skimming this now, but we have studied every frame of this video. That man never came in or left by any door. No evidence of him exists anywhere. It's like he appeared out of the blue."

"That's our Iranian agent!" Andy shouted. "Amazing! Have you put out an APB for him? Is anyone looking for him?"

"That man is dead," Stan replied. "We analyzed the photos and even lifted a few prints from the wreckage. He does not appear in any of our systems anywhere."

"What makes you think he's dead then?" Andy asked.

"His body is in a morgue in San Diego, California. The eyewitness reports did not make much sense, but that's all we have."

"Go on, I want to know it all," the vice president said.

"Make I sit down? This might take a while."

"Please sit down, but give me the Reader's Digest version, son. I don't have all day," Andy replied.

"When we compile the various accounts, we end up with this. This man was trying to run down another man in a strip mall parking lot in San Diego. Some reported that the other man was struck and flew through the air, although no body was ever found. This man got out of his car carrying a weapon, apparently to finish the job. When bystanders started to come to help, he leveled his gun on them and they backed away. He looked around for a few seconds for the man he ran over. Just then, another man appeared and shot this man in the temple at point-blank range. The other man exchanged his gun for the dead man's and then disappeared and is still at large."

"So, no one ever found the man hit by the car, and the shooter disappeared too," Andy confirmed. "All we have is this dead guy, and he's the one who sabotaged Air Force One."

"Sir, I mentioned that the reports didn't make much sense," Stan replied.

"Is that it?" Andy asked.

"Almost, Mr. Vice President," Stan replied. "The man was also seen at the site of the cartel gunfight in Mexico and also attacked the Sacred Life Tranquility Retreat in Maui. It seemed he had a grudge on Ezekiel Thompson, but somehow Thompson got the better of him."

"You see, Frank, I told you Thompson was in this up to his neck!" Andy exclaimed. "Thank you, Agent Morgan."

"There is one problem sir. Air Force One was sabotaged on November 14. This man was shot dead in San Diego on October 4. The faces match, but we don't know what to make of the time anomaly," Stan said.

"There has to be a mistake somewhere?" Andy asked.

"We are still checking, sir. Thank you, Mr. Vice President and Mr. Secretary," Stan said and then walked out of the room.

When they were alone, Frank asked, "Andy, if this saboteur was trying to kill Thompson, doesn't that mean Thompson is innocent?"

"Don't be stupid, Frank," Andy growled. "I think Thompson and that man were partners. If they fought at all, it was probably for deniability if they got caught. I think we need to send Thompson to hell with his buddy very soon."

"Andy, he is on US soil. He is entitled to justice."

"Just like the justice he offered to the people in Brazil or those on Air Force One, right? That bastard deserves to die and the sooner the better."

"But how could that man sabotage the plane when he's in a morgue in San Diego?" Frank queried.

"I don't know what is going on anymore, Frank, and I don't really care. The time to act has arrived."

§

Zeke sat chained in a metal chair facing the two CIA agents across the small table. This was the same room where the vice president had cajoled and threatened him just yesterday. "Good morning, Mr. Thompson," Agent Brian Lewis said. "I trust you slept well."

"No, I did not sleep at all. Your boss has already told me I'm going to die here, so why should I tell you anything?" he replied.

"What are you talking about, Mr. Thompson?" Agent Tom Bradley asked.

"Were you two on the other side of the mirror when he interrogated me yesterday?" Zeke asked. Both men nodded. "Obviously you know he turned off the microphones and sat with his back to the mirror so you couldn't read his lips."

"Is there a point to this, Mr. Thompson?" Lewis asked.

"He accused me of being an Iranian spy and said I would be killed by lethal injection very soon. I didn't do anything and there is not one shred of evidence that I was involved in any wrongdoing," Zeke said.

Lewis and Bradley exchanged worried glances. "Excuse us a minute, Mr. Thompson," Lewis said and the two walked out of the room and closed the door. Zeke sighed and hung his head. "Do you think Thompson is serious, Tom?"

"Look at this guy, Brian," Bradley replied. "He's a young kid just out of college. Everything he has said had checked out. There are no records of him leaving the country other than when the two cartels kidnapped him from federal custody."

"Tom, when the vice president muted the microphone, everything was still recorded, wasn't it?"

"Of course, everything is captured on tape. That's the only way we can be sure there are no double-agents here," Bradley answered. "But if you think the brass will let us listen to a private conversation by the vice president, you're crazy."

"Well, I have to try to get someone to listen to that conversation, even if it's only the director," Lewis replied. "If what Thompson said is true, we have a real situation on our hands."

"Let's finish our interrogation and then you can do whatever you want, Brian. Just keep me out of it, okay?" The two walked back into the room and sat across from Zeke.

"The director won't listen to the tape for days, and I'll already be dead," Zeke said.

"Could you hear us from in here?" Lewis gasped.

"No, but I know that Tony won't listen to the recording for a week. There's too much red tape to expedite anything around here."

"But how do you know that?" Bradley asked.

"I see things in the future sometimes," Zeke replied. "If you understood what that means, you'd know why I'm in this mess right now."

"Let's drop that discussion where it is," Lewis said. He picked up a manila folder on the table and leafed through the papers inside. "Mr. Thompson, we have proof that someone did tamper with Air Force One, leading to the catastrophic crash. These images were taken from a security camera inside the hangar." He put three photos on the table facing Zeke and asked, "Do you recognize this man?"

Zeke was flabbergasted by what he saw. "Untor?" he squeaked.

"What does that mean, Mr. Thompson? Is that a name?" Bradley asked.

"Yes, his name was Fola Untor, but you won't believe me if I tell you about him," Zeke replied.

"Why did you say his 'name was' instead of 'name is,' Mr. Thompson?" Lewis asked.

"He's dead, right? Shot in the head in San Diego a month ago."

"I'm not going to follow that line right now. Why would this Untor fellow want to kill the president of the United States? Was he a nut case of a foreign agent?" Lewis asked.

"He was both actually," Zeke chuckled. "I was told he came from another galaxy." The two agents frowned but kept taking notes. "He came back in time to change our history and start a global nuclear war sooner than it is supposed to start."

Bradley glanced at Lewis and then turned to Zeke, "There is supposed to be a nuclear war? What evidence do you have of that?"

"None. Someone told me those things. So far, everything she told me is coming true."

"I suppose this female you mention also comes from the future?" Lewis questioned.

"Of course," Zeke replied. "But the police in San Diego can get the evidence you need to corroborate my story. Have them do a full autopsy on the body including DNA screening. What they'll find will blow everyone's minds."

"Why should we believe you about this man?" Bradley asked.

"I guess I don't really care since the vice president is going to kill me soon," Zeke sighed. "But when the missiles land in Iran and the Russians and Chinese retaliate, then you'll understand. But then it will be too late for Earth. Within a few years, every sign of life will be gone."

The two agents looked at each other. Lewis said, "Mr. Thompson, clearly you are either a prophet or clinically insane. Since there is no evidence of life on other planets or time travel, I suppose you can guess which way I tend to believe."

"Mr. Thompson, where are your parents?" Bradley asked.

"What? What happened to them?"

"They were at their home in Maui. Two FBI agents were sent to take them into custody. When they got no response, they entered the residence and found it vacant. Where did they go?" Bradley asked.

"How would I know? I've been locked up here with no visitors or access to a phone," Zeke complained.

"You have to understand that their sudden disappearance is not good for your chances," Bradley continued. "What country do they work for, Mr. Thompson?"

"They don't work for anyone! My dad was just laid off from his career at Reliant Industries and my mother doesn't work outside the home," Zeke said.

"Let me guess," Lewis interjected. "Did they go into the future?"

"I suppose that is possible," Zeke replied.

The two agents laughed and stood up. "That's enough of your crap for today, Mr. Thompson. We'll take you to your cell now," Lewis replied.

"Get Tony to listen to the tape and have the police do the autopsy," Zeke said as they unchained him from the chair. "I'll be dead, but at least there is a chance that the war can be stopped if the evidence comes out."

"We'll see what we can do," Bradley said as they led him out of the room.

§

Zeke sat at the small table in his cell, pushing the food around on his plate with a plastic fork. He reached out to Bea with his mind. "Bea, are you there?" he thought.

"I'm here, Zeke," she replied.

"Are my parents safe?" he asked.

"Yes, they're at the Maui house with me in my time," she replied.

"Why did you do that, Bea?" he asked. "You know that gives them another reason to kill me right away. Do you want me dead?"

After a moment of silence, she thought, "I love you, Zeke. I will do everything I can to help, but things are complicated right now. Your time is spiraling toward war. If that happens, everyone will die and my future will cease to exist."

"What can I do, Bea? I'm just one man."

"Zeke, I'll come to you tonight with a surprise," she said. "Like I told your parents, the time line you're living through is different from what I was taught in school. In my history, President Nelson was not seriously injured in the crash and nobody else died. I'm surprised I still remember my education. After all of these changes, my memory should have changed as well."

"Well, Bea, the universe is a much more mysterious and magical place than most can imagine" Zeke said. "I do know why your history changed though."

"What?"

"It was Fola Untor again," he replied. "When I was being interrogated today, they showed me security camera images of him inside the wing of Air Force One."

"Oh my God, how much longer do we have to deal with that sick bastard?" she asked.

"He's dead now," Zeke replied. "Hopefully, there will be no more changes. I also have a theory about your history books. So much of the future is in flux right now that there is no definitive course. Once things normalize, your memory and the books will come into line."

"You could be right, Zeke. Sometimes, I think time travelers get so intertwined in different time lines that their brains hold on to bits that no longer exist."

"Tell me about the surprise, Bea," he said.

"You know they want you dead, right?" she asked. "We have to make them think they succeeded. Once they stop guarding your body, you can help me save the president's life and stop the war."

"You mean delay it."

"Yes, Zeke. We will delay the war. It's up to you and the rest of humanity to avoid it. There's only so much I can do."

"Thanks, Bea. Please give my love to my parents."

"I love you, Zeke. Goodbye."

Zeke looked at his plate and realized he had no appetite. What would happen next was anyone's guess. All he knew for certain was that he was about to die. He walked over to his cot and lay down, pulling the covers over his head.

# Chapter 18

At 8:00 p.m., Zeke was led back to the interrogation room and chained down again. A television had been rolled in on a cart and an agent was fiddling with the controls. Zeke wanted nothing more than to end this nightmare. He prayed Bea would take him to her future as well, even though that might be short-lived. Somehow, she thought he was the only one to stop the vice president from starting a war, but he was nobody, locked up in a secret prison and about to be killed for doing nothing. His stomach growled and he also regretted missing his lunch. The door opened and the CIA director and the attorney general entered the room and sat down on either side of Zeke. The agent working the controls changed the channel, handed the remote to Tony Marshall and left the room. "I'm sorry about the shackles, Zeke, but those are the rules here," Tony said. "By the way, this is Attorney General Cynthia Travers. She's on our side too."

"I met the attorney general in Alaska. It's good to see you again, Cindy. I hope you pardon me for not getting up or shaking your hand," Zeke said demonstrating his limited range of motion in his shackles.

"Zeke, it's nice to see you again, too," she said. "Tony and I wanted to watch the vice president's address and get your thoughts."

Tony pressed the mute button as the newscaster announced the vice president. The scene switched to the Oval Office where Andrew Lake was seated at the president's desk. "Doesn't he have his own office?" Zeke asked. The others frowned at him and then turned back to the screen.

"My fellow Americans," Andy began. "I apologize for disrupting your evening again, but there is much new information I must share with you. I am certain many of you have seen the jubilant reaction of the Iranian people to their country's assault on President Nelson. I have never been more disgusted in my life. This rogue state must be held to account for its actions. Today, I was shown the following images of an Iranian agent inside the wing of Air Force One while it underwent standard maintenance." The picture changed to the photos Zeke had seen earlier. "It is now clear that this man sabotaged that plane as part of an Iranian attempt to kill the US president. The leadership of that government has not denied it. In fact, they held rallies all over the country in support of the attack. Justice will be served.

"This saboteur was part of a sleeper cell of Iranian agents led by a man named Abraham Thompson of Hawaii. Mr. Thompson and his wife disappeared while under house arrest at their home and remain at large. Their son and daughter are currently in custody and being interviewed for more information. The son, Ezekiel Thompson, did identify the saboteur as Fola Untor. We are still working to find more evidence of their involvement, but rest assured, they are guilty and will be punished along with their leaders in Iran.

"Now I speak to the leadership of Iran and ask you to cease your campaign against the United States. If you do not, we will use military force, possibly including nuclear weapons to stop you.

"My friends, none of us want war, but we cannot sit idly by while terrorists attack our homeland. I urge each and every one of you to contact your representatives in the Congress and tell them to support us in this effort. May God continue to bless the United States of America. Good night." Tony turned off the set.

"Shit, we're in a lot of trouble!" Zeke exclaimed.

"Where are your parents, Zeke?" Cindy asked.

"Did either of you review my meeting with your agents earlier?"

"Yes, Zeke, but please don't expect us to believe your parents jumped into the future," Tony said. "This is reality, not some science fiction novel."

Zeke laughed. "Okay, let's do it your way. The house was surrounded by a lot of your agents. How many?"

"Twenty or so, I imagine," he replied.

"Neither of you are stupid. You have been briefed on my parents' backgrounds, travel history, income tax returns, and everything else. You know they are just normal, middle-aged people. How could they leave without anyone seeing them?"

"That's a good point," Cindy offered.

"Not really," Zeke interjected. "I've already been kidnapped twice because the federal agents in charge of me were crooked. Perhaps all of your agents at the house are on the Iranian payroll, or yet another drug lord. Maybe they sold my parents to the North Koreans in order to get me? Have you considered all of that?"

"We're performing an investigation of every possibility, Zeke," Cindy said.

"Personally, I think it's improbable that all of them are double agents," Zeke replied. "What are the odds that twenty crooked agents would randomly be assigned to guard my parents, one in a billion? You may not like my story of time travel, but compared to having a massive infiltration of enemy agents into the FBI, CIA and NSA, my story isn't so bad."

"He has a point, Cindy," Tony noted.

"That's just the tip of the iceberg, Tony." Zeke gestured toward the screen and continued, "Not only do you have mass numbers of double-agents in your teams, but that sick bastard had the audacity to call me an Iranian agent when there is zero proof."

"That's pretty strong language to use about the vice president," Cindy said.

"Did Lewis or Bradley ask you to review the audio of my meeting with Lake?" Zeke asked. "Both of you should listen to it. He threatened to kill me and will likely fulfill that threat in the next day or so, maybe even tonight while I sleep. When someone threatens me like that, I think I have the right to say whatever I want about them."

Cindy sighed heavily and said, "Tell us what you think is going to happen, Zeke."

"You won't know this, but the team of doctors helping President Nelson was changed. The original lead doctor refused to continue the induced coma and said Nelson needed to be conscious to get better. Lake fired him and found another doctor who would recommend continuing the coma for at least two weeks. That gives Lake the time to launch a nuclear strike on Iran."

"How do you know any of that?" Tony asked.

"Check it out. Ask the original doctor before Congress subpoenas him. It doesn't matter because Lake is insane now. He thinks the Russians and Chinese won't intervene, but he's wrong. He will strike Iran. Then other countries will start with lots of saber rattling and arguing. Then the North Koreans will nuke Honolulu, the only major American city in their range. We'll retaliate, the others will jump in, and voila, instant Armageddon."

"You're just making this up," Cindy argued.

"It doesn't matter whether you believe me or not," Zeke replied. "I'm pretty sure Lake will kill me tomorrow. If that happens and you want to stop the end of the world, you have to wake the president. If he regains control before the first missiles are launched, he will stop it. Once the first rocket smashes into Tehran, the rest is set in stone and the end of the world is now."

"Zeke, I don't know whether you're a kook or a prophet," Cindy said. "I pray to God that you're a kook. Tony, check on what he told us and let me know as soon as possible."

"Okay, Cindy, I'll get on that right now. Zeke, the guard will take you back to your cell."

§

After returning to his cell, Zeke was too exhausted to think about his hunger. He sat with his head in his hands wondering how he got into such a mess. A part of him looked forward to death. If the world was about to be destroyed, it was better to die here before the mushroom clouds filled the skies and millions of innocents succumbed to radiation sickness. He climbed into bed and promptly fell asleep. At the guard station, a solitary agent watched Zeke sleeping, as there were no other prisoners in this facility. It was absolutely quiet and the guard's eyes closed for a moment.

A siren sounded for half a second and fell silent as the power failed throughout the compound. The guard fumbled through the drawers of the desk until he found a night-vision headset and put it on. Its battery pack was drained. He fumbled through more drawers until he found a flashlight. He left the station to check on his prisoner.

"Zeke," Bea whispered in his ear. "Wake up, I'm here."

Zeke's eyes opened but he could see nothing in the blackness. Then he felt her lips on his and kissed her. "There's no power, Bea. I can't see you." She slipped a pair of special glasses on his face so he could see.

"It couldn't be helped, Zeke," she continued. "You're the only prisoner and the guard will be here soon. I placed a few obstacles in the way to slow him down." Just then they heard the sound of someone tripping and falling to the floor.

A sharp pain rushed up Zeke's arm. "Ouch, what the hell was that?"

"Be quiet," she whispered. "Sit up and drink this." She handed him a small vial.

"What's going on?" he whispered.

"Just drink it. It's going to taste real bad."

He drank the noxious liquid and felt vomit rising in his throat. "Ugh, are you poisoning me now? I think I'm going to throw up."

"Ouch, shit!" shouted a voice down the hallway.

"Don't throw up, Zeke. You need that stuff inside you," she said. The shot and liquid should counteract any lethal injection they give you."

"Should? That doesn't sound very reassuring," he replied. She jabbed him with two more needles. "Would you stop doing that?"

She kissed him and wrapped her arms around him. "This is everything we have to help you, Zeke. We researched all lethal materials available at this time, and that stuff will counteract everything we found. It's the best we can do right now."

"Who is in there with you, Thompson?" the guard's voice said a few feet from the door.

Zeke whispered, "I trust you, Bea."

"I'll see you tomorrow," she replied and then stood up. She took the glasses from his face and stepped through the inky black portal. As it collapsed, a brilliant flash of light filled the room and Zeke had to close his eyes to avoid blindness.

"Freeze!" the guard shouted as he stepped inside with his revolver drawn. "Where is the other person, Thompson?"

"I have no idea what you're talking about," Zeke replied.

The siren wailed and the lights came on. The guard pressed a button on the radio on his shoulder and said, "Thompson is secure. What the hell happened here?"

"Power failure, as best as we can tell," a voice on the radio said.

"I thought we had a backup generator," the guard replied.

"It must have failed too," the voice said.

The guard put his gun into its holster and said, "Good night, Mr. Thompson. I expect you'll be interviewed tomorrow about this incident."

"I bet you're right."

§

Vice President Andrew Lake was pacing back and forth in the Oval Office. He had barely slept the previous night as he tried to formulate the last pieces of his plan. The disappearance of the Thompsons was the perfect linchpin, tying up all the loose ends. Not only did that prove they had something to hide, but vanishing while surrounded by federal officers was virtually impossible without prior espionage experience. There was a knock on the door and the secretary of defense walked in. "Thanks for coming, Frank. Are the warheads ready for launch?"

"We have a situation, Andy," the other replied. "Let me turn on the television." He picked up the remote and pressed the power button. "This is live on Fox News."

"We are here today with Abraham and Sarah Thompson, the heads of the family called out as Iranian agents yesterday by Vice President Lake," the reporter said. "Folks, why did you request this interview?"

"Bill, we are not agents of any government," Abe began. "I've been an accountant my entire career, most recently working for Reliant Industries. Sarah has raised our children and kept our home for the twenty-five years we've been married. There is no evidence that we are aligned with any spy ring. The vice president is making that up to convince our country to go to war."

"The vice president also said you two disappeared from your home in Hawaii while being in the custody of the US Government. What do you say to that accusation?"

"As far as we knew, those guards were protecting our family. Since we had not been arrested or anything, we just left," Sarah replied. "Our son, Zeke, has been kidnapped by drug lords twice while in federal custody. FBI agents also planned to sell him to North Korea."

"But how did you get out without them seeing you?" the reporter asked.

Abe chuckled and replied, "Bill, as Sarah said, we've encountered crooked agents before, so it's no big surprise that there are incompetent ones as well."

"Just a couple more questions from me," the reporter started. "First, why are these people so interested in getting your son?"

"We really think you should talk to Zeke about that," Abe said. "Unfortunately, he is being held without charges in a secret Defense Intelligence Agency compound in Washington, D.C. We believe the vice president will have him murdered in the next twenty-four hours."

The reporter sat stunned for several seconds. "Wow! That's quite a revelation. Let's just let that accusation stand as it is. Mr. and Mrs. Thompson, what do you want to tell the vice president?"

"Obviously, first we want our children released. They have not done anything wrong and no charges have been filed. Second, we implore the vice president not to use nuclear weapons unless there is real evidence that a foreign state was involved and the escalation is approved by the Congress," Abe concluded.

"Well, there you have it, America. This brave couple is standing up and telling the Administration to stop the saber rattling and provide real evidence to back up the vice president's assertions. That seems fair to me," the reporter concluded as the secretary turned off the television.

"That was inconvenient," Andy said. "Are the warheads ready?"

"Andy, did you hear what they just said?"

"Frank, I'm not going to sit back and allow terrorists to take over. Those two will be old news once the first bomb detonates. We have to stand strong or we risk losing this great country," the vice president said.

"Please be reasonable, Andy. We can't launch nukes because you have a hunch the Iranians were behind the Air Force One crash. And once the Thompsons start testifying in front of Congress, you'll never be able to get a consensus to act."

"Do we know where those two are?"

"No, but we can have the FBI find them."

"I'll tell Carl to get on that right away," Andy replied. "Frank, in my position as acting president of the United States, I order you to arm ten nuclear missiles and set their guidance for the nine largest cities in Iran and one for their uranium mining area.

After I take care of Zeke Thompson, you will meet me at Walter Reed where we'll give the launch authorization from Ben's room. That will be the perfect photo op with us showing the world what happens when you attack this country." Frank sighed, turned around and walked out of the room.

§

Zeke pushed the scrambled eggs around on his plate while his mind contemplated the future. There was still a chance that he would really wake up and find it had all been a dream. But something was different today and not in a good way. Rather than eating in his cell, he had been brought to the interrogation room for breakfast. His legs were chained to the chair, but his hands and arms were free. Also, rather than two eggs and a piece of toast, today he also had crispy bacon, hash browns, and a cup of steaming coffee. The notion of his final meal slipped across his consciousness and he fought to subdue it. The door opened and Agents Stephanie Marshall and Brian Lewis entered and closed the door behind them. They sat across from Zeke quietly.

"Is there something I can do for you?" Zeke sat after taking a sip of coffee.

"What happened here last night, Zeke?" Brian asked.

"Power failure," Zeke replied looking down and fiddling with his food.

"Zeke, the night guard reported hearing two voices in your cell," Stephanie noted. "There were also obstacles placed in the hall to slow him down as he came to check on you. Who did that?"

"Stephanie, as you should know, I was locked in my cell and the only view outside I have is through the door panel, which was locked from the outside," Zeke complained. "I can't help it if your facility is poorly maintained and sloppy."

"Mr. Thompson, this is for your own good," Brian stated. "For all we know, North Koreans could have compromised our security and will come again to kill you."

"I suppose that could happen," Zeke said. "So far the FBI and CIA have proven themselves either incompetent or crooked. Why wouldn't they just pay one of you to shoot me?"

"Perhaps they are paying the vice president to give you a lethal injection," Brian suggested.

"I'm glad you said that instead of me!" Zeke laughed. He considered the two agents and continued, "I know you both are just trying to do your jobs. I'm sorry if I'm picking on you. It's just facing death in a couple hours is not a comfortable place to be."

"Zeke, we won't let anyone kill you," Stephanie replied.

Zeke touched her hand softly. "I know you don't want me to be killed, but that is out of our hands now." He removed his hand and said, "Brian, do you really want to know what happened last night?" The agent nodded. "Okay, I'll tell you everything so it is on tape for posterity. But don't interrupt me or question me. You don't have to give a shit for what I say, but let me say it. Grant a dying man his last wish."

"You're not dying, Mr. Thompson," Brian said.

Zeke smirked at the agents. "You can believe that if you like, Brian. Last night agents from the future, the year 3267 to be precise, traveled through a portal in time to this location. They cut off the power and disabled the backup generator. The woman I love, Bea Watson, was one of them. She came to my cell and gave me some injections and a tonic that are supposed to keep me alive if I'm given a lethal injection. She or the others set up the obstacles to keep your agent from catching us. Then they slipped back through time and restored power."

"So, that's it," Brian smirked. "You expect us to believe that?"

"No I don't, but that is what happened," Zeke replied.

The door opened again and Vice President Andrew Lake walked in. "You two cuff Thompson's hands and then take his food and get out."

Stephanie flashed a look of panic at Zeke and he smiled back, mouthing the words, "Don't worry." The agents walked out of the room and locked the door behind them.

"Zeke, I guess you know I was in the room next door while you were talking to those agents," Andy said.

"No, I didn't know that, but I'm not surprised, Mr. Vice President. Did you hear what you wanted to hear, sir?"

"Frankly, no, I did not. Why do you keep up with the silly story about time travel? None of that is possible. It contradicts physical reality, son. Tell me the truth if you want to save your life."

Zeke could barely hide his contempt for the man across the table. Images of other harbingers of doom flashed through his mind, including Genghis Khan, Alexander the Great, Adolf Hitler. There were several other faces he did not recognize, but his mind told him those people were from his own future, the war. "Mr. Vice President, please let me go. You have no proof I am involved in anything. This country is a land of laws. Please respect the laws of the nation you currently lead, sir."

"You don't have a clue about what's really important, do you, Zeke?" Andy asked. "I am going to end the war on terror with one forceful strike! All of your speculation is meaningless crap. If you were in my position, you'd do the same thing!"

"No sir, I don't think I would," Zeke replied. "For starters, I would have followed Doctor Hampton's recommendation and ended the president's induced coma." Lake's face was contorted in anger. "I think you forgot to press the mute button, Mr. Vice President."

"How dare you question me?" Andy growled. "You know nothing of Ben's case, and using that against me is not helping your chances for survival, you sick bastard."

"I don't care, Andy," Zeke replied.

"What? You think you're my friend and can disrespect my position?"

"Frankly, Mr. Vice President, I think you've done enough already to degrade your position all by yourself," Zeke replied. "Please sir, for the love of God, do not launch nuclear missiles for this. The world will end if you start this. Wake the president and let him decide. The people elected him to lead, not you."

Lake jumped to his feet and brought his arm back as though ready to strike Zeke dead on the spot. His face was twisted and red with anger. Soon, his arm fell limp by his side and his grimace turned into a smile. "It was your choice, Zeke," he said and then turned to the mirror. "Director Marshall! Get in here now!"

Seconds later, the door opened and Tony Marshall walked in. "Yes, sir."

Andy reached into a pocket in his jacket and withdrew two syringes, handing one to Tony. "Director, I order you to administer this injection to the prisoner."

"I'm sorry, Mr. Vice President, but what exactly is this?"

"Mr. Thompson is going to pay the ultimate price for his crimes, Tony. Now do it!"

"I can't do that sir," Tony said. "Federal regulations prohibit all domestic CIA facilities from handling punishment of American citizens." He handed the syringe back to the vice president.

"This man is a terrorist, Tony."

"Mr. Vice President, I have sworn to uphold the laws. There's nothing we can do," Tony said.

"No, you're right, Tony. I was wrong to have suggested it. Please have some men take Zeke to Walter Reed. Put him in a secure room in the basement, preferably near the morgue. Then call Doctor Forsyth and have him meet me there in twenty minutes."

"Sir, are you certain you want to go through with this?" Tony asked. "You're breaking the law by taking this into your hands."

"Are you going to arrest me, Tony?" Andy laughed.

"No, but I wish you would reconsider."

"Just do it and do it now!" Lake exclaimed and walked out of the room, slamming the door behind him.

Tony motioned toward the mirror for others to come and help. He walked over to Zeke and said, "I'm sorry, Zeke. I don't know what to do."

"It's okay, Tony. It will be okay, I promise," Zeke smiled back at him. "But if something goes wrong, you have to give the recordings to the press. If I can't stop the vice president from starting Armageddon, you have to do it." The door opened and Brian and Stephanie reentered the room.

"Take Mr. Thompson to Walter Reed," Tony said. "Turn him over to a Doctor Forsyth. I believe he's the one currently in charge of President Nelson."

"With all due respect, sir, this is wrong!" Stephanie exclaimed.

"I know, but we have our orders," Tony replied.

"I don't know about you two, but I could give a damn about any orders," Brian complained.

"It's okay," Zeke replied. "This is what was meant to happen. Please pray that the medication Bea gave me works."

"Is there another way?" Stephanie begged with tears in her eyes.

"Wake up the president," Zeke smiled.

# Chapter 19

Alice Nelson stood by her husband's bed, holding his hand in hers. Tears streamed down her cheeks. Doctor Allen Forsyth was checking the president's vitals on a tablet. The secretary of defense was sitting on a couch looking through e-mails on his phone. "Mrs. Nelson, your husband is improving nicely now," the doctor said. "We may be able to wake him in a week or so." Frank Albright heard the comment and looked up at them.

"Thank you, Allen," she said. "So, I guess it was better to keep the coma for a week or so longer."

"Every case is different, and any number of physicians will have any number of different diagnoses, but in my opinion, we did the right thing."

"How are his broken bones?" she asked.

"That is a bit of a problem," the doctor reported. "Until the president is awake, we cannot really judge the progress. We will need him to move about and even try to walk before we can know for certain. You know that both arms and legs were broken and his spine was cracked in several places. That level of injury can take many months to improve. But he does not need to walk and shake hands to fulfill his duties. We will check his mental state when he awakens, and I will be ready to let him resume his duties, God willing."

"God willing indeed," Frank said as he walked over and stood next to the First Lady. "Alice, you know that Julie and I have you both in our prayers every day."

"I know, Frank, and thank you both for that," Alice said.

"May I ask a question, Doctor?" Frank asked. The doctor nodded. "Does a person in a coma hear what everyone is saying around them?"

"I would have to say yes," Forsyth said. "Many coma patients respond to the physical presence of loved ones. In some cases, they recall each person who visited and what they said, although that is quite rare."

"That's an odd question, Frank," Alice noted.

Frank put his hands around the First Couple's hands and squeezed. "Ben, this is Frank, I want you to know that Julie and I are praying for you every day." Then he released them.

"I'm sorry, Frank," Alice said. "Now, I know what you meant, and I know that you come here often to be with him. You and Andy are great friends."

"You two will always have places in my heart," Frank replied.

The door opened and the vice president walked in. He was smiling and waved to the group. "What a wonderful day!" he exclaimed. "How is our patient?"

"Improving quickly, sir," Forsyth replied. "Perhaps the coma can end sooner than I predicted."

Andy's face had turned hard and tight. "What wonderful news," he replied. "If I may, I need to speak with Doctor Forsyth about another issue. It won't take too long." The two men left the room.

"What do you think that's about, Frank?" Alice asked.

"It's definitely not about Ben," Frank said. "You make those decisions."

"Do you think we did the right thing switching to Doctor Forsyth? I wonder sometimes. Doctor Hampton is a world-renowned physician."

"As long as Ben is improving, that's all we can hope for, Alice," Frank replied.

§

Lake and Forsyth exited the elevator on a basement level in the hospital, accompanied by two Secret Service agents. Lake led them to a small door halfway down the hallway. He inserted a key into the lock and turned it. "Mike and Ted, you two wait outside. I only want the doctor with me."

"Mr. Vice President, I should at least check the room," Mike replied.

"It's already clear. Wait outside," Lake barked. He and the doctor walked in and the door locked behind them. Lake turned on the light switch. The room was bare, except for several storage boxes in one corner and the stainless steel gurney in the center. Zeke was strapped down to the gurney with a bag over his head.

"What is the meaning of this, Mr. Vice President?" Allen asked.

"I need you to take care of something for me, Allen." Lake led the doctor to the gurney and pulled the bag off Zeke's head. "This man is a convicted mass murderer and is responsible for the attack on the president." He removed the two syringes from his pocket and handed one to Allen. "I order you to carry out the sentence and administer this lethal injection."

"What? No! This is very irregular, sir," Forsyth said as he backed away. "This isn't the job I signed up for. Who is this man, and why is he gagged anyway?"

Lake dragged Forsyth to the corner of the room farthest from the door and whispered, "Allen, we both know why you're here.

You want a lot of money and you need me to help you overcome some legal issues, right?"

"But you said I just had to keep the president asleep for a few weeks," Forsyth complained.

"Well, the price just went up," Lake noted, poking the doctor in the chest with each word. "Listen, if word ever got out about our deal, we're both finished."

"You're asking me to murder a man I don't even know."

"The drugs in the syringe are not traceable. There will be no evidence, just another John Doe body in the morgue."

The doctor was trembling as he said, "Sir, why is there a second syringe?"

"You just leave that to me, Allen."

"You're going to assassinate the president, aren't you?"

"Depending on how things go, that is a definite possibility," Lake admitted.

"What if I just go tell those agents what you're asking me to do?"

"Either I'll jab you with the needle myself, or I'll tell them you were trying to kill me. Believe me, they love their job and would have no problem blowing your head off," Lake smiled.

Forsyth considered his situation and realized he was in a corner. If he wanted to stay out of prison, he had to kill this young man. If he refused, he would die. "Please reconsider, sir."

"Just do it," Lake growled.

Forsyth began to walk slowly toward the gurney. He could see the man on the gurney watching him. He did not seem to be frightened or squirming for freedom. Forsyth wondered what he would do in that circumstance, facing his imminent death. He shivered and his hand began to shake.

"I don't have all day," Lake said. "I have a full schedule after this."

Forsyth removed the shield from the needle and looked at the man who still showed no emotion. What was he thinking, he wondered. Forsyth took the man's hand. The man squeezed his hand and his eyes smiled back at him. The doctor focused on the man's arm and promised not to look in his face again. The needle slipped into the man's flesh and he pressed the plunger, releasing the poison into the man's bloodstream. He removed the needle and replaced the shield and walked over to the vice president, who was smiling from ear to ear. "Here."

"Good job, Allen," Lake said. "Go check on Zeke and tell me when he's dead."

Forsyth looked in disbelief at the vice president. How could any man be so cold and heartless, he wondered. He walked back to the gurney, took Zeke's wrist and felt for a pulse. There was none. A few tears slid down the doctor's cheeks, and he brushed them away. He realized he had failed to uphold his Hippocratic Oath in the most horrific way. "He's dead, sir."

"Go ahead and remove the restraints and leave the body here," Lake said. "I'm sure an orderly or janitor will find it later. I'll let you see yourself out." The vice president walked to the door, opened it and walked away with his protective team.

After removing all the restraints and the gag, Allen said, "I am so sorry. I don't even know who you are. Wherever you are, I hope you can forgive me." His eyes welled with tears and he said, "Forget I said that. I don't deserve your forgiveness. I only hope God can forgive me someday." He opened the door, turned off the light and walked outside. He closed the door and headed to the closest tavern for a drink.

§

The motorcade approached the open gates of the White House. The guards saluted the vice president's limousine as it passed. It pulled to the doors, and Andrew Lake exited and headed directly to the White House briefing room where the press had gathered for a press conference. He walked in with the secretary of defense right behind him. Lake took the podium and said, "Good evening, folks. I am here to make a few comments and answer a number of questions. First, I want you to know that I just came from Walter Reed and saw the president. His doctors are continuing his induced coma but see continued improvement and will review his status every few days."

"Mr. Vice President, there are reports that the team of physicians helping the president was recently changed. Do you know why that happened?" a reporter asked.

"Jay, all health decisions for the president are controlled by the First Lady. She did consult with me and others, and I told her she could get better care from another team. But she made the final decision."

"Sir, are you aware that Congress has issued a subpoena for Doctor Hampton, the original physician in charge?" Jay replied.

The vice president flinched, but quickly recovered and said, "No, I was not aware of that. The Congress will do what they do, but I think it's wrong for the government to get involved in a family's medical concerns. But I would prefer to focus on our Iranian problem. You are all aware of the interview of the Thompson family that aired this morning. You should be skeptical of such propaganda. I heard their comments about their escape and want you to know they were in custody when that occurred, regardless of what they said. They continue to hide to avoid real questioning. Also, their son, who was being detained in Washington, has now disappeared as well."

"Sir, is there any evidence that the Thompsons were involved in the attack on Air Force One?" a second reporter asked.

"Yes, but that evidence is top secret at this time. You will be advised when it is available through FOIA," Andy said.

"Mr. Vice President, the Thompsons claimed their son was kidnapped twice from federal custody by drug cartels. Is that true?" another reporter asked.

"No, of course not. It is patently absurd to believe that drug lords or North Koreans have taken over elements of our government. Frankly, it is an insult to those brave women and men to even consider those allegations," Andy growled. He was beginning to sweat heavily and regretted his decision to speak.

"I meant no disrespect, sir, but I don't think I mentioned anything about North Korea. Would you care to comment further on that?" the reporter asked.

Andy was panting for air, trying desperately to calm himself down. He took a long drink of water and looked to Frank for support. The secretary's head was in his hands and he looked at the floor. "I'm sorry for my anger. It's been a difficult day for all of us. We have been dealing with the attack on the president for a long time and the strain is getting to everyone. There is nothing I want more than for Ben to wake up and get back to work." He put his hand over his heart to appear sincere, but he could feel the second syringe in his pocket. "You did this to me, Thompson," he thought. "Please let me say just one more thing tonight. The Iranians will pay for this and all their years of terror. Now, I'm going back to Walter Reed to talk to Ben. I often sit at his bedside and ask his advice. Every day, I pray he will answer me. Good night." He walked out of the briefing room alone. Frank was still sitting with his head down. Lake murmured, "I don't need you anyway, Frank, you're nothing but a damned coward."

§

Zeke sat straight upright and gasped for air. His entire body was stiff and sore. The site where the doctor had jabbed him stung like a bee sting. It was completely dark, except for a sliver of light under the bottom of the door. He tried to stand and almost fell, grasping onto the gurney for support. His knees and ankles creaked and ached. He started toward the door to find a light switch. After a couple of steps, his hair began to stand on end and the room felt full of static. He turned around and thought he could almost make out the event horizon of the portal. Suddenly, a figure appeared to step through the blackness and into the room. A long arc of static shot from the gurney and stung his back. A brilliant flash filled the room for an instant and then was gone. "Bea?" He felt her arms wrapping around his neck and her lips on his. "It worked, Bea, I'm still alive!" She jabbed a needle into his arm. "Ouch! What the hell is that?"

"It's just a little something to help with the pain and stiffness," she whispered. "God, I was so afraid it wouldn't work."

"Yeah, your whole world would end in a flash," he replied.

She kissed him again and said, "No, because I love you and you'd be dead, Zeke." She kissed him again. "You have to realize that I'll never know if the past changes for my time. Once the change takes place, everything is just different."

"I'm sorry, I didn't mean to doubt you, Bea," he said, caressing her cheek.

She took his hand and pulled him to the door and switched the light on. "I hate to keep saying this, but we're running out of time." She pulled two small devices from her pocket and handed them to Zeke. "These will automatically dispense the medication that the president needs."

"What's in this stuff?" Zeke asked.

"I swear it will cure all the president's injuries and wake him up. The green one is the cure. The blue one wakes him. Please inject him in that order. You just press the pointy end into his skin. It self-injects with no needles. Do you trust me?" she asked.

He kissed her. "Yes, I trust you, Bea. If not for you, I'd be dead. But why don't you or your team do this? Why me?"

"Zeke, you are the key to everything. When you save the president and delay the war, you'll be a national hero. No one else would dare try to kidnap you, and Ben Nelson will become your good friend. You'll be able to help him stop the saber rattling and keep things calm for two hundred years."

"But then the war comes anyway," Zeke noted.

"According to my history, yes, the war will come. However, none of this is written in stone. It is possible that mankind will be different than I've read about. Everything that happens from now on is up to each person. You know that now, don't you?" she asked.

"Yes, Bea, I know that. Do you think my dream of marrying you will ever come true?" Zeke asked.

She blushed and looked down. "So that was the dream you didn't want to tell me about! Well that depends on whether you ask me or not, and also the carats of the engagement ring." He looked into her eyes and saw only love. He wanted to ask then and there, but she put her fingers to his lips and said, "Now is definitely not a good time for a proposal, Zeke. There's not much time. Let's go."

They left the room and hurried up the hallway. She ran past the elevators to the stairwell and opened the door. They headed up several flights of stairs. Zeke stopped to catch his breath, and each time she grabbed him by the arm and pulled him along. After another flight, she stopped and motioned for him to be quiet and stay in place. She opened the door and closed it again. She walked up a few steps very slowly and without a sound and then came back. "You wait here," she whispered. She removed a small device from her pocket and headed back up the stairs. Zeke heard the sound of static electricity and she came back to him. "Follow me," she whispered.

At the next floor, two men were lying on the ground. "Are they dead?" Zeke asked.

"Just stunned," Bea whispered. "They'll be fine in a half hour." She cracked open the door, looked around, and closed it again. "Take a peek to the right. You'll see two men standing there. That's the president's room that they are guarding." Zeke did as he was told. The room was the fourth on the right. He closed the door. "Okay, you stand here behind the door. I'm going to draw their attention. I'll shoot one and the other will chase me. I'm coming back here and running downstairs. When the agent goes by, you hurry to the room and do the job, got it?"

"Frankly, I'm scared out of my mind, Bea. Is this the only way?" he asked.

"To accomplish our goal to wake the president and delay the war, yes, this is our only chance," she whispered. "Put your arms up to block the door when he flies by. I don't want you getting knocked unconscious by it." He complied and stood silently with the two devices in his hands. She kissed him and whispered, "Wish me luck." He smiled back at her.

The door opened and she strode out into the corridor. Her weapon hand was behind her. "What the hell is going on up here? Where's the party, dudes?" she shouted.

"I'm sorry, ma'am, but this floor is closed," one of the agents said as he drew his revolver and moved to stop her. "Call for backup, Mark."

"We've got a situation up here. Please send backup," the other agent said into his microphone.

In the blink of an eye, Bea's hand came from behind her and a flash of light shot forth, striking the approaching agent in the chest. He crumpled and fell to the ground. "Officer down, I'm in pursuit," the other agent said as he drew his revolver and took chase. Bea had already started to run and pushed through the door and headed downstairs. She was pounding her feet to help the agent know where she was. The door slammed open onto Zeke's arms. The agent stood for a fraction of second, inches away from Zeke on the other side of the door. When he heard her footfall, he started flying down the stairs. Zeke hurried around the door and down the hallway, stepping carefully over the fallen agent. He turned the knob, expecting other agents to shoot him when he entered. Gathering his courage, he opened the door and stepped in.

President Nelson lay quietly in the bed. Doctor Forsyth stood at the foot of the bed. "What is the meaning of this?" the doctor shouted and moved toward Zeke and then froze when he recognized Zeke's face. His lips moved for a moment before he could articulate any words. Finally, he said, "You, but you're dead." The doctor fainted and fell to the floor.

Zeke knew more agents would arrive any second. He pressed the green device on the president's exposed arm and said, "Sir, this will help you. People have come from the future to make sure you survive." A small light flashed for a few seconds and then turned off. He took the blue device and did the same.

The door flew open and Vice President Lake and two more agents rushed into the room. The light was still flashing. "Get that assassin!" Lake shouted. Zeke could feel them on him. The light stopped flashing and they threw Zeke to the floor. "Cuff that bastard and let me see his face!" Lake screamed. They pulled Zeke to his feet and turned him to face Lake. The vice president stumbled, but caught himself on a chair. "This isn't possible," he groaned. "You're dead! I saw Forsyth inject you myself."

"I'm not quite dead yet, Mr. Vice President," Zeke growled.

"He's killed the doctor too," Lake moaned, pointing to the other man on the floor, who as if on cue began to stir and groan.

"We'll take care of this man, sir," one of the agents said.

Alice Nelson, Frank Albright, and Tony Marshall came into the room with three other Secret Service agents. "What's going on?" Marshall asked.

"This man administered something to the president," the agent said. "The doctor apparently fainted."

"Don't you see," Lake said in a dazed voice. "Zeke Thompson has poisoned the president. You have to let me help him." He pulled the other syringe from his jacket. This will cure him, I guarantee it."

"Don't do it!" Zeke shouted. "That's the poison."

"He's right," Tony said. "The vice president asked me to administer that to Zeke this morning."

"You're a goddamned liar, Marshall! How dare you say that?" Andy screamed, his face contorted in anger.

"No, enough is enough," Doctor Forsyth said from the floor. "I administered that shot to that young man only hours ago. He was dead, I swear it."

"I want Forsyth and Marshall arrested!" Lake screamed again. "This is an Iranian plot!"

"Just shut up, Andy," said a voice behind them. They all turned to see President Nelson sitting upright in the bed. "I want the vice president and secretary of defense kept under house arrest, pending a full investigation. Andy, one thing Doctor Forsyth told Frank today was true. I remember everyone who came to visit me and everything they said. Also, release Mr. Thompson. He is a hero, not the villain." He moved his legs over the side of the bed as everyone except Zeke, Tony, and Alice were led out of the room.

"Darling, the doctor said your arms and legs were broken," Alice said. "You should stay in bed."

He kissed her and replied, "I'm feeling fantastic." He stood up and stretched to ease the ache out of his joints. "So, your name is Zeke, Zeke Thompson?"

"Yes, Mr. President," he replied.

"You said people came from the future to save me. You have to know that's hard to believe, son," Ben replied.

"Sir, I've been through too many things in the last weeks to believe, but here I am. Whether they came from the future or not, at least it all worked out."

Alice Nelson hugged Zeke and kissed his cheek. "This is truly a miracle, Zeke. Thank you and thank your friends."

"Mr. President, I think Andy had the FBI holding Zeke's sister and tracking down his parents. Perhaps you should make them stand down," Tony suggested.

"I can't wait to hear the story behind this!" Ben exclaimed. "I'll call Carl after you two leave." He stepped up to Zeke and put his arm around his shoulders and said, "Thank you for healing me, Zeke. I owe you my life. I would be honored if you would come to the White House for lunch tomorrow, just you and me. We have lots to talk about."

"It would be my pleasure, sir," Zeke smiled.

"Thank you," the president said. "Now, if you don't mind, I have to call the FBI and then spend some quality time with my wife. I'll send a car for you tomorrow, Zeke. Where are you staying?"

"Mr. President, since Mr. Thompson has been in town, he's been held in a DIA detention facility," Tony noted.

"Tony, please get him a suite at a local hotel and then let the office know where he is," Ben replied.

"Yes, sir."

"Thank you again, Mr. President," Zeke said and then he and Tony left the room.

# Chapter 20

Zeke Thompson was exhausted. Once he arrived in his hotel room, he pulled off his clothes and climbed into bed, falling asleep immediately. He dreamed about Bea Watson, the mysterious woman from the future who had come to save the world. He ached for her and longed to hold her again, but in the dream, she was an apparition, dissolving to smoke at his touch. A flash of light filled his room and he was shocked awake. And there she was. Bea stood at the foot of his bed wearing nothing but her underwear. She climbed on the bed and crawled to him, pulling back the covers and sliding next to him. "Am I still dreaming?" he whispered.

"What do you think?" she purred as she ran her hands up and down his body and then kissed him passionately.

He woke again, hours later, finding himself alone in bed. He looked around and saw her standing by the window, looking out on the city. He rose and walked up to her, wrapping his arms around her waist and squeezing her tightly. "Bea, I love you."

She turned around and kissed him. Zeke noticed her eyes were red and puffy. "I'm sorry, I didn't mean to upset you."

"Zeke, you don't understand," she said, taking his hand in hers. She pulled him over to the bed and they both sat. "What I have to say now is very hard for me. I wish more than anything else that I could stay here . . ."

"Then stay!" Zeke begged.

"It wouldn't work, Zeke. I have no identity here. There is no record of me because I won't be born for more than a thousand years," she said. "Plus there is no mention of me after the first volume of 'A Simple Life.' I am not meant to be here."

"But you said yourself that history hasn't been written yet," he noted. "Maybe the real books will be full of words about you."

"We can't take that chance, Zeke. This is a lot more than a love story about us. There is the world to consider, this world and the world of my future. Forcing more changes will make me worse than Fola Untor, and look at the havoc he unleashed. If not for you, my future would evaporate."

"So, just like that it's over?" Zeke gasped. "What about my dream? What about our wedding and our future together?"

"Zeke, do you trust me?" she asked.

"Of course I do. I'd have to be pretty stupid not to after everything we've been through."

"I will visit you as often as I can, but you have to promise not to write about me or tell anyone who I am. It has to be a private thing between you and me," she said.

"That's not a life, Bea. We were meant to be together always. I don't know if I can live like that, waiting weeks or months to see you for a few minutes or hours."

She smiled and patted his hand. "I know you're right, Zeke, but that's the best I can do. The Temporal Command won't allow me to do more than that. My grandmother, Aria, is already bending too many rules in order for me to do what I've done. If you trust me, I know it will work out." She stood and walked over to the window and glanced outside. Then she turned and said, "We all make choices, Zeke. You can find someone in your own time and have a long, happy life together with her. I won't be jealous, in fact, it might be better for you."

He rose and went to her, holding her tightly in his arms and kissing her face. "Bea, I do trust you. Let's just do what we both have to do and see how things work out."

"Okay, Zeke. I couldn't say it better than that," she replied. "Unfortunately, I have to get going." The room felt electrified. Static charges jumped off the carpet and stung their feet. A tiny black spot appeared and began to grow until it was seven feet in diameter and hung like a painting of death in the air. "Zeke, my love, there is so much more to tell you. If I could tell you everything, I'm afraid it would freak you out." She kissed him and then pulled herself away and moved toward the event horizon.

"Bea Watson, I love you and want to marry you!" he shouted.

"I left you a present on the table. I think your last phone is gone forever," she said. Bea smiled, turned and walked through the circle. A flash of light forced him to look away and then was gone, leaving Zeke alone in his room again. He went to the table and looked at the phone, searching the contact list. He sighed with relief when he saw her name. He set the device down and walked to the bathroom to prepare for his day.

§

"You have to admit that's an unbelievable story, Zeke," the president said. "Time travel, kidnappings by drug lords, a villain from the future sent to kill you and me. If I hadn't lived through it, I'd think you were crazy."

"I know what you mean, Mr. President," Zeke smiled. "Sometimes I have a hard time believing it myself."

"Zeke, I owe you my life. When you and I are alone, please call me Ben. In public, I know everyone has to respect my position, but here, we're just two men enjoying each other's company, okay?"

"Thank you, Ben. When I think about what happened, I try to cling to the things that made it all work, like those two injections I gave you. Those things give me clarity."

"You're right. Doctor Hampton was shocked that all my organ and bone injuries were suddenly healed. There's not a physician on earth today who could do anything like that. So, what are you going to do now, go live in the future with that girl?"

"I wish it could have been that easy, Ben. I begged her to stay here or take me with her, but she said I have a job to do in my time. I guess I'll do that."

"And what job is that, Zeke?"

"Well, you'll find this hard to believe too, but I want to help you stop nuclear war, and I want to help people by telling them the future."

"Ah yes, Tony told me about your prognostication ability. Did that come from the future people too?" the president asked.

"No, that's just me. For most of my life, I thought it was a curse. When I was arrested and kidnapped, arrested and kidnapped again, chased by a man from the future, and then killed, only to come back to life, I realized my gift is a true blessing. Ben, I don't know the future any more than anyone else. But I can sense what could happen if a person keeps doing what they're doing. I think that gives me the chance to help them make better choices."

"That's a noble goal, Zeke, and I would be honored to be your friend and first client. What do you see for me?"

Zeke gently touched the president's hand and closed his eyes. After a few seconds, he opened them and sat back. "Whew! You're a busy guy!"

"It comes with the job title. What did you see?"

"You won't get much sleep for the next few weeks as you deal with the Iranians and convince the Russians and Chinese that there is no risk of nuclear war. That will negatively affect your relationship with Alice. You'll give a eulogy for the vice resident who will commit suicide in the coming days. Further down the line, I see a second term."

"What? I don't want to hurt Alice or see Andy kill himself," the president said. "Those things can't be true?"

"Ben, that is my point," Zeke began. "I sense the ways things will go if you don't work to keep them from happening. Now that you know, you can spend more time with Alice. She has been by your side every day since the accident. And you can find support for the vice president and try to help him through this too."

"I'll do my best."

"That's all any of us can do, Ben. Please remember that Alice, Andy, and everyone else make their own decisions on how to feel. The vice president needs serious help, but while there is life, there is hope," Zeke concluded.

"Thank you, Zeke. I appreciate your advice. Let me put my direct line into your phone. I know I'll be calling you from time to time," the president said.

"It is my honor to help you, Mr. President."

# Chapter 21

Zeke traveled back to Hawaii where he was reunited with his family. Abe went back to writing books while Zeke traveled from city to city and country to country, trying to help world leaders and individual people understand their lives and be empowered to change things for the better. Bea did her best to visit him at least once per month, and somehow with his travel and schedules, that was okay for Zeke as well. He began to realize that she had been right all along. This was the role in life he was meant to pursue. El Tigre's men assumed the security for the Maui house while his family built an estate near the Sacred Life Tranquility Retreat.

After a few years, Peter Smith left his job in New York and joined Zeke. Peter arranged the travel and schedule while Zeke focused on the people he met. Later, Stephanie Marshall did leave the government and moved to Hawaii where she and Peter became a couple. Eventually, Peter and Reverend Paul Isaac discovered their own ability to foretell the future, and the three split to cover more people and places to dispense their knowledge. When it was winter in the Northern Hemisphere, they would all return to Hawaii to relax and celebrate the holidays together, eager for the coming spring and the opportunity to work again.

The years flew by, until one day Zeke found himself in the Oval Office again with President Jack Lancaster and Peter Smith. He smiled as he recalled the painting he saw of this meeting in the college in the future. It struck him again how old Peter looked. For some reason, Zeke had not aged very much. He had even taken to dying his hair gray so he wouldn't look so young.

"I don't know how you do it, Mr. Thompson," the president said. "You look as young as ever, while Peter and I are old men."

"Thank you, Mr. President," Zeke replied. "I can't believe it's been fifty years since my first visit to this office. I feel young, but the calendar says I'm seventy-two years old."

"Frankly, Zeke, I think you're Dorian Gray and I'm your painting," Peter laughed.

"Personally, I hope you both keep doing what you've been doing," Lancaster said. "You both have done a lot to keep the peace for the last half century."

"Thank you, Mr. President," Zeke said. "It's been a great joy for all of us. It's just hard to deal with the passing of so many dear friends. I suppose that's the price of age."

"Zeke, do you realize it's been ten years since Paul passed away," Peter said. "God, I miss that man every day."

"Me too, Peter. That man saved my life," Zeke replied.

"And you made his by telling him about Judy," Peter said.

"Gentlemen, I'm afraid we have to get going," the president said. "We're due at the ceremony soon. Let's get one last picture here in the office and my car is waiting outside."

"Yes, sir," Zeke said. "And thank you again for the honor tonight." The cameras clicked and the men left the Oval Office.

§

A week later, Peter Smith passed away. His wife and children were by his side when he slipped away. Zeke was trying desperately to get back from Africa on time, but arrived hours late. He cried for hours that night, holding Stephanie and praying with her. Now it was just him, he thought. "I'm sorry I wasn't here," he apologized.

"Zeke, do you remember the first time we met?" she asked.

"Yes, you were on the team that took me into custody and flew me back to San Diego."

"Zeke, you save my life that night. You told me to put on a second vest."

Zeke smiled. "Well, I actually put you in danger too. It was me El Tigre was after."

"Zeke, everything you told me came true. Peter and I had a wonderful life together and have three children and eight grandchildren so far. Thank you." She kissed him on the cheek. "Thank you for my life, Zeke."

§

Three days later, the rain poured down on Peter Smith's funeral. He was laid to rest near the graves of Reverend Paul Isaac and his wife, Judy. Stephanie and the entire Smith family filled the area under a sea of black umbrellas. After paying his respects, Zeke moved away from the crowd to be alone with his thoughts. Everyone was gone now, although his team had recruited and started a new generation of prophets to follow their path. Soon it would be his time to pass, but he was okay with that. It was Nature's way.

"Hello, Zeke," a voice said behind him. He turned to see Bea Watson standing under an umbrella. "I'm sorry for your loss, my love."

He walked over and put his arms around her and hugged her. "I can't believe he's gone. I don't know what to do now that I'm alone."

"Come with me to the future, Zeke," she said.

He looked back at her with a stunned look on his face. "What? I thought you said I had to be here. What changed?"

"Nothing, my love," she replied.

"But I'm an old man now, Bea. I'm seventy-two years old. What good will I do in your time?"

"Did you finish volume seven?" she asked.

"Yes, it goes to print next week."

"Then your work here is done, Zeke," she said. "Now your life can begin in my time. We can get married and be together. Isn't that what you wanted?"

"Yes, but that was so long ago. Didn't you hear me say that I'm seventy-two?"

"You're still a young man, Zeke. If you didn't dye your hair, you'd still look like you're in your mid-twenties. Did you ever wonder why that happened?"

He looked at her and she looked as young as ever, which seemed illogical. Suddenly, a thought struck his mind like a ton of bricks and he shouted, "The green pills!"

"Bingo!" she exclaimed. "Medicine is highly advanced in my time thanks in large part to the Kalideans. Zeke, I'm seventy-four years old."

"So, you were twenty-four when we met."

"I never said that. Zeke, I was seventy-two when we met," she stated. "Do you remember the shot I gave you after you woke from the lethal injection?" His mind was fumbling for thoughts or words, but he could not assemble anything meaningful to say. "I told you it would help you with the aches and stiffness, but that wasn't true. That shot contained nanobots that traveled through your body correcting your DNA. Both of us can live to be a thousand years old or more!"

"Huh? I don't know what to think. How did you age two years while I aged fifty? That's not logical."

She hugged him and kissed his lips lightly. "I know that time travel boggles the mind. But you remember how I came to you every month to spend a day or night together?"

"Of course, I'll never forget one of those visits."

"Zeke, in your time, you saw me once a month, but I actually came to you every night of my life for the last year and a half. You were always in my arms and my bed, even though it seemed rare to you," she said.

"Why?"

"Because you are the love of my life, Ezekiel Thompson, that's why!" she smiled. "I want you to come with me to the future and be my husband, if that's what you still want."

"Can any of this be true?"

"Do you trust me, Zeke?" she asked, smiling from ear to ear. "You told me before that you did."

"Until the end of time, Bea Watson," he replied. He knelt down and took her hands in his. "Bea, will you marry me?"

She pulled him up to his feet and kissed him passionately, and then said, "I suppose that depends on the carats." The air felt warm and electricity crackled as though a storm was approaching. "That's our ride, Zeke."

He turned to see the black circle suspended in the air two feet from them. "So, this is it. I won't be in my time ever again."

"You can come from time to time if you want," she said. "But you'll have to get clearance from Aria first, and I won't even ask her for you until after the wedding."

"Sounds like a deal to me," Zeke said. He kissed her and took her hand. They walked slowly up to and through the event horizon. The circle exploded in a flash of light.

# About the Author

**Karl J. Morgan**

Karl Morgan has a lifelong fascination with stories in the science fiction and fantasy genres, whether it was the Tom Swift novels by Victor Appleton he read as a young boy, or television like *Lost in Space* and *Star Trek*, and especially films like *Star Wars*, *Harry Potter* and *Lord of the Rings*. All of those tales put the protagonist in terrible situations where the odds are against them and, yet, somehow they prevail. The reader/viewer is always left with a sense that something greater than ourselves is watching over us.

The reliance on Divine Providence, the power of friendship, and the desire to learn and grow are cornerstones of the author's Dave Brewster and *Heartstone* series. That continues in the Modern Prophets series, only the unseen forces are now out in the open.

These are tales of reluctant heroes who have been given powers they do not yet understand, and challenges that would seem overwhelming. Still, the hand of Fate is firmly on their shoulders and friends arise just when needed most to prevent the most despicable of evils.

Karl lives in the San Diego area with his wife, Aida, and their beloved puppies. Their two grown children have fled the nest and started their own adventures in life.

    To read more about Karl and his projects, please visit his website and blog: www.karljmorgan.com
Facebook: www.facebook.com/karlmorganauthor
Twitter: @karljmorgan.

# Other Books By
# Karl J. Morgan

### *The Dave Brewster Series*

*Showdown Over Neptune*
ISBN: 978-0-9860270-0-0
(Book 1)

*Second Predaxian War*
ISBN: 978-0-9860270-1-7
(Book 2)

*The Hive*
ISBN: 978-0-9860270-2-4
(Book 3)

*Tears of Gallia*
ISBN: 978-0-9860270-4-8
(Book 4)

*The Accord*
ISBN: 978-0-9860270-6-2
(Book 5)

### *Heartstone*

*Heartstone: Sentinels of Far Sun*
ISBN: 978-0-9860270-3-1
(Book 1)

*Heartstone: The Time Walker*
ISBN: 978-0-9860270-5-5
(Book 2)


## *Modern Prophet Series*

*Two Doors*
ISBN: 978-0-9860270-7-9
(Book 1)

*Hand of God*
ISBN: 978-0-9860270-9-3
(Book 3)
Available for sale early 2015


## *Individual Book*

*Remembrances: Choose to Be Happy and Embrace the Possibilities*
ISBN: 978-0-9826461-9-9